LEAHBELLE BEACHY
AND THE
BEINGS OF LIGHT

AMISH TERROR

LEAHBELLE BEACHY AND THE BEINGS OF LIGHT

by Stephen Beachy

✴

Vapor Books
SAN DIEGO

This is a work of fiction. Names, characters, places, and incidents either are the product of the author's imagination or are used fictitiously.

Leahbelle Beachy and the Beings of Light

Copyright © 2018 by Stephen Beachy
Published by Vapor Books
SAN DIEGO
Cover art)) by D-L Alvarez
Cover design by James Salas
Interior Design by Vapor Books

ISBN-13: 978-1-7321289-2-7
ISBN-10: 1-7321289-2-8

I. LEAHBELLE

ONE

Leahbelle was up long before sunrise, sitting high in her favorite oak, listening to the first birds and the drones and the elaborate symphony created by their responses to each other. She listened to the rustling of the pork bushes in the neighboring fields and the rustling of the small creatures that were attracted to their smell. A chain clanking against a distant gate. A dog barking. And then a noise at first so faint it was like a tickle, the rumble of a motor, some kind of vehicle gradually coming nearer, but not too near, maintaining a certain distance from Leahbelle, circling her but never passing by.

She'd been hearing that sound throughout the day, for several days, but hadn't realized it until just now.

The pork bushes all shimmied together, creating a sound like a breeze, although there was no breeze. They were synchronized, connected to each other and to the Grid; in unison they sprayed their poisons at the small creatures that were attracted to their smell, so that the squeaks of the dying creatures seemed synchronized too.

Zeke Yoder had been gone for two weeks. Fifteen days, actually. Somewhere in Nebraska, he'd been captured by a mad scientist. According to the rats, he'd be rescued from her underground bunker any day.

In Iowa, the night was calm. Leahbelle was wearing her nightclothes. She descended from the tree and walked barefoot to the road that ran past the house. No cars, no buggies, nothing, but in the distance to the north, the rumble of that motor.

She got her shoes and walked alone along the road toward the intersection with Redwood Avenue. The noise of the motor was moving up Redwood and then cutting east on 105th over to Red Oak. She could barely hear it as it rumbled west and then south all the way to G16 and back east again, crossing the river and forming a huge circle or a rhomboid, with her home in the center.

At the intersection, she waited. It was coming closer and closer.

Gonzalo looked right at her as he passed by on his motorbike. He didn't seem surprised to see her, but he didn't slow down either. From the sound of it, he kept going east on 105th, perhaps heading back to the ruined orphanage where he lived with other assorted off-the-Grid types: rebels, political radicals, and homeless kids.

She'd only really met Gonzalo once, although she'd seen him around; he was Zeke's friend. Kind of skinny but strong, with tattoos on his skull, and one of his arms was a machine. A couple of years older than she was, he was crazy and sinful and kind of violent. Kind of full of himself too, she always thought.

She wondered if he was waiting for news of Zeke's rescue too.

Leahbelle walked on home and got started on her chores.

That afternoon her mother told her that one of the piglets was missing. She told Leahbelle's sister Ruth to watch the younger children so that she and Leahbelle could walk down toward the creek.

I'm sure it just dug out and went for a bath, said Leahbelle.

That's what I figured, said her mother. But there wasn't any path dug out of the pen. There wasn't any hole.

Leahbelle's mother was a solid woman with dark hair, quick to laugh and smile, but also quick to fret. Leahbelle had been taller than her mother since she turned thirteen. Sometimes, more and more lately, Leahbelle felt like she was the adult in the relationship.

I didn't sleep so good last night, her mother confessed.

Me either, said Leahbelle. I was out walking around, maybe I woke you. We're all a little nervous since Zeke left.

Since the rats came, said her mother. And whatever else is going on out there.

Her mother stopped walking.

What's this?

The dirt along the path glittered, sprinkled with a shiny metallic substance scattered in bits. Leahbelle leaned over to look more closely. Some of the sparkles were moving. Some quickly disappeared, as if they'd burrowed into the earth.

Don't touch it! her mother said.

She grabbed Leahbelle in a ferocious hug.

I love you, Leahbelle, she said. I love you, you're my baby.

Mother, said Leahbelle. It's okay. It's okay.

Her mother was crying.

Probably just some drone waste, Leahbelle said.

We've never seen it before.

Everything changes so fast for the English, said Leahbelle. It's nothing. I'm sure it's nothing to be alarmed by.

A couple of weeks ago, the Genetically Modified Rats had told the Kalona Amish that the new government wanted their land and that war was coming. Zeke and his grandmother had set off to find new land for the community. Since they'd left, Leahbelle's mother had seemed a little bit crazier every day.

We'll find out, Leahbelle said.

She picked up a flat stone and scraped some of the dirt and the sparkles into her bonnet, then tied it up tight and put it in her pocket.

Mother, look.

Little hoof prints took off from the trail, leading down toward the water.

You see? she said, leaving her mother by the trail, descending down through the weeds along the muddy bank. She heard it again just then, in the distance. Gonzalo's motorbike. She tried to figure out what direction the noise was coming from. It was so faint, and while she was outside of herself in this way, concentrating, she noticed the little tail sticking out from a weedy patch. It wasn't moving. She stepped closer.

Mother, stay back.

The piglet was dead, flat on its side among the marshy plants. Its head had been smashed or cut open, and she could see its little brain, open to the atmosphere. She'd seen a pig's brain before. It didn't look so different from her own. But this one was glittering. The shiny metallic sparkles were all over it, moving as if they were alive, or as if they wanted to be alive.

The sun was setting. Leahbelle stood again at the intersection of Redwood and the old highway that ran past her house. This time Gonzalo did look surprised to see her. He slowed, but went on past. She waved for him to stop, so he turned around and pulled over, but didn't get off the motorbike.

What's up? he said.

I need to show you something.

She opened up her bonnet.

What's the shiny stuff? she asked.

Gonzalo examined it, then shrugged.

Hard to say. Where'd you find it?

Down by the creek. Along the trail. The same stuff was all over the brain of a dead piglet. Like maybe it got inside the pig's head and killed it.

Locusts were getting louder in the Amish fields. In the Foodco fields there was just a kind of dead hum and the synchronized rustle of the plants. Gonzalo stared at her, visibly thinking. The motorbike made a kind of ticking noise while he idled there. Gonzalo had an interesting face, she thought, but she also figured he knew that some girls would think he was handsome.

Leahbelle didn't trust guys like Gonzalo.

Maybe it's the other way around, he said. Maybe it was inside the pig's brain and it got out.

She thought of Zeke trapped inside that mad scientist's bunker somewhere in Nebraska.

But what could it be? she asked.

Robots maybe. Tracking devices, surveillance systems. Agricultural control systems that got loose from their original hosts. I'd have to analyze it, but I won't take it back to the orphanage. Too risky. Put your bonnet in here.

He materialized a clear metallic container from somewhere, maybe inside his own body, and held it out to her.

Then where? she asked.

I know a place. But first, show me where you got it.

He smiled at Leahbelle. The smile was too much.

Climb aboard, he said.

She didn't.

You scared?

Not at all. I just don't like boys telling me what to do.

That's not very Amish.

Yeah, well. I've always been that way.

She made a motion with her hand.

Scootch up, she said.

She climbed aboard.

Speed changed the world. It changed the way things sounded and it changed her sense of being in control. In control of herself, of her body, of her space. She had to hang on tight to Gonzalo, and she wasn't wearing her bonnet. Her hair flew loose. She could sense the way he loved it—the speed of the motorbike, the motorbike itself—and she thought that it was crazy, just a little bit crazy, but she wasn't sure crazy was such a bad thing.

She had never before felt the wind in her hair like this.

There was no trace of the glittering substance in the dirt. It had burrowed deeper or moved on.

Or maybe somebody cleaned it up, said Gonzalo.

She took him to the shed where they'd taken the piglet's body.

I didn't think we should eat it, she said. But my father couldn't quite get to wasting all that meat.

Most of the glitter was gone from the piglet's brain, but a few sparkles remained. Gonzalo ejected a cable with a sharp blade from one of his mechanical fingers and prodded the brain. The sparkles lit up and slowly squirmed away. He cut into the piglet's side, a small rectangular incision. The chunk of meat had glitter inside.

Don't eat that meat, he said.

What is it?

I don't know. How many pigs do you have?

Just the mother and the one litter. Seven more piglets.

He looked absent for a moment, like he was counting the piglets inside his own daydreams.

Why have you been riding around here all the time? she asked.

How do you know what I do?

I hear you. I hear you all the time.

You have me under surveillance?

He laughed.

You might want a vet to take a look at those pigs, he said. Or maybe the rats, I'm sure they could figure it out.

I thought you were going to figure it out.

I'll take it to my lab tech, but you can't come along.

I never said I wanted to come along.

Take what you've got to the rats, he said. If it's a surveillance device, my lab tech will destroy it. If it's an infectious agent, it won't be able to escape from my fingertip or your container. But be careful. Don't carry it around more than you have to.

You're telling me what to do again.

He laughed.

You want my help, but I don't think you like me very much, he said.

That's not true.

He raised a mechanical finger in the air as if he was about to make an important point. The finger whirled like a drill.

Do they teach you about quantum entanglement in Amish schools? he asked.

No. What is it?

Well there's a bunch of different ways that systems can get entangled, said Gonzalo. Once that happens, entangled particles remain connected, and anything you do to one affects the other, even if they're separated by a huge distance.

Okay, said Leahbelle.

It's supposed to be what causes time, said Gonzalo. The mystery of time.

Why are you telling me this? Does this have something to do with the piglet's brain?

Time is just a side effect of increasing correlations, said Gonzalo. You have to be inside the universe to experience it. For an outside observer, it doesn't exist.

For God, said Leahbelle.

Gonzalo shrugged.

I just thought you'd think it was interesting, he said.

She did think it was interesting, but she didn't want to tell him that. She thought he was showing off.

You think I'm a bad influence, Gonzalo said. On him.

I don't even know you.

Don't worry, he said. You will.

The lights were out at the Miller farm, but Anna Miller was still sitting on the front porch, rocking, wearing her day clothes. She was becoming more nocturnal, Leahbelle figured.

Hi, Anna, said Leahbelle.

Leahbelle, said Anna.

They'd known each other their whole lives, but they'd never been friends.

I need to talk to the rats, Leahbelle said.

I figured, said Anna.

The entrance to the rats' underground lair was located in the ditch between the road and the Stoltzfus farm, about a half mile down the road toward Kalona. Anna made a gesture for Leahbelle to go first, so Leahbelle crouched and crawled into the narrow entrance of the tunnel for a few feet until it opened into a larger cave where she could stand. The cave was dimly lit with luminous living jellies stuck to the walls.

A shadow scurried along the wall, and she jumped.

Oh, she said.

It was Willard. She still couldn't quite get over the creepiness of the rats. Whatever it was that gave her the creeps. Their smell? The way they moved? Anna scurried in after her.

Is Lilith here? Pazuza? Leahbelle asked, and Anna translated. Anna had volunteered to take the medicine—pills or machines or DNA fragments or whatever it was, Leahbelle wasn't sure—that allowed her to understand the rats. It was the sort of thing that Leahbelle imagined herself doing or that she thought other people imagined she might do—take a leap into the unknown. When it came down to it, however, the thought of becoming part rat was too much. Whatever Anna said was too high-pitched for Leahbelle to hear it, but she could see Anna make an unattractive grimace every time she squeaked.

They've gone to Nebraska, said Willard. For the rescue tomorrow. And then to Colorado.

Leahbelle didn't know Willard. He was less obliging and gloomier than Pazuza and Lilith, like a stern Amish bishop. She wanted to tweak his little tail.

I'm in charge here, he said.

For the first time, it occurred to her that the rats weren't actually one thing. They must be like the Amish, she realized: a group of individuals with different opinions, different levels of authority, different personalities.

Tomorrow, said Leahbelle. Will you come to me, please? As soon as you know if Zeke is safe.

Of course, said Willard. I'll come personally. I know where to find you.

The rats seemed to know everything.

I need to show you something, she told him. It was inside one of our piglets and in the dirt. I'm wondering if you can tell me what it is.

She presented the container with her bonnet and the dirt and the sparkly stuff still inside.

The piglet is dead, she said.

He examined it for a moment and then stepped back. A couple of smaller rats scurried out of a side tunnel and collected it in a larger container they snapped tightly shut. Leahbelle wondered who put Willard in charge. Who put Willard and Lilith and Pazuza in charge.

We'll check it out, said Willard. We'll let you know.

Leahbelle found herself wide awake still at two o'clock that morning. At three she got out of bed and went out to sit in the tree. It was quiet. She went in and tried to sleep again, but soon it was time for chores. By that afternoon she was beginning to feel really weird, even before the government exterminators showed up at the door.

There were two of them, both mostly female, one young and one older. The older one wore a red cap, the younger one a blue scarf.

We're here to enlist your help in the campaign to eradicate the Genetically Modified Rats, the younger one told Leahbelle and her father.

As you have probably heard, the older one said, these mutants are a great risk to the health and food security of the nation.

We know the GMRs are active in this area, the younger one said. We'll need access to your farm to set traps and poisons and to utilize our cyborg-feline scouts.

We haven't seen a single rat, said Leahbelle. Not on our farm.

Just because you haven't seen them, said the younger exterminator, it doesn't mean that they aren't there.

We know they're there, said the older one.

Here, there, everywhere, said the younger one. They hide in the dark. They build tunnels. They scurry away from humans, and yet, in general, the sighting of one rat usually indicates the presence of dozens.

The exterminators were creepy. The red cap and the blue scarf just called attention to the weird emptiness of their eyes. As if they didn't have souls, she thought. Leahbelle found it difficult to focus on what they were saying. Whatever it was they wanted from her, she felt sure that she should do exactly the opposite.

We have always had an understanding with the powers that be, said Leahbelle's father, that we would be left alone. I don't know that we'll participate in any government campaigns. It goes against our beliefs.

Then we'll be forced to take action, said the younger one.

We are asking for very little in the way of your cooperation, the older one said. Just an hour or so to do some reconnaissance and set some traps, and we'll be on our way.

And if we say no? said Leahbelle.

We'll return with a court order, said the older exterminator.

And weaponized agents, said the younger one.

I'll need to discuss it with the community, said Leahbelle's father.

You have seventy-two hours.

What would it be like to go crazy, Leahbelle wondered. Never before had it seemed like such an easy thing. Such a small gap between normal everyday life and total chaos. Leahbelle couldn't just sit around waiting for the exterminators to come back. She couldn't do nothing while she waited for Willard to come tell her if Zeke was free or imprisoned, alive or dead. She hitched up Fern to the one-seater buggy and rode the buggy out to the ruined orphanage, the East Liberty Home for Boys. Bot-cars zipped past her, and one particular dragonfly drone flew alongside her, as if it was watching her, until something larger swooped down and swallowed it. A flexi-screen or a bot-bird.

She figured Willard would know where to find her anyway. The government probably knew too. Maybe even Gonzalo. Thank God her parents were Amish, she thought. At least they couldn't keep her under constant surveillance.

It was dusk. She hitched Fern up by the creek and stepped carefully across the crumbling bridge that led to the ruined orphanage.

Well, well, well, came a voice from the darkness.

It was the girl, Gonzalo's friend or comrade or whatever, Aeren.

I'm here to see Gonzalo, Leahbelle said.

No shit. Gonzalo isn't here.

Where is he?

Hard to say. Gonzalo gets around.

Around and around and around, thought Leahbelle. He was orbiting or maybe spinning erratically. But maybe if you could see him from above, the pattern of his movements would mean something. Maybe it would be a message from God.

She didn't know where this thought came from. Craziness.

You ride horses? asked Aeren. Or just buggies?

I've ridden, said Leahbelle. But those aren't the kind of horses we keep.

I know, said Aeren.

She stepped closer to Leahbelle, and Leahbelle could see that her face was kinder than her voice, that she was more of a child than she wanted anyone to know. A lost child, perhaps, wearing a synthetic leathery jacket that was so black it was like a hole in space and time.

It's cruel, I think, said Aeren. Riding a horse. I hate the politics of it—breaking the horse, dominance, obedience, all of that. But I still love riding. It's been a while.

You think it's cruel? said Leahbelle. It's a horse. It's what a horse is for.

Aeren shook her head.

A horse is designed, has become designed, over hundreds of thousands of years, to run free, said Aeren. Without saddles, bridles, whips, or people up on top.

Aeren stepped closer.

Like a girl, she said. Exactly like a girl.

Leahbelle blushed, she didn't know why.

But what are we standing around in the dark for? Come on into the compound.

Aeren led her across the yard full of odd sculptures and rusting metal, through several dark rooms and hallways, and down into the basement and an interior room where two older boys were sitting in the dim light, playing some sort of game with a hologram between them.

This is Crash and Spider, said Aeren. Guys, it's Leahbelle.

Crash was skinny and bald with strange googly eyes that didn't seem to focus much. Spider was short and muscly and bearded, with bright orange hair and a tail like a monkey's that made lazy circular movements, as if it was restlessly looking for something to do. They both grunted at her, barely looking up from the hologram.

Aeren knows my name, Leahbelle realized.

Where's Helios? asked Aeren.

Down below, said Spider. Working with the cadavers.

Leahbelle said, Cadavers?

For spare parts, said Aeren.

Leahbelle decided to just pretend she understood what that meant.

Gonzalo was doing some tests for me, she said. I was just wondering how it went.

Aeren took off her black jacket and tossed it into a corner of the room. The darkness of that jacket had to be quantum or something. It seemed to bend the space around it, remove the light. It looked like a cave had settled into the corner, a deep pit hiding something vicious with razor-sharp teeth.

Some sort of agricultural robots most likely, said Aeren. Introduced into the pork bushes for crop control.

She was wearing a white tank top that showed off her muscles. She looked more like a person that way, not so much like an idea.

Not so surprising if they found their way into an old-fashioned pig, she said.

Gonzalo told you that?

On the other hand, that might just be what it's supposed to look like. Could be doing surveillance. Could have some other military purpose we can't figure out yet. Or maybe they're purposefully destroying your livestock as part of the Amish Eradication Campaign.

Amish Eradication Campaign, repeated Leahbelle.

AEC, said Aeren. That's what they actually call it. We've deciphered some of their communications.

They, said Leahbelle. Who is *they*?

The government, said Aeren. Foodco. Same thing, more or less.

It was too much information. Her brain couldn't process it all. But then again, it could. Leahbelle trusted her own mind, most days. I'm Leahbelle, she reminded herself.

I have to go, she said. Thank you, Aeren. I'll see you again. I know the way.

She made her way up the stairs, out through the yard full of sculptures and clicking motion detectors, and back across the ruined bridge.

Fern had collapsed, right there where she'd been standing. She wasn't dead, but dying, panic in her eyes. A seam in the horse's forehead had opened, and Leahbelle could see a metallic liquid oozing out.

And little sparkles. Fern was looking straight at her, as if begging her to help. It was the worst look Leahbelle had ever received.

She ripped a sleeve off her dress and tied it around Fern's eyes as a blindfold. She grabbed the biggest rock she could find and she raised it with all her strength, brought it crashing down to smash Fern's head. Again and again. She made sure that Fern was dead, and then she walked back to the road, toward home. And then she began to run.

TWO

Leahbelle was miles from home. She ran and she ran, and then she stopped running and knelt by the ditch at the side of the road and threw up.

I need to calm down, she told herself. No point in panicking.

She walked, and as she walked she became convinced that Zeke was dead, that the piglet and Fern were just signs or precursors, an escalating series, one, two, three: piglet, Fern, Zeke. As soon as Willard could find her, he would tell her that Zeke was dead.

She began running again, and she heard the familiar rumble of the engine, the sound of technology and the world and the future tightening its noose around her throat. This is the future, she thought. Desperate, suffering, meaningless, and suffocating. It was bearing down on her, and she stopped and looked up, and there was an Amish boy sitting on a motorbike, waiting for her to climb aboard.

It's Zeke's ghost, she thought, stupidly, crazily. He smiled at her, but in a different way this time, like she was a skittish colt and he was trying to calm her down.

It wasn't Zeke's ghost. It wasn't even an Amish boy. It was Gonzalo, wearing an Amish shirt and pants and suspenders. He'd even cut his hair in an Amish style, or maybe it was a wig, or maybe he could grow some sort of pseudo-hair whenever he wanted with his implants and whatnot. Who knew? She felt a profound relief at seeing his face, as if he was the only friend she had left in the world. At the same time, his outfit enraged her.

Why are you wearing those clothes?

Doing some reconnaissance, he said. You'd be surprised how much you can get away with when people think you're Amish.

I am Amish.

Right, but you don't have anything to compare your experience with. The world trusts you, or at least it's barely threatened by your existence, so you think that's how it is for everyone, right?

Where'd you get that outfit?

Where do you think.

Her hallucination had been true, in a sense. These were Zeke's clothes—they had faded and creased in response to his body, they contained his history in some way—like a ghost or a spirit, an empty shell where a boy had once been. But now another boy had stepped in to take his place.

I have to get home, she said. I have to get my family. We have to get out of here.

Leahbelle, said Gonzalo.

What?

Take a deep breath.

She took a deep breath. And then another.

Why didn't you tell me? she asked. About the Amish Eradication Campaign?

What's the news? asked Gonzalo. The rats already told you the government was out to get you.

No, no, that's not true, she said. They told us they wanted our land. They never told us they had a plan to exterminate us. Plus, they're rats. It's different. You're …

Not human either, said Gonzalo.

Oh, whatever, you're close enough, said Leahbelle. Post-this, post-that, fancy gadgets and silly toys all over your body, you're just a boy, Gonzalo. You're just a kid.

Nothing's changed, said Gonzalo. Eradication and extermination, not the same thing.

They killed Fern. That glitter stuff—what if it gets inside me or my family? What if it already is?

It's in the pork bushes, said Gonzalo. We sampled the bushes from the Foodco fields. It's not in all of them, but a few. Experimental, maybe. Maybe tested for human safety.

It got out of their crops, said Leahbelle.

Or maybe that's all just what they want us to think, Gonzalo said. Still, I don't think they're trying to kill your family with tiny robots. Wouldn't make sense. There's easier ways to do that, if they want.

Great.

It might be aimed at the rats. It might be aimed at my organization. It might be aimed at your animals.

I don't understand, Leahbelle said. What can I do?

Climb aboard, said Gonzalo. I'll take you home. You need to sleep.

I can't sleep.

You can sleep, said Gonzalo. Trust me.

For some reason, she did.

He parked just down the road from her house and let her off.

I'll come by tomorrow, he said. I need you to take me to the rats.

Okay.

She was going to ask him why, but decided it didn't matter.

You like music, right? he said.

You know a lot about me.

Just what Zeke said. Here, listen to this.

He handed her some earbuds that seemed to be connected to his chest.

Just what *isn't* connected to your body? she asked.

Wireless isn't secure.

She didn't know what he was talking about.

Just listen, he said.

The music was beautiful. It was sad, and yet it soothed her. It was energetic, and yet she felt more and more relaxed. It seemed like more than music. Like love or dreams, and it seemed to come from inside Gonzalo's body.

It ended. She hummed the melody, the part where it changed most movingly. She didn't want to forget it.

Go to bed, said Gonzalo. Everything else can wait until morning. You'll sleep now.

He gave her a hug and actually kissed her forehead. Like I'm a sleepy child, she thought. It could have offended her. But she *was* a sleepy child, she realized, and soon she was in her nightclothes and fast asleep.

She dreamed about History. It wasn't a scary dream, but History was the name of a monster. In the dream, this mutant creature covered with eyes and udders and beards lived in a dank cave on a mountain. Men from the community climbed the mountain and then descended into the cave to feed the monster stories about the past, from the Bible and the genealogies and *The Martyr's Mirror*. Leahbelle was napping next to History, but she was also wide awake. After loudly digesting the pages from all these books, History would lean over and whisper something into Leahbelle's ear, but the whispers were toxic smoke. She was calm in the dream, none of this disturbed her, but she also realized that if she didn't find History something different to eat, the toxic smoke from his digestion was going to kill her, maybe kill everyone. It occurred to her that the music from Gonzalo's heart was more nutritious.

She woke with the feeling that her hand was being licked. Her hand *was* being licked. It was Willard.

He stood there gazing at her. How long had he been there, she wondered. She wondered how he'd gotten into the house. The rats were getting into everything.

Not the rats, plural. Just Willard. Willard was alone, with nobody to translate, but he handed her a note.

Zeke Yoder is safe and free, it said. He'll be in Longmont by morning.

After she read it, Willard ate the note and disappeared. It reminded her of something, but she couldn't put her finger on it, the way he chewed up information and the way he disappeared into the darkness like smoke. It didn't matter. Zeke was okay, everything would be okay. Leahbelle fell into a deep and dreamless sleep.

In the morning, she felt calm but energetic. She didn't think she'd ever had such a restful sleep. She wanted to see Gonzalo again, and she wanted to listen to more of that music. Her own stupid grin seemed profound somehow. Her father's stupid grin, however, was making her crazy.

The sleeve was ripped off her dress. She knew what she'd done to Fern, but she couldn't quite remember it. She explained to her father, but he didn't seem to understand either. She told him about the Amish Eradication Campaign, but he snorted like it was a joke. It was like he refused to understand.

We need to leave here, she told him. We can't wait for Zeke to come back. We can travel through the tunnel like he did.

Silly, said her father.

He ruffled her hair.

My little baby girl, he said.

They're trying to kill us. The exterminators, they're probably a part of this. They want us all dead. The rats and the Amish both.

I'll speak with some of the menfolk after church, her father said. The menfolk will help us decide whether or not to cooperate with the exterminators.

Leahbelle rolled her eyes. Her father didn't seem to notice.

We will pray on it, he said.

For the first time in her life, the familiar idea seemed crazy. When had God ever helped them or even told them what to do? It seemed to her that God was like a nice feeling—a feeling of peace, a feeling that everything was small and insignificant, a feeling that time would wash all the pain and suffering away. But what did that have to do with a murderous government, the death of their livestock, the coming war? If God had a plan, it didn't seem like their safety or well-being was a part of that plan.

It was Sunday. After chores and church services over at the Fisher farm, the menfolk stood in a circle and gossiped and shuffled their feet. Nothing was decided, as far as Leahbelle could tell. Afterward, back at home, Leahbelle's mother and the older kids sat in the front room playing Bible Lotto. Her father sat with a puzzle. Aunt Ethel and her cousins would be over to visit in the afternoon. Everyone was acting like it was a perfectly normal day.

When she first noticed the approaching rumble of Gonzalo's motorbike, however, her whole body felt suffused with a warmth and happiness that was completely unfamiliar to her.

It feels like love, she thought. Like they talk about love.

She was probably just confusing her intense relief that Zeke was safe with some other feeling. She wasn't even sure she liked Gonzalo. But when he pulled up in front of the house and said, Climb aboard, flashed that ridiculous smile, she felt even warmer and happier.

You changed your outfit, she said.

It was just a disguise.

You sure you don't want to be Amish for real?

She was trying to tease him. His Amish hair was gone, his head shaved, scalp tattoos visible again.

Disguises are lonesome, he said.

More praying, less rumbling, she said. That's all you'd have to do.

Too many noises keep me awake at night, he said.

It suited you, she said.

The shirt he was wearing now seemed like it was made of some sort of flexible metal, luminous and almost black. It looked like it would be cold to the touch.

Cries and screams, he said.

Made you look more honest and peaceful, she insisted.

Disguises are lonesome, he said again. I'm not like you. I need to get some of this crap out of my brain.

What kind of crap is in your brain?

The violence of liberation. Disorder as a strategy. And what happens to the whole freaking earth.

Violence, she said. Not a good idea.

She climbed on board the motorbike. The metallic shirt actually gave off a comforting warmth and a subtle but pleasing vibration.

Who's crying and screaming at your place at night?

Gonzalo shrugged.

Violence, passion, whatever it is.

Leahbelle held on tight. He rode her to Anna Miller's house just up the road, but for a minute she wrapped her arms around him, right there on his chest where the music had come from.

Anna Miller's mother said that Anna was sleeping. In a dark corner of the barn. In the straw.

I guess she's a real night creature now, her mother said, and shrugged.

Leahbelle tried to wake her as gently as possible, but Anna hissed at her, bared her teeth, and scurried away.

Oh, you again, she said. It's too early. Everyone's asleep.

We'll wake them up, Gonzalo said.

Anna looked Gonzalo over, a little too closely. She stood up, brushed herself off, and put her bonnet on, leaving a wisp of her curly hair peeking out from underneath, in a way Leahbelle knew Anna's mother wouldn't approve.

For you, I'll do it, she said, staring at Gonzalo shamelessly. She didn't even look Leahbelle's way.

In the rats' tunnel, Willard was almost as disgruntled as Anna.

He needs a minute, Anna said.

Willard vanished down a narrow tunnel. While they sat there in the cave, waiting for Willard to return, Leahbelle watched the luminous living jellies throbbing on the wall. She remembered her dream about History. The colony was all around her now, thousands of them, more and more babies born every day, all of them burrowed into crevices in the earth, sleeping and dreaming.

Do rats dream? she said out loud.

You asking me? said Anna.

Do you know?

They dream, said Anna.

Leahbelle remembered sitting up with Zeke the night before he left, listening to Lilith tell the history of the colony. Why had she assumed that the opinions of the leaders was the opinion of all the rats? Why had she assumed that the history they told was the history the younger rats would tell? What had been left out?

Anna had scooched up next to Gonzalo and looked to be *sniffing* him. She said something Leahbelle couldn't hear, and Gonzalo laughed.

Gonzalo, said Leahbelle.

Yeah?

She couldn't think of anything to say. The idea of Gonzalo had seemed so pleasant and warm, but now he just seemed gloomy and annoyed and easily distracted. Willard returned, looking more annoyed than Gonzalo. He greeted them rather formally and got right to business. Even after Leahbelle explained about the exterminators, he delivered his information through Anna briefly and directly.

Cooperate with the exterminators, he said. We're in no danger from their traps, poisons, or cyborgs, and they must know this. We've constructed highly visible entrances to our tunnels, and yet they haven't been breached by surveillance devices or infectious agents. If they want access to your farm, it isn't about us. It's about you and your family and the Amish community.

They wouldn't need access just to keep them under surveillance, Gonzalo said.

True, Willard said. Perhaps they're looking for an excuse for military action. An excuse to appropriate the land. This is why you should cooperate.

The government can see and hear whatever they want with their drones, Gonzalo told Leahbelle.

As for the substance you brought us, Willard continued, it is primarily an agricultural control element designed to coordinate bio-activities within the pork bushes. There are secondary capabilities, however, for both intra-corporeal surveillance and control, and for low-level detonation.

It can read minds and control behavior, said Gonzalo. And blow things up?

If it gets inside, yes, said Willard.

I need to get home, said Leahbelle. I need to warn my father.

You go on, said Gonzalo. I need to discuss some other issues with Willard.

Anna Miller seemed delighted at the idea of being left alone with Gonzalo and the rats. Who cares, she told herself. She didn't even like Gonzalo.

Come by when you're done, she said. I need to talk to you, okay?

It was after supper, after she'd spent an hour trying to convince her father that cooperation was the only possible choice, that she began to wonder not only what Gonzalo might be doing with Anna Miller, but what it was that he needed to discuss with the rats.

Was it really true that the government wasn't worried about the rats? Had the doctors at Absolute Genomics assured the government that the rats' auto-destruct feature would take care of them? She didn't quite trust Willard. She wasn't sure if she trusted Gonzalo. What had his music really done to her? She needed to talk to somebody she trusted completely. But Zeke Yoder was six hundred miles away.

Everyone else was asleep when she finally heard the motorbike approaching. She was waiting on the front porch, and she hurried out to the road.

Where have you been? she demanded.

Busy, he said. Sorry. There's a lot going on.

A lot going on. Right. I can imagine.

I'm not sure you can, said Gonzalo.

What's Anna Miller doing?

You two don't like each other much, do you?

We've known each other our whole lives.

And?

And she liked Zeke, said Leahbelle.

Everybody likes Zeke Yoder, said Gonzalo. Why is that?

He's jealous, too, thought Leahbelle. But there was something backward about it, something that didn't make sense.

Zeke is kind and gentle, said Leahbelle, and handsome and smart. He'll make somebody a fine husband.

Lots of people are kind and handsome and smart. I don't think that's it.

Really?

I think Zeke seems like he's wandering around in a dream half the time, said Gonzalo. So his head seems like a really weird place to be. Everybody wants to walk inside his head, take a look around. Join the party.

That's a really weird thing to say.

But is it true? You think?

You aren't kind and gentle at all, said Leahbelle.

So you think I'm handsome and smart.

I didn't say that.

What's so important it couldn't wait until tomorrow, anyway?

What's so important? What's so important?

He just sat there on his motorbike, waiting for her to finish.

I need your help, she said.

I know, he said. I'm going to get the tools to check out your live-stock. Check out you and your family too.

He'd changed his shirt, she realized. It was plain and black and kind of green.

My father doesn't want to cooperate, she said.

I don't know what to do about that, said Gonzalo.

She wanted to slap him, she didn't know why. Violence. Where did it come from?

Oh, forget it, said Leahbelle. I just need a good night's sleep. Let me listen to some more of that music.

Gonzalo gave her a funny look.

Better not, he said finally. It's pretty addictive.

Leahbelle felt an intense rage, and then it was as if a strange flood of information was revealing a completely different reality. Gonzalo was her enemy.

Some people are more susceptible than others, he said.

I've only done it once, she said. I'm not an addict. Come on.

I get it, said Gonzalo.

Get what? Just let me listen. Now. Please.

He just stood there thinking, or pretending to think. What was actually going on in that head, she had no idea. Maybe nothing.

Kind and gentle is for people who never had to fight to survive, said Gonzalo finally. We'll see how that's working out next time we see Zeke Yoder, I guess.

Gonzalo.

No, he said.

She didn't love him. What had she been thinking? She hated him. He was like all the rest of the men and the boys.

Stupid, she said. Controlling. Egotistical. Childlike.

I'll give you a pill instead, he said. It'll help you sleep and help with the cravings.

Cravings? You …

But he slipped a yellow pill into her hand and sped away on the motorbike before she could finish the thought.

THREE

The next day, Leahbelle still felt restless, but clearer in the head. She couldn't understand why she'd been so angry. She was under a lot of stress, she reminded herself. The day passed in a dull haze of chores and silly games with the children.

After supper, her father headed off in the large buggy to meet with the bishops and the other men from the community. Shortly after he left, she heard the motorbike and hurried out front. But it wasn't Gonzalo on the bike.

Hey, girly girl, said Aeren.

She'd fastened the one-seater buggy to the motorbike and towed it along.

Girly girl? said Leahbelle.

You don't like my nickname for you?

I don't think of myself as very girly, said Leahbelle. Some even call me a tomboy.

Maybe you're not girly by Amish standards, said Aeren, but for the rest of us you read like a total femme.

Leahbelle sighed. She unhitched the buggy and parked it in the drive.

You people confuse me, she said.

Where I'm from, Aeren said, the girls are all tough and ornery.

Really, *all* of them? Where's that?

Nothing matters, their families are shit, the boys are another species, brain-dead and obsessed with animated porn-games, and so the girls are all free.

That doesn't sound very free.

There's no place as hopeless and butch as the ruins of Tulsa.

So why'd you leave?

Aeren gave a little snort.

Gonzalo asked me to bring you this pill, she said. And to tell you he'll come by to check out the animals as soon as he can.

Where is Gonzalo?

Busy, said Aeren.

A busy little bee, said Leahbelle.

Gonzalo's a good comrade, said Aeren. But probably not a guy any girl would want to get hung up on.

Nobody's hung up on anyone. There's a lot going on. I need to talk to him, that's all.

There's a lot going on, Aeren agreed.

That's it?

That's it, said Aeren.

She handed Leahbelle the pill. It was lemony yellow.

I already had one of these.

You looking for something to do? Aeren asked. I'll take you for a ride.

Maybe, said Leahbelle. So what was it like there in the ruins of Tulsa?

Aeren made a sour face.

Like, she said. Some things aren't *like* anything. Some things don't resemble anything else.

I've never been outside Iowa, said Leahbelle.

I know, said Aeren.

Leahbelle just waited.

Bad tremors, said Aeren. Bad storms, bad air, bad heat. Bad mom.

Then I guess it was bad.

The worst, said Aeren. Are you getting on, or what?

She rode smoother than Gonzalo, but just as fast. Holding onto Aeren felt nice, without the nagging question of sin. Leahbelle discovered that she was growing accustomed to speed. Maybe speed was addictive, like the music, maybe the pills, like everything the English did, every sin and vanity and pleasure, the world itself. Was the world an addiction? Was the world like a drug? She'd heard stories of Amish kids who got into everything during Rumspringa: sex and tech and interactive holographic simulations and fluid genders. The Kalona Amish didn't let their children run around like that. But up and down the hills, racing across the back roads, the familiar land-scape of Leahbelle's life was made new and exciting. Like all you needed to change the tired old world into something beautiful was a new perspective. Distance and speed.

Aeren pulled over in Riverside next to the commemorative hologram of the Starship Enterprise. The hologram shimmered; it was surrounded by colorful planets and infinity. People came here every year to celebrate the birthday of a famous space explorer, a man named Captain Kirk. Aeren was watching little drones and bot-birds fly through the air.

I miss secrets, she said.

Secrets?

I get tired of them watching and listening all the time.

Them, said Leahbelle. Who's *them*?

Nobody's happy this way, said Aeren.

Really, nobody?

People want things, that's all. Impossible things, things that aren't real. They've figured all that out, how to give us nothing, so that we keep on wanting something. They know that I want to destroy them, and it doesn't bother them at all.

You think the government is watching you?

They're watching everyone. They're watching you, too. Everything goes through the Grid into the supercomputer out in Utah. This conversation is being fed into it right now, and it's being analyzed by machines, and maybe one day they'll have enough little red flags in my file and the algorithm decides to kill me. Or maybe they'll just sell me some sort of brainwave simulacra of femme revolution or butch apocalypse to keep me pacified and I won't be lonely anymore and that's it. I'm done.

You make it sound like Earth is just some kind of prison, said Leahbelle.

Everyone on Earth is lonely. The alternatives are even worse.

What are the alternatives?

One of the colorful planets in the hologram exploded into meteors and dust. Another one leaked a sort of mist.

You wanna be a part of my femme revolution?

I don't even know what that means, said Leahbelle.

She watched the greenish mist slowly swirl into the cosmos like a poisonous gas.

We wouldn't love ourselves only in the mirror of our own impossible desires anymore, said Aeren. We wouldn't need to own each other unless we wanted to.

What about out there somewhere? asked Leahbelle. Mars or one of the moons.

They have a file on everyone, said Aeren. You can't escape from a modern prison.

What about this Captain Kirk?

You have to destroy it.

They say he spread freedom all over the universe.

He's not a real person, Leahbelle.

What are you talking about? He was born here. They celebrate his birthday every year.

In the future. In 2228.

Nothing made any sense to Leahbelle. The English world was stranger than she'd imagined.

I'll take you home, said Aeren. Climb aboard.

At breakfast, her father told her what the menfolk had decided. They would refuse to cooperate with the exterminators.

Father, no. They'll kill us. They'll kill us all.

If that is God's will.

Her whole life long, until now, she'd been able to get her father to do pretty much whatever she wanted. Now she felt doomed.

The deadline came and passed that afternoon, and the exterminators didn't show up. Leahbelle wasn't sure if that was a good thing or a bad thing. But she was calmer and calmer. She had to be calm. She could see that she'd been acting crazy with Gonzalo.

After supper, she went out back to shoot at dragonfly drones with her slingshot. They'd always just seemed like annoying pests in the past; she'd never imagined they were watching her or listening to her, conspiring with someone to kill her.

She only got one of them.

Just after dark, from her perch in the tree, she saw Anna Miller walking along the road toward her. The glow from the data vapor overhead was brighter than usual tonight, and she could see a small creature rustling the grasses beside Anna as she cut through the ditch and back up across the neighboring field. It was Willard.

Leahbelle jumped down from the tree.

There's been a murder, Anna said.

Leahbelle didn't understand. The word *murder* didn't make sense. It was the strangest word, bloodless and moist.

Zeke, she said.

Willard held up a paw to silence her.

Anna explained that an Amish boy was wanted for murder in Colorado. His robot had incinerated a Gstate engineer with its death ray. Nobody knew the boy's name, not yet.

Where is he? asked Leahbelle.

We are in communication with the grandmother, said Willard. They are safe for now. It is best that you not know any more than that.

She didn't like the idea that ignorance was good for her, but she didn't want the government opening up her brain somehow either to find out where Zeke was hiding.

The sky overhead brightened and dimmed again.

My father won't cooperate with the exterminators, Leahbelle told him.

That's a problem, said Willard.

Yes. What should I do?

Willard typed something into a flexi-screen and handed it to her. It was filled with sentences she could only read from a very precise angle, words that disappeared as soon as she read them. In a few weeks, it said, if everything went according to plan, a window of possibilities would open up. One option, in order to get to that point, was to go into hiding. On her own or with as many Amish as she could convince to come with her. In the rats' tunnels or in the unmonitored ruins of the former retail world.

I don't know anything about surviving in English ruins, said Leahbelle.

Perhaps Gonzalo could help you with that, said Willard.

Where is your friend Gonzalo anyway? Anna asked Leahbelle.

Probably riding around in circles, said Leahbelle.

She turned back to the flexi-screen. Another option: she could disobey her father and talk to the exterminators directly and try to appease them.

Or, option #3, she could simply wait and see what developed.

While some sort of action from the government was almost certain, the device told her, the timing was impossible to predict. The rats were keeping abreast of the anti-Amish propaganda being spread through popular culture and the news. There'd been a slight uptick in the juxtaposition of the words *Amish* and *terror*, the phrase *radical Amish*, and crime show villains with beards and hats and suspenders. But so far it hadn't reached the level that would suggest imminent action.

As much as she resented the rules and the prying eyes of all the busybodies in the Amish community, she'd never seriously imagined that she might leave, as others had done, and live in the darkness and terror outside. Leahbelle knew she wouldn't go into hiding without her family. She would never abandon her parents or her brothers and sisters.

Will you update me tomorrow? she asked.

Certainly, said Willard. One more thing. There is a letter for you.

He handed her an envelope. It was from Zeke.

Isn't that sweet, said Anna. Does Zeke know what you're up to back here with your new *friend?*

Leahbelle tucked the letter into the waist of her apron and handed Willard his flexi-screen.

Goodbye, Willard.

She turned and went into the house.

She had just opened the letter with her mother's letter opener when she heard the motorbike out front.

You gonna stab me with that thing? Gonzalo asked her.

I'm not like you, she said.

Violent, he said. Crazy? Full of sin?

Everybody's full of sin, she said.

You got that right.

He'd brought a diagnostic imaging device he could use to look inside the livestock. The wand created a light ring he would pass over each animal, creating a holographic image with the insides visible. Sailor and Lady, the other horses, were clear. While he checked the piglets, she read Zeke's letter by the dim glow from the wand.

> *Dear Leahbelle,*
> *I don't know if you will ever read this letter, as I'm currently imprisoned by Dr. Brockton, and I don't know if I'll ever get free.*

She watches everything I do and seems to be unaffected by the suffering she is causing. But perhaps this isn't so. She doesn't have a heart, but I don't believe that means she can't have sympathy for a conscious being under her control. As for me, I'm going crazy it feels like, but I think about you, out there on the farm, free and mobile under the sky, in the tree, on the road, moving about, and it makes me feel better. If I never see the sky again on Earth, I trust that I will when I'm dead and in heaven. But I don't really know if that's how it works. Dr. Brockton refers to my "silly folk superstitions," and while I don't think Dr. Brockton is as smart as she wants to be, it's hard not to doubt when all you can see is white walls and white floors and white ceilings that stretch on to infinity.

Grandma is doing fine. She is reading a lot, she's into political theory these days.

I was going to write you about all the things I saw and experienced out here in the world. But I've seen the tunnel and the darkness, and for a minute the wide empty plains and some buffalo, and then some robots, some mist, and this horrible white basement. And that is all.

Despite the anguish that my confinement causes me, the sleeplessness and headaches, the craziness and upset stomach caused by my confinement, I hope that you are safe and well and that the Amish community, with all its unique genetic information, is also safe and well. I have asked Gonzalo to watch out for you. Maybe I should have asked him to watch out for me. If he'd like to come smash his way into this basement and rescue me, that would be fine. Please tell him that I need to see him again. It's very important.

I have these dreams.

I know that I will see you again and I must believe it, Leahbelle, because you are my heart. I'm wandering around like Dr. Brockton—well, maybe pacing in this depressing room is more accurate than "wandering"—separated from my heart. I guess my heart's supposed to belong to Jesus or whatnot. But nothing seems so simple. Good and evil and all that. Do I even have free will? Does anyone? You do, I'm pretty sure. Not so sure about the rest of us. The rats? Are they acting on their own or just doing what the doctors designed them to do?

The letter became more and more rambling and erratic. It described dreams about chess games and dreams about flight, more philosophical digressions about the nature of freedom and the human mind, old movies, and someone named Jello. He began using the word *smash* in almost every sentence. He was wanting to smash everything he could name, it seemed.

> *Now the doctor's given me some pink powder. I don't know if I'm human or if I ever was. Set the animals free, smash all the cages, because I'm just one of them. You see, my thoughts are ... like that. Unfinished and smashed up and all over the place. They want to gallop off the page and smash against the wall. You need to find your music. I need to find my sky. I hope that what we long for isn't just some kind of a trap. Somebody somewhere must know everything, but I am pretty sure that the more you know, the less you understand.*
>
> *Let me out! Let me out, Dr. Brockton! I'll smash you. You're hurting me.*

At the bottom of the page, the writing actually ran off the page and became so messy and erratic that she could only decipher a few words: *Jello, bones, apocalypse*, and something that looked like *alphabetical*. Then, at the bottom, in clear script:

> *PS I am free now and I'll try to get you the letter. I miss you.*
> *Love, Zeke Yoder.*

It was cute that he wrote *Yoder*, as if she might confuse him with some other Zeke. It annoyed her that he imagined Gonzalo rescuing him, but not her—as if only boys could smash things. It worried her that he'd been feeling even crazier than she had. And it touched her that he told her to find her music, that he called her his heart, and that even so far away, trapped in a basement, he seemed to be traveling the same kind of journey she was and receiving the same kind of messages—like those entangled particles Gonzalo had told her about.

All of the piglets were clear but one. She and Gonzalo quarantined it in an old cage a bit further out that her father had used for his puppy mill. Like many of her father's business ideas, that one had failed. Nobody wanted the old-fashioned dogs anymore, they wanted dogs that glowed in the dark or spoke a few words or had indestructible heads. Gonzalo gave Leahbelle some animal pain medicine so that she could put the piglet out of its misery when the time came. She tucked it into her apron pocket along with the yellow pill.

Thank you, she told him.

No problem.

I mean for the other night. For keeping me away from the music.

He shrugged.

My fault, he said. It can be really addictive. I didn't think you'd be so sensitive.

That music, she said. Does it come from inside of you somehow?

Sort of, he said. It's a soporific program, but it makes use of my own heart rhythms and stuff. It doesn't have to be mine. Anyone could give you that kind of music.

I see. Still, it was smart to stay away.

Yeah, I didn't really want to.

Zeke asked you to watch out for me.

Yeah, it's no big deal.

They were far enough away from the house now that nobody could see them. Nobody from the family at least. The government or the rats, who knew?

It was sweet to send Aeren, Leahbelle said.

I didn't exactly *send* her.

No, I don't suppose Aeren likes to be *sent* anymore than I do.

Aeren likes you, Gonzalo said.

I like Aeren too.

Aeren *likes* you.

I don't know what you mean.

Really?

Oh, she realized. Yes, she did know what he meant. She blushed.

That letter I was reading, she said. It's from Zeke.

Yeah? What's good old Zeke Yoder got to say?

He wanted you to rescue him. He said he needs to see you again. It's very important.

That's it?

She thought he was trying to look like he didn't care.

The rest was for me, she said. And some crazy stuff. He's free now, so no need for the rescue.

Okay, said Gonzalo.

He waved the wand.

Now you, he said.

Ugh, no, said Leahbelle.

Come on. We gotta check you out.

It's like being naked.

It's nothing like being naked, said Gonzalo.

You probably would know.

The difference between a holographic X-ray and a naked body? he said. Yeah, I do know the difference. You can *touch* a naked body, it's warm …

Stop it.

… it kind of pulses, you can *squeeze* it or *rub* it or give it a little *smack* …

Stop it I said, said Leahbelle. I don't want to know about your smutty adventures.

He made a little smacking gesture with his real hand against the mechanical claw.

I don't want to know about your life, I don't care.

One of the tattoos on his scalp seemed to grow larger; it almost seemed as if it was about to burst into flame. She'd never seen the tattoos mutate before. Was he angry?

I haven't lived my life dressed in a plain shapeless bag and a bonnet, if that's what you mean. You think that makes me a bad, sinful person, fine.

He'd never talked to her like that before—like he cared what she thought about him.

But this is life or death, he said.

She was acting like a spoiled brat.

I'm sorry, she said. Do the test. Please.

There was a dim hum as the light passed over her, that was all.

It was strange to see this transparent image of herself, like her own ghost. Was this what her soul looked like? A hologram?

All clear, said Gonzalo. Now you need to check your family.

Gonzalo showed her how to use the wand.

I'll come back by tomorrow, he said, and check out your results.

After dinner the next noon, she played a game with the little ones, pretending the wand was the staff of Moses and she'd use it to bestow God's blessing if they could answer a quick Bible quiz. She made the questions easy enough that everyone got blessed. As far as she could see, none of the children showed any sign of infection.

She found her mother in the kitchen, staring out the window.

I need to do a quick test, she said. Make sure you don't have any of that glitter inside.

Inside? said her mother. Inside me?

Just to make sure, said Leahbelle. Don't worry, Mother, please. Nobody else has it. We just need to make sure.

She made the hologram and quickly looked it over.

Looks good, she said, although she wasn't actually sure. She'd need to show it to Gonzalo.

Where's Dad?

Napping, said her mother.

Perfect.

She walked quietly into his bedroom. He was stretched on his back, fully clothed, his mouth wide open, his beard rustling every time he snored. As she finished up, she heard the rumble of the motorbike outside. Her father stirred, so she hurried out to see Gonzalo.

Gonzalo took the wand from her and led her to the barn, but instead of inspecting the holograms, he changed the setting somehow and created a dark bubble of shadow around Leahbelle and himself. She could see the rest of the barn only dimly. Only her body and Gonzalo's were bright and clear and close. She didn't think she'd ever seen colors so bright, their skin so intensely warm and beautiful and vibrating.

What are you doing? she said. Let me out.

It's just a privacy bubble, said Gonzalo. As far as we know, there's no way to break the encryption. I have to tell you something.

He's going to kiss me, she thought. What am I going to do if he kisses me?

We're attacking the Grid, he said.

It took Leahbelle a moment to process that.

I don't know what that means. How can you attack the Grid?

In two weeks, said Gonzalo.

Who's this *we*?

A loose alliance of anti-government factions is coordinating attacks on the programming, on the material infrastructure, and on the coherence of the global network. The rats are involved, I'm involved, some old friends in Colorado, a lot of others I don't know.

That's why you were dressed like an Amish boy.

Yeah, that's part of it.

And what's the point?

The point is *time*. We're buying time. Time for a second wave of attacks. Time to replace the Grid's brainwashing and break through with real information.

Why are you telling me this?

I thought you should know.

Yeah, well Willard already told me. Pretty much. He said *a few weeks*.

Plus I have to leave for a while. I have some missions.

Okay. Whatever.

I won't be able to watch out for you.

I can watch out for myself.

I know.

He waved the wand and the privacy bubble disappeared. He pulled up the holograms of her mother and father. She noticed it before Gonzalo did—a shiny smudge floating in her father's brain.

We have to get him to a doctor, she said.

I don't think a doctor can do anything about that.

Don't be stupid. He'll die. They put it there, somebody can get it out.

He won't die, said Gonzalo.

It killed Fern. It killed the piglet. Willard said it can explode.

Animals and humans aren't the same thing, said Gonzalo. Think about it. It's in the crops. It's either designed to be eaten by humans or designed for us to think so.

Leahbelle thought she would scream. She needed to think clearly.

It's keeping watch on him, she said. From the inside. That's why the exterminators haven't come back. They already know.

Are you going to tell him?

I can't tell him.

Think, said Gonzalo. Has he shown any symptoms? Has he acted strange?

They're controlling him, she said.

Leahbelle could see it clearly. His refusal to cooperate—with the government and with her.

They don't want him to cooperate, she said. They want him to refuse.

That can't be good, said Gonzalo.

I need to talk to the men, said Leahbelle. Bring the wand. We need to talk to Zeke's father.

In the Yoder home, Zeke's father shook hands with Gonzalo but as if it caused him pain. Gonzalo was looking around at the furniture, the homey sayings in cross-stitch on the walls, the devotional books on the shelf, and the grandfather clock, as if memorizing every detail.

I would have expected my son to go gallivanting about with the English and their motorized vehicles, he said. But I thought better of you, Leahbelle.

Zeke's mother sat next to him with her hands in her lap.

I'm sure Leahbelle's got a good reason for whatever she does, she said. Leahbelle, tell us what's on your mind.

Gonzalo ran some medical tests for us, she said.

She explained about the piglet, about Fern, about the exterminators and the substance in her father's brain. Gonzalo stood quietly as she explained her theory that the government was manipulating her father.

It's true that he was quite forceful in arguing against cooperation, Zeke's father said. I'd never seen him like that. He isn't normally so ...

He seemed to be searching for a word that wouldn't be taken as an insult.

He's normally so easygoing, Zeke's mother offered. Never riled up.

Not so much one for serious discourse, Zeke's father said.

He likes to joke, doesn't he, said Zeke's mother. More than to argue.

That's just it, Leahbelle said. I'm sure it's because of the glitter in his brain. They want an excuse to take action against us, all of us. I'm sure of it.

Zeke's father pondered this conclusion.

It makes sense, said Zeke's mother. What can we do?

People will listen to you, Leahbelle said to Zeke's father. Everyone respects your opinion.

I'll talk to the men of the community, Zeke's father said. God will help me find the words, I'm sure. If I can convince the others, we can notify the government of our cooperation. We'll give them free rein to come and go as they please. Anything they want in their attempt to exterminate those critters.

Leahbelle wondered if he really believed what she said, or if part of him was just happy to be working against the rats.

At supper, Leahbelle's father was in such good spirits, so much like his usual self, that even she began to doubt the story she'd just told. Her father told stupid jokes, and her mother was the only one who laughed. It was so nice to see her mother smiling again, not so nervous. Their good humor filtered down to the children, the nine children gathered around the big table, gobbling up the ham loaf and potatoes, all on their best behavior. Ervin told of a lucky five-legged toad he'd found out by the windmill that afternoon, and Hannah shared some gossip she'd heard at the store in town, that Anna Miller's older sister Miriam was being courted by Richard Stoltzfus.

Everything seemed so normal.

It was while she was washing the dishes that it occurred to her that there might be another explanation she hadn't considered. What if the substance in her father's brain didn't come from the government at all? She was taking Willard's word for it, mostly. Gonzalo and Aeren, but how could they know? Maybe it only looked like a government plot. *Maybe that's what they want us to think,* Gonzalo was always saying. What if it had come from the rats? It was Willard who'd told her the government didn't care about the rats, but what if he was lying? They'd changed Zeke's grandmother and they'd changed Anna Miller. They knew how to do all kinds of complicated things. It was the rats who always said a war with the government was coming. It was the rats who seemed to want the war to come.

Then she thought about Zeke's letter. What if somebody else was controlling the rats? What if it was the doctors who made them? All of the possibilities began to make her dizzy. What if it was Gonzalo?

She whispered to her mother that she had to go out and take care of some things.

You be careful, her mother said, and gave her a hug. I know you can take care of yourself, but there are things in the world … things that none of us can comprehend.

Like how her mother understood so much when she seemed to understand so little, Leahbelle thought.

Don't you worry, Mom, she said.

She slipped out the back and walked up the road a ways and waited for Gonzalo.

FOUR

Gonzalo rode her straight out to the ruined orphanage. She had come to enjoy the speed of the motorbike, but if people spotted her riding around, they'd start talking.

The spot by the bridge where Fern had died was cleaned up. They'd incinerated the body and used a robot to dump the ashes in the Foodco fields. Aeren wasn't around. Nobody else was up and about either. Gonzalo took her to the top of the building, what used to be the attic. But the roof was missing and most of the walls, so that it was now more like a deck.

The night seemed to be whirling around her. The warm breeze and all of the night's sounds. Some faint rhythmic music from off in the trees, and further, what sounded like a flute. The wind rushed through the tops of the trees. Some bot-cars hissed down the highway. Gonzalo's breathing. He was flat on his back, looking at the sky.

They say you used to be able to see the stars, he said.

Sure, my mom told me about it. It must have been beautiful.

It was reality, said Gonzalo. We could see reality then.

It was quiet for a minute.

Where we are, in space, he said.

Tell me more about your plans. You said you're leaving.

He put his finger to his lips.

The night has ears, he said.

Make us a bubble, she said.

I had to return the wand.

You don't have one of your own? You, Gonzalo?

It's being used.

They lay in silence. She began to talk about Zeke, but in a kind of code.

You heard about that murder? she said. In Colorado?

Yeah, they say a robot did it. And some Amish.

Nobody can find them.

Not the killers, no, said Gonzalo. But the rats know a lot of things.

I do too.

The rats tell you?

No, I just know my friend really well.

She laughed.

We used to play hide and seek. We had to be on the same team, always, or it wasn't any fun. We could always find each other.

You miss your friend.

It's not even like that. It would be like missing your own self.

I could show you something.

Something what?

Things even you haven't seen. I could show you Zeke.

What do you mean?

I have it on file. When we plugged in for our trip to Mar-shalltown. Plug in with me, and I'll share it with you.

No way. We don't believe in plugging in. It's not what God intended.

That's what Zeke said. But he did it.

He had to do it. To save his grandmother.

True. But you're different.

Different.

You hate for men to tell you what to do. What not to do. What to think. You're curious. You're tough. You want to know.

What will I know?

Zeke. Zeke from the inside.

I don't get it. I don't know how it works.

It was a filtered connection, said Gonzalo. And the file is my perceptions, but my perceptions are connected to his. You see? If you plug into me, you can plug into my connection with him. You can touch him from the inside.

Not just Zeke.

I suppose. But you love Zeke, right? I'm not sure you like me at all.

I do like you. I just don't trust you.

She thought she saw the ghost of a smile on his face.

Why do you care? she asked. What's in it for you?

I don't know, he said.

That wasn't good enough, but she figured he knew that. She waited.

You're my friend, he said. Zeke's my friend. I need friends.

That's funny. You don't act like you do.

I want to show you things.

You want to change us. Corrupt us.

I want you to come into my world.

That's what you said about Zeke. That he made people want to get into his world.

His head. I said his head, not his world.

Okay, whatever. Head, world, same thing. So which is it? You want to come into our world, or you want to bring us into yours?

Why does it have to be one or the other?

Why does it have to be either one?

She thought that she was hurting him, but she couldn't help it. When he made that sad, vulnerable face, just for a minute, she thought she could stay with him forever.

Look at this ruin, he said.

You have friends here.

Sure, he said. Everybody loves Gonzalo. I have comrades from Mexico to Colorado, from Marshalltown to Des Moines. But I'm all by myself, do you see? I've been alone my whole life, as long as I can remember. Can you get that? With your eight brothers and sisters and your hundred cousins and your mother and father and uncles and aunts. You even had a horse named Fern.

Fern's dead.

I've never lost anyone, Leahbelle. I never had anyone to lose.

Leahbelle felt like she was playing a game and she had won somehow, she wasn't sure why. She knew it wasn't a game. But she knew she wouldn't let this chance pass by.

Okay, she said. Okay, I'll do it.

It was deep in the night. Gonzalo involved himself in various elaborate preparations that seemed too much like religious rituals. Music for before, during, and after. Water and snacks. Comfortable pillows and blankets. Candles, and he even lit them. She'd thought she could ride her impulse, her *yes*, immediately into this strange experience, but Gonzalo had turned it into something else. She was afraid he was making too much of it. She was afraid she'd be disappointed. She was afraid she'd change her mind.

You didn't do all this with Zeke, she said.

Different situation. That was an adventure. A leap into the unknown.

And this isn't?

Different situation.

She was only becoming more confused. What was he really after? What did he expect her to discover? Did any of this have anything to do with Zeke?

He had her settle back on the pillows, right there on the deck or roof or whatever it was, out in the open air.

You'll get hallucinations, he said. It isn't just like watching a movie.

I've never watched a movie, she said.

But you get the idea, he said. It's like a movie from your own mind. With pieces from mine, pieces from Zeke's. But most of it, what you see, it comes from deep inside yourself.

I'm ready.

You're trembling.

I'm okay.

You'll feel a little stick.

Everything was brighter, as if illuminated from inside. The hazy sky. The crumbling wall.

No was her first thought. Not now. She needed to turn back.

It was too late.

Don't fight it, the voice said. Let it carry you along.

She wasn't sure if the voice was even Gonzalo. It was more like Zeke.

I'm going to die, she thought.

She knew that it was true. Not tonight, perhaps.

It didn't matter.

Time was all around her. There was so much of it. Endless time.

The atmosphere was alive with ghosts. The spirits of dead and ruined boys. Ruined, what did that mean?

The orphans who had lived here. In the previous century, or whenever.

She thought she could see their faces emerging from the intricate patterns of the concrete wall. Organic patterns that seemed to cry out to her. Everything connected like stick figures and letters from foreign alphabets. Their cries for love or feeling or perception were inscribed into the patterns of the wall. A winged mutant flying. A happy monster made of shadow. A naked, blobby, bald, mannish creature. A transparent alphabetic structure like light.

Whoa, she said.

Right, said Gonzalo.

Music was playing. It was happy music, like from outer space.

They were both laughing. She didn't know why.

The haze in the sky was like the concrete wall. In every way. She didn't know what that meant.

It was full of life forms or of images of life forms. Within the pale, shining haze of the data vapor, another pale, shining, transparent haze was branching out in every direction. Directions that couldn't be perceived, directions that didn't exist. These aren't my thoughts, she said out loud. She could feel Zeke's presence in the haze, in the wall, within *everything*. Had Zeke's thoughts entered her mind? This transparent, alphabetic structure like light, but not light, was emerging from inside everything—the palm of her own hand, the bark of a tree, the old tombstones she could see scattered just beyond the trees, the fabric of Gonzalo's pants.

There were creases in Gonzalo's pants that seemed to be trembling, and underneath was his body, and she wanted to touch it.

She stood up. She could see the wire running from the back of her own neck into Gonzalo, flat on his back, looking up at her, totally calm and kind of *elsewhere*.

I need to move, she said.

You can go as far as you want, he said. The cord will stretch.

As far as I want.

Up to a mile, I think.

He was laughing again.

You always find the thing once you stop looking for it, he said.

She thought he was crazy. Completely insane.

And now I'll be crazy too.

She was in a kind of a maze. Hallways and doors. She moved in the direction of creaking noises, soft murmurs, shadows. A thin cord trailing behind her like the breadcrumbs in that fairy tale. The brother and sister, abandoned in the woods.

This was the world, and there was no end to it. It didn't frighten her, it made her want to know.

Every time she came to a stairway, she went down.

In the basement was a weird echoey room and something that had once been a swimming pool.

She didn't see anyone. But she thought she heard someone breathing.

Maybe it was only her own breathing. Or Gonzalo.

She didn't want to think about Gonzalo's breathing. He was breathing inside her, right now. His breath was warm. His body. It was full of oxygen and it kept going in and out and in and out.

She came to another stairway. She went down.

Don't open that door, a voice said.

Of course I'll open the door, the other voice said.

Both voices were her own.

A sign on the door said *Medical Research: Stay Out*.

It was cold inside. Several gurneys were situated at grotesque angles, covered with sheets over lumpy things that looked like they might be bodies.

They *were* bodies. And they were dead.

Oh, right, she thought. The cadavers.

She wanted to get out of there fast. But she paused and looked at the body in front of her. It was human. Cold and bluish. There was no breath. No warmth. No life. No soul. No energy. Just dead matter. No vibrating pulsing nothing nothing nothing. What did this mean? It meant *something*, she was sure of it. That's *me*, she thought. It's the future. And where are they now, these people, and where will I be?

It wasn't horrible yet, her thinking, but it was about to be.

Don't panic. Just walk away. You can think about death later.

In another hallway, higher up, there were doors and doors and doors. It seemed that she could open one particular door and she would no longer be Amish. Behind one of these doors, she would control her own life, her own body, she would make choices and become something that she hadn't even yet imagined. She was finding her way back up to the top, where Gonzalo's body would be waiting. But she couldn't think about that either.

She was too warm. She took off her bonnet, dropped it somewhere, set her hair free. *Without saddles, bridles, whips, or people up on top.*

Like a girl.

On one of the doors was a poster, some sort of science chart it looked like. Things were connected together. Lines and words and balloons, stick figures, chemicals, molecules, genetic information. She didn't know if any of this was true. The molecular substructure of everything, she thought. That's what everything looks like underneath. A pulsating cartoon. It made perfect sense, or it didn't. The Book of Life. She was staring at the face of God, and it was incredible. It had male parts and female parts and parts that were anything but. It wasn't what she'd been taught. She began laughing. God was not a man. Wasn't male. Didn't have a long white beard.

Gonzalo's eyes were closed. His shirt was off and he was sweating. He wasn't moving, but his body was in motion—his torso. Changing colors and shapes and exploding with pictographic images. His tattoos. It was like a dirty movie. Porn, they called it. The smutty English. Filthy lucre, somebody had said once, in a sermon. It was incredible, and she couldn't stop looking. For a minute, it wasn't Gonzalo or anything like Gonzalo. It was Zeke, and Zeke was throbbing and naked. Underneath everything, he was throbbing and naked. He had slight creamy muscles, and nipples, and light hair on his calves. Inside his pants were his private parts, and she wanted to see them.

No, she said.

She closed her eyes.

But all she could see was Zeke. Zeke changed, not like the boy she'd grown up with, not at all. More like a man. Still a boy, still a man. Conscious and powerful, and his body was warm. Hot even, too hot to touch. The word she kept thinking had never been in her head before, never. Fuck. She wanted to fuck.

She opened her eyes.

Fuck, she said.

The world was in flames.

Gonzalo blew out the candles.

Like stars, he said.

He said, Are you okay?

He said, I'll make it stop.

She said, I don't know.

I'm not me, she was thinking. I'm somebody else.

As soon as he broke the connection, she rushed back into herself. Leahbelle was back in some sort of configuration she recognized. This was her dress, at least, plain and blue. These were her hands, her hard black shoes. She was still shaking.

Sit, said Gonzalo.

He gave her a sip of water.

She was exhausted. Where had she been?

Just rest, he said after a while. Breathe deep.

It would be okay.

Tell me, he said. Tell me what you saw.

She was angry.

You made it seem like friendship, she said. Not like …

Like what?

Like sex, she said.

He laughed, like it didn't matter.

I said you'd go deep inside yourself, he said. Not my fault if you got a dirty mind.

No, she said. You did it. You did it to me. That thing with your body.

My body? he said. My body's not always me. My body's got a mind of its own sometimes.

He waved his finger at her.

Part of that mind might have been yours, he said. Or someone else, who knows?

No, she said. I saw Zeke. I saw him all … sexy and … animal-like.

Yeah. And?

I never thought of him like that before.

Really? Why not?

What do you mean *why not?*

Who do you think of that way?

Nobody. Nobody.

I don't believe you.

I don't get it, she said. Are you his friend or his enemy?

Not his enemy, he said. No way. Everybody's complicated.

Some people are simple.

Not you.

Simple enough.

You think? I don't get *you.* Are you his girlfriend or his sister?

She wanted to slap him. Why did she always want to slap him?

Look, he said. I'm always trying to … do the right thing. It doesn't always come natural. All my life, you know, I had to do things. I couldn't do the right thing sometimes. I had to survive. I had to get what I needed.

I don't believe you, she said. What is it you need?

He didn't say anything. He seemed elsewhere again.

You want everyone to think you're so bad, she said. So violent. Ready to kill someone at the drop of a hat.

You think I'm fronting, he said, and he laughed.

She'd learned a new verb today. The way he laughed, it helped. It wasn't so serious. It wasn't real.

It was just visions, hallucinations. Everybody had sin inside them. Even Leahbelle Beachy.

He gave her a bowl of fruit.

I'm not hungry.

You will be, he said.

What time is it?

Sun'll be up in a while.

She rested. For a minute, she even dozed off. There was too much to think about, but she also realized she could let it all go. When she woke up, there were pancakes with real maple syrup. Soft bubbly music was playing.

They were delicious. She was hungry, hungrier than she'd ever been.

I told you what I saw, Leahbelle said as she finished her plate. What about you?

My own stuff, he said.

That isn't fair.

No, no, I just mean it's hard to explain. But I saw Amish stuff too. I get a lot of historical suffering from you guys. Your ancestors were tortured and imprisoned a lot, right?

Sure, she said. But I didn't see that stuff at all.

Sometimes your own genetic memory is invisible, he said. It's just like the atmosphere. It's what you take for granted, who you think you are.

She wondered. Who did she even think she was anymore?

What happened to you? she asked. When you were a kid? What happened to your family?

I don't know, he said. I don't remember.

There were dim memories, he wasn't even sure if they were real. A mother. Some video games. The streets of Tegucigalpa. He's sure they were really poor. And then he was with strangers. He was traveling in the back of a truck, but maybe that was later. Maybe he was on a train, maybe it was a bus.

His earliest perfectly clear memories are from Tijuana. He lived in the garbage dump, digging through the trash for the valuable bits, for scrap. There was a gang of kids. He was one of them. It was there, in the garbage dump, that he came across the portal.

A portal to what?

I don't know, he said. I don't think I went in. I think something stopped me or I stopped myself.

Is this a memory? Leahbelle asked. Or a dream?

It was real. It was the realest thing. They hadn't mapped the Tijuana garbage dump, you know? The dump is huge. The Gstate Maps, if you ask for the dump, it'll only direct you to the edge. There's a gap, and that gap is what's real. Outside the consensual reality. It's Aztlan.

Aztlan?

Once you Map something, you imprison it, you turn it into the consensual reality.

I'm not sure I understand.

They've Mapped almost all of the portals out of existence. Doorways to other dimensions. Doorways to our dreams, the dreams that are realer than this world.

God is what's realer than this world, insisted Leahbelle.

But when she said the word *God*, she thought of what she'd just seen, or what she'd thought she'd seen. It wasn't just reality, and it wasn't just the law. It was more like a structure, but it was the gaps in the structure too.

They still haven't Mapped the dump, said Gonzalo. The portal must still be there.

But what's Aztlan?

It's a country. A real country made of dreams.

It was just after he found the portal that he crossed over to this side. He was in the meat towns: Bakersfield and then Longmont and then Marshalltown.

And then you escaped, Leahbelle said. How did you escape?

Long story, he said. Better save it for another day.

He pointed toward the eastern sky.

Sun's coming up, he said. We better get you home.

Before they left, he played one more song. It was called *Good Feeling*. It was sad and it was also kind of happy, and some man with a rag-gedy voice sang: *Dear lady, there's so many things that I have come to fear / Little voice says I'm going crazy to see all my worlds disappear ...*

At the end, the singer asked somebody, or maybe just the feeling, to stay. The song made her happy and the song made her sad. It interested her, the way it moved more ways than one.

Who is this? she asked.

A twentieth century band. The Violent Femmes.

Violent, of course, she said.

But she laughed. Aeren had told her she read like a femme. A total femme. Was Leahbelle secretly a member of this band?

Just a name, he said. Words don't always mean what they think they mean.

But sometimes they do.

Sure, he said. Sometimes they do.

My family must be wondering where I'm at, she said.

They won't know you've been out all night. They'll think you just got up early.

My mother will know. But she trusts me. She knows that if I stayed out all night, it was for something important.

Oh yeah? What was that?

The question confused her. Wasn't she trying to find a way into the future, a way to save them all? Wasn't that why she'd been here? She realized that wasn't why she'd been here at all.

On the motorbike, she began to feel sleepy. She felt good, speeding along in the early morning, resting her head on Gonzalo's back. It wasn't until they rounded the bend of the road before her home that she noticed all the commotion. There were news drones circling up above and all kinds of vehicles pulled off along the road. Bot-cars and buggies, everything mixed up together, and as they neared the house, the people were everywhere.

But the house wasn't there.

As Gonzalo pulled over, she could see the charred, burning pit where her home used to be. People were screaming and crying and the sky was falling apart.

Leahbelle, wait, said Gonzalo.

But it was too late. There was just her own cry of horror as she tumbled off the motorbike and rushed into the crowd.

FIVE

It was like she'd left her body. She was watching herself from a distance. There's Leahbelle being passed around among the Amish, being comforted, hugged, and petted like a dog. There's Leahbelle with a cracked and shattered look on her face. Leahbelle who isn't really there. Look, it's happening, it's happened: Leahbelle, going crazy.

A miracle, they kept saying. A miracle she wasn't killed. A miracle that even one member of the family had survived the missile shot from the government drone. It was insane, she thought: a miracle? the hand of God? She could trace back all of these decisions she'd made, things she did or didn't do, a fuzzy network of paths leading backward in time, and she could never quite figure how they all mixed together. Wandering the ruined orphanage with a wire tied to her, through a maze of death and cadavers and a sick, sinful pleasure buzzing in her mind. When exactly, she wanted to know, had she taken the wrong turn? When had she made the decision that murdered her family?

Ethel Miller had come by to pick up some eggs. Instead of Leahbelle, Ethel Miller had died. Ethel Miller had wandered through her life making silly little choices with life or death consequences. Ethel could have woken up ten minutes earlier that morning or ten minutes later and picked up the eggs ten minutes earlier or arrived at the farmhouse to pick up those eggs after the missile had already struck, like Leahbelle, and gazed upon the charred remains of her own destiny. Now Leahbelle watched herself being fed and bathed and put to bed.

Not a miracle, but a curse. Everything was over.

It was night, and she was in Zeke Yoder's house. She was in Zeke Yoder's bed. It felt like a stranger's bed after all. The evil was inside her and everywhere, evil and death, and him too, she thought. Maybe all the tangled paths that led back to her own stupidity, her evil and sin, her mistake, her bad choice, maybe it also led back to Zeke and his stupid adventure, the despicable rats, the tunnels underground, maybe it was all his fault, the boy who seemed gentle and kind.

Shadows on the wall. She didn't sleep, but she dreamed.

Music emerged from a black, smoking pit in the earth. Rivers flowed deep beneath the surface of things, and boats sailed down those rivers. It was Leahbelle's job to navigate those rivers, because she was neither dead nor alive. Only Leahbelle could read the maps, the secret maps, the maps that were written in blood. If she could find the way out, where the underground river flowed into the sea, there, in the west, maybe they would let her die.

Children sleeping. A voice outside the door.

They might be looking for her, somebody said.

We have to hide her, said a woman.

A woman. Zeke's mother.

If they figure out she's still alive, somebody said.

When they figure out, said somebody else.

But I'm not alive, Leahbelle wanted to tell the voices in the shadows. Can't you see me? I'm right here, crazy in my tomb.

In the morning, she walked out the door in her nightclothes, across the Yoder fields to the west. Dusty fields covered with an intricate pattern of footprints and hoofprints. When she kept walking, further and further away, they came to fetch her.

Terrorists, people kept saying. A terrorist cell was wiped out. Plotting a terror attack. Terror, terrorist, terrorize, terrorism, territory, territorial, terrestrial, terrible, terrify, terrapin, terrain …

The daylight was excruciating.

They're coming, somebody said. They're from the government.

Zeke's mother took Leahbelle to the barn.

Just stand here quietly, she said. Next to the horse.

From inside the darkness and warmth and heavy animal smell of the barn, she could see them: the census takers, here to count the Amish. One, two, three. Two womanish creatures were doing the counting, she'd seen them before.

They carried little square machines. They told Zeke's mother and father to bring everyone out, everyone who lived in this house. The older one had a red cap, the younger one a blue scarf.

Leahbelle smiled because it was true that she didn't live in the house. She was not exactly alive. She wasn't dead yet, but she wasn't alive either.

The children came out and were scanned with the machines. Their names were taken down.

It was the exterminators. Nobody else seemed to recognize them, but then maybe nobody else had ever seen them. There weren't that many people in the world, it just kept changing their outfits, switching them around, so it would look like the world was full. Somebody was tricking everyone, but not Leahbelle. She had everything figured out.

That night she was back in Zeke's bed. But she never slept. All around her, the children slept. She counted them. One, two, three, four …. She counted them again, over and over again, convinced that she was missing something, that somebody was missing.

Much later, still wide awake in that bed, she heard a sound she'd heard before. Long ago and far away. It was her murderer, she remembered. Coming to kill her at last, to put her out of her pain. She slipped out to the road and waited barefoot in her nightgown for death to carry her away. Her hands discovered a pill in her apron, and a bottle. It was the medicine she'd been given to put something out of its misery. She opened the bottle and peered deep inside. That's where she needed to go.

When she saw Gonzalo's face, however, she felt something break open inside. He took the bottle from her hand. She was shaking.

They killed them, she told him. Over and over again. Every last one.

He held her. He held her and then looked at her from a distance. She could tell that he saw her now, saw her craziness, saw that she was already dead.

We have to get out of here, he said. It isn't safe.

No, she agreed. It isn't safe.

Can you get your shoes?

I don't have any shoes.

Where do you keep them? Your shoes?

She just waited for him to realize that dead girls didn't need shoes. He seemed to figure it out, but then ran up to the barn and went inside. He came back with a pair of rubber galoshes and made her put them on her feet.

They don't fit, she said. Too big.

They'll have to do, he said. Here put this on.

He took off his jacket for her.

They were riding through the night. It didn't matter where they were going. She watched from a distance: Leahbelle in her nightgown, holding onto this crazy sinful boy like some sort of a harlot. Racing through the night on a ludicrous machine. Surely, God did not approve.

God made her ill. She felt electric with her newfound hatred for God. If she could murder God, she'd spit on God's corpse. God could rot in hell forever.

Back roads, they were sticking to the back roads. They were traveling further than what she knew, obliterating her life, and at some point, just before dawn, they stopped and met a pale, greenish, glowing boy in a stand of trees off the road, near an abandoned gas station. The boy was smooth and round like a big baby. He was naked except for a kind of bubble around his private parts.

Wait right here, Gonzalo said. Don't even move.

He went off with the boy, who knew where, and when he returned he had clothes for her, English clothes. Pants and a shirt and a jacket, but still no shoes because she wasn't alive. Dead girls had to wear galoshes.

We'll get you some real shoes in Des Moines, Gonzalo said.

The city was full of trees and buildings, but where were all the people? It was hot already and everything was melted, melting. Gonzalo drove past the Mars Cafe and past an old university, turned down a narrow driveway, and parked behind a crumbling brick building back a ways from the road. He took her up the rotting back stairway into a hallway with a door and another door and another door, and knocked quietly.

Something let them in, something very old.

Gonzalo was talking and talking, but she couldn't hear another word. Talking to this person or creature, Squidboy he was called, but he told Leahbelle to call him *Cousin*, she didn't know why.

Squidboy is a musician, Gonzalo told her.

He had two normal arms, normal meaning human, Amish, whatever, it exhausted her already. He had several tentacles with tough little plastic bits on the end—picks for his atomic guitar. He didn't seem to have legs. They'd been converted into something with even more fingers, and so he rolled around his apartment on a kind of scooter. He was mostly head and guitar-strumming appendages. His apartment was stuffed full of musical machinery. Where did the machinery end and where did Leahbelle begin?

We'll be safe here for a minute, Gonzalo told her.

How long was a minute? A minute lasted forever. He put her to bed. What would she do if he kissed her?

Scream. She would scream.

Voices were talking about her

I can't just leave her.

You can do what you want.

I made a promise.

Your precious Zeke Yoder. This is the revolution, asshole. This is the real shit.

Leahbelle burrowed beneath her pillow. She didn't sleep, but she woke up. And when she woke up, she was screaming.

Make her stop, said Aeren. You have to make her stop.

She opened her mouth wide, wider, she couldn't believe what was inside her. Where did Aeren come from anyway?

Gonzalo held her, Shhh, shhh, quiet.

But she wouldn't be quiet.

He slipped the earbuds in her ears, and that did the trick. He gave her the music. It was so beautiful. It came from his heart, and it washed over her. It felt so good. Let it go. Let it all go. What a marvelous boy.

She lay back, and she closed her eyes, and she slept.

When she woke up, Gonzalo was gone. So was Aeren. It was just Squidboy. He was strumming his atomic guitar. On the Grid-screen behind him, a rocket was shooting through outer space. Behind it, Earth.

It doesn't bother the neighbors? she asked.

Nobody complains. It isn't the sort of place where people complain.

She liked the music.

Mostly Syrian refugees who fled the Sonic Devastation of the thirties, he continued. They hear through computers anyway, so they just tune me out.

It's different, she said. Different than the English music I've heard before. Is it the guitar, or is it you?

He said, Studies have shown that certain musical tones inhibit human spiritual and emotional development. Those are exactly the tones that dominate contemporary music.

The Grid-screen flashed the words *Mad Scientist on the Loose*, and there was an image of a bald woman with wires running into her head. It's me, thought Leahbelle. She'd become a machine, a mad scientist, an image on a screen.

It isn't an accident, said Squidboy. They want to keep the population in a state of stunned, acquisitive non-contemplation.

He shrugged. The Grid-screen flashed the words *What Terror is Dr. Brockton Plotting Against the Earth?*

Where's Gonzalo? she asked.

He'll be back.

And Aeren?

Her too.

Everything was calm. Her family was dead, and in the space of her calm she could see that fact now, as if at a distance. Her own life was over, and she could see that too, but she could see that she'd need to keep moving, to keep going, all the way to the end of the line.

Are you a part of their organization? she asked.

I'm not sure organization is the right word, he said.

What's the right word?

Maybe a … conglomeration?

Okay. Are you a part of their conglomeration?

Loosely associated, let's say. I'd like to say I'm not political, I'm an artist, but then music is a social phenomenon, and so music is political, and so every chord is a political position, isn't it?

If you say so.

His walls were covered with pictures of musicians. They were all doing the same thing, more or less. Holding a guitar, singing or shouting. But the attitudes and the styles were all so different. Like there was an infinity of poses a musician could adopt.

How do you live?

I haven't left my apartment in years, he said. Local live music was abolished for health reasons. Same forces that create the soul-crushing tones of contemporary music were behind that law. I do it all from here now, give virtual guitar lessons to rebellious teens enamored of the "authentic" musical past.

You teach people to play music.

Yes. That's what they pay me for.

Can you teach me something? Something simple.

Cousin, he said, you're a natural.

Maybe he said that to everyone. Once she got the basics, he asked her what kind of song she wanted to learn.

A sad song, she said. The saddest song you know.

The song was sad, sadder than sad, devastatingly, beautifully sad, and it helped, but as the day dragged along and Gonzalo didn't return, she started to feel crazy again.

The music he gave me, she said to Squidboy. Do you have some of that?

I don't keep that sort of song, he said. My music isn't sleep-inducing. More like it's supposed to wake you up.

Oh, Jesus, she said.

Was she praying or cursing? She'd never cursed. She started slapping herself, harder and harder.

Squidboy wrapped his tentacles around her and squeezed, immobilizing her.

I'll scream, she said.

You don't have to scream, he said. I'll make you some herbal tea.

Herbal tea, she thought. She could give that a try. She waited while he prepared it, and then she took a sip and waited some more, to see how it would make her feel, and then she hurled the cup against the wall.

I'm horrible, she thought.

She had become a horrible, violent person. Plotting terror against the earth. Light it on fire, watch it burn, a pretty light visible from space, sending a little bit of warmth to the coldest edges of the solar system—out where Leahbelle lived now, the outer limits, where the solar wind had ceased to blow and everything was still and cold.

She curled up in the bed.

She was wide awake early the next morning, listening to the Syrian children playing in the hall, just outside the door. She heard a familiar voice talking to the children, making the children laugh. She was already on her feet when Gonzalo finally hustled in.

We have to move her, he said to Squidboy. It isn't safe here anymore.

It isn't safe here? said Squidboy.

We don't know. They might be paying attention.

Will they come here? Will they come to my apartment?

I don't know.

Leahbelle was on her knees, holding onto Gonzalo's legs.

The music, she said.

Gonzalo looked at her, sad.

Don't look at me that way. I'll scream.

Shhh, it's okay, Leahbelle.

Give me the music. Please.

Here you go. Just a little bit. Listen to this.

It was a brief song, but it was pure bliss. Her heart exploded with love. She loved Gonzalo. She loved him completely. She was sprawled on the floor, staring up at the water-stained ceiling. The stains were beautiful. They looked like robot butterflies or kissing piglets or a fantasy of what clouds once looked like.

You're turning her into a junky, said Squidboy.

Do you have a better idea?

It's a crime against free will.

It's just until we get her to a safer place.

He crouched down next to Leahbelle.

Aeren's going to take you to Marshalltown, he said. My friends there will look after you, but I can't go to Marshalltown.

Don't leave me, Leahbelle said.

I'll come see you as soon as I can.

I love you, Leahbelle said.

I'll send you some music, he said. I'll send it with Aeren.

Do you love me?

He gave her that sad look again. He's going to lie to me, she thought. Go ahead, she thought. Tell me a lie.

Of course I love you, he said.

He kissed her on the forehead again. She was still a sleepy child.

The ride to Marshalltown on the motorbike with Aeren kept Leahbelle awake, just barely. It was like she was dreaming in the daylight. The back roads. The dried-up rivers and shimmering trees. The fields of pork bushes and monster-soy and thousand-eared maze-corn. She was still wearing those galoshes, and it occurred to her that Gonzalo had said he'd find her real shoes. Gonzalo, what a liar. She rested her head against Aeren's back.

She remembered that everyone she cared about was dead. Everyone but Leahbelle was dead, and she didn't care about Leahbelle. But surely there was somebody else, someone she was forgetting.

The streets of Marshalltown were the most decrepit and depraved she'd ever seen, full of dazed and hallucinating creatures lurking in the shadows or unconscious in the sunlight. Crumbling brick buildings, partial walls where buildings had once been, vacant lots revealing century-old advertisements for nonsense, the shimmer of crime and addiction and ruined architecture. She thought it was beautiful.

Aeren parked in back of an enormous warehouse and knocked softly on the backdoor. They were greeted by a man and a wooden doll. A kind of puppet—the man's left arm was lost inside the doll's body. How wonderful to be like that, to have given up completely. No will of your own; just somebody else pulling the strings.

Efron was the security guard. He lived there, but he wasn't always on duty. When he was on duty, he mostly sat in a little hut out front dealing drugs, gadgets, medicines, and life forms. Zeke had told her about this man, and about Merle, the puppet.

Another human, said Efron.

Has it come to stay? asked the puppet.

For as long as it lasts, said Aeren.

Tell Gonzalo he owes me, said Efron.

Does it do any tricks? asked the puppet.

Leahbelle was led through a tunnel lined with shelves. On the shelves were hunks of meaty substances shrink-wrapped and meticulously labeled. The perfect place for me, she thought. A hunk of un-living flesh hanging out with the rest of the dead meat.

As if he could read her mind, Efron told her that some of the packaged meat was technically still alive. It stayed tastier that way. Some of the packages actually trembled as she walked past. They could sense her presence somehow. Without eyes or ears, with no brain or nerve endings at all—somehow they could sense that she was one of them.

She was put to bed in a back storage-room that held nothing but a cot and a blanket, a mop and a microwave oven. Aeren tucked her in.

She fell into dreams that were like the memories of dreams she'd had as a child. In her dreams, she pretended that time and death were not real. She was resting in the glow, the afterimage of the music from Gonzalo's heart. But then the glow would begin to fade, and in her dreams she would see children digging through the wreckage of her home, the charred earth and blackened remains of the structure, searching for some small piece of a body for the mass funeral. They were looking for a chunk of her mother or her father, of Hannah or Ruth, Ervin, Elvin, or Ivan. A finger, a toe, a smear of cells on a blackened doorknob, a bit of DNA burnt into a fragment of pale blue cloth.

Supposedly the government wanted to kill her. A safe place meant a place where nobody could see her. A place where nobody was watching, where nobody cared.

She was all alone in a tiny room in a building where brainless things were grown and butchered and packaged. But it wasn't just that. It wasn't a case of Before and After. She'd always been alone, always lived in such a place, she'd just never realized it before. The government missile had simply peeled back the layers of illusion and revealed the stark reality: alone, and alone forever, floating in a dark cage, separate, unreachable, lost in fantasy and delusion. Leahbelle, alone.

She would sink into that voidy feeling. She would explore the parameters of the cage, while lying absolutely still, eyes wide open. She'd never really been anywhere except her own mind. Nobody could get in, and she couldn't get out. She understood that the boy she told herself she loved wasn't real. He was an idea, a phantom, lost in his own fantasies and delusions. A handsome face was just a mask, a pretty picture that allowed her to imagine the beauty of unlimited depths underneath. She'd been imagining a kind of bottomless pit of affection and joy. She'd placed it in the future. But the future would never come. One would want the accompaniment to that face as a grandiose music, reaching backward and forward through time, redeeming everything, every moment of loneliness and loss, a music that would bring together all of the animals, all of the stinking lumps of conscious flesh just waiting to be butchered, bring them all together into the most beautiful image, an impossibly elaborate arabesque that would cohere for just a flash, an instant of pure love, before dissolving into nothingness forever.

She thought about faces, handsome faces, beautiful faces, and she touched herself, and for a few minutes the pain went away. But there was nothing underneath anything. She was trapped on the surface of her own mind. Separate, unreachable, lost in fantasy and delusion. Leahbelle, alone. She didn't know if time was passing. She was drowning in time. And then inevitably she would begin suffocating, gasping for breath, and then she would begin to scream.

When she screamed, Aeren would come. Aeren's voice, nurturing but stern, reassured her that she hadn't been floating in empty space forever. It calmed her down a bit. Leahbelle would make a sad, pouty face and tell Aeren how much it hurt.

Poor little girly girl, Aeren would say.

She brought her food. She made her eat. Spoonful by spoonful.

If I could listen to just a little bit of the music, Leahbelle would say.

She didn't call it Gonzalo's music with Aeren, only in her own mind.

Try to wait just a little bit longer, Aeren would say. You shouldn't need that much. You're a tough girl.

I'm not.

After a few minutes, Aeren would give in and play the music, and then Leahbelle would look up at her with such joy and relief, such trust and love, that Aeren's face would light up too—her chemistry was also being changed, Leahbelle realized, and it was the most beautiful thing, that smiling face. It was amazing how well she'd come to understand everything, how every little thing worked. She'd become so good at getting people to give her what she needed. She would dream again in a golden haze, everything and everyone blurring together, everything calm and everything okay.

SIX

One day or one night—Leahbelle had no way to tell what was what—she got up before the music had worn off completely and decided she needed to take a look around. She had no idea how long she'd been there—weeks or maybe months or maybe just one endless night. Even if it was all just a lonesome dream, she needed to try and understand where she was in the dream.

Outside of the storage room, nothing looked familiar. There was a short hallway she didn't remember. She chose one door at random and found herself in a vast room, warm and humid, with greenish lumps slowly revolving on a circular conveyor belt from one heatlamp to the next.

Beyond that was a small room with a desk and about fifty tiny video screens on the wall. They seemed to show what was happening in every part of the warehouse, which wasn't much. On one of the bottom screens, she could see herself making her way through the room she'd just passed through, pausing to watch the greenish lumps slowly revolving. Some sort of time lag, she supposed, unless the video was the real present and she was watching herself from her own future. Had she somehow slipped ahead in time? Come unsynchronized from her own self? Gonzalo had told her that time had something to do with entangled particles. She wondered if she could communicate somehow with the Leahbelle who was now making her way past the greenish lumps. Could she keep the future from happening?

Bored with this little thought-experiment, she searched for her own room on the screens. The tiny storage room with the cot and the mop and the microwave oven. It wasn't there.

Nobody was watching her. Just as she'd thought.

She scanned the screens, looking for Aeren. Aeren wasn't anywhere. She couldn't find Efron and Merle either. Other than the living meat, the only organic life was a little girl who was playing in front of a tiny pink cottage surrounded by a picket fence, all within a vast room within the vast warehouse itself.

She set out to find the little girl.

Most every room offered a different form of edible matter that, on its own, would serve to expose the fundamental horror of existence. All together, they just settled in under the umbrella of a concept: the new meat. And yet several hallways and even some rooms contained nothing at all.

After passing through a malodorous carpeted hallway, with only a few bloodstains soaked into the carpet, she arrived in the vast cavernous room that housed the little cottage. The girl had long hair in a braid and enormous brown eyes. She waved her hand, just once, slowly from left to right, and then just stared at Leahbelle, waiting for her to come closer.

Hello, said Leahbelle. What's your name?

Valkilmer, said the little girl.

That's a pretty name, said Leahbelle. Is it … a Syrian name?

I think so, said Valkilmer. I like your name better.

You know my name?

Leahbelle. It's very pretty.

You're all alone here? Where is everybody?

They're out destroying the Grid.

Gonzalo and Aeren?

I've never met Gonzalo. He's a fugitive from justice. A wanted man.

How do you know all of this?

I listen.

What about Efron and Merle? Leahbelle asked.

Working on the generator.

Where is that?

In a different building, said Valkilmer.

Are you Efron's daughter?

I'm a war orphan.

The girl tossed a tiny pink ball into the air. It disappeared somewhere up above.

How did you get here? Leahbelle asked.

A trade.

A trade.

Yes, you know, Efron gave somebody something. They gave him me.

What for?

I remind him of his happy childhood.

Leahbelle thought she should do something. She should be a mother for this child.

Would you like me to take care of you?

I'm fine, thanks.

But don't you get lonely?

Sometimes I'm allowed to play with the others.

Other children, said Leahbelle.

Something like that.

The girl pulled another ball from the pocket of her dress and tossed it in the air.

But you don't have a mother, Leahbelle said.

Merle's kind of my mother.

Merle's just a puppet.

The lights went out. Everything was quiet for a moment. A pervasive and dim humming noise that Leahbelle had barely noticed in the background had disappeared. The warehouse remained quiet even when the lights came back on.

There goes the Grid, said Valkilmer.

What do you mean?

I guess it worked. The emergency generator will only keep the lights on, nothing else. The meat will go bad. Some of it might even come back to life. I don't wanna stick around and see what that's like.

What do you mean? repeated Leahbelle.

They took out the Grid, said the girl. Duh.

Leahbelle had lived her whole life off the Grid, and yet its disappearance seemed as impossible as the disappearance of the sun or the air. What might possibly come next?

Where will you go? Leahbelle asked.

Wherever Efron and Merle take me. Where will you go?

Leahbelle was confused. She hadn't thought that she would ever leave this place. She thought she'd just float alone in nothingness forever.

You're a fugitive too, said Valkilmer. The government wants to kill you.

I'll find Zeke Yoder, said Leahbelle. That's where I'll go.

Are all the Amish fugitives? asked Valkilmer.

Colorado, said Leahbelle.

He'll be long gone by the time you get *there*.

Who told you that?

She had to think.

It must have been the rats.

The rats? You know the rats?

We manufacture things for them. Medicine. Drugs.

From beyond the despair and hopelessness, the utter meaninglessness she'd been feeling, a different feeling returned, one she remembered from before the catastrophe. The feeling that she was trapped in a sinister web, that things were profoundly meaningful, but that nothing was what it appeared to be.

She clung to that feeling. Paranoia felt better than the void she'd been dreaming in.

Where is Zeke going? she asked.

West, of course. Probably California.

The door to the cavernous space opened, and in walked Efron. Merle was badgering him about something—his incompetence with the generator and his lack of imagination in general.

Some people can only imagine a future that's a continuation of the present, said Merle. Their boring daily lives. But what about those futures that destroy the present and create a complete break? A future severed completely from this tedious Now. That's the sort of future I'm looking for.

The bitter apocalyptic dreams of someone who can't accept he's just a puppet, said Efron.

Merle rolled his eyes.

You'll see. One of these days ... goodbye Merle.

Nice to see you again, Efron said to Leahbelle.

Have you packed your bag? Merle asked Valkilmer.

Of course.

We're leaving, Efron told Leahbelle. You can stay as long as you'd like.

It didn't make sense.

Stay ... alone?

Maybe alone, said Merle. Maybe not. Things could get pretty animate around here.

What time is it? asked Leahbelle.

Six thirteen, said Merle.

AM or PM?

It's still daylight outside.

I can't stay here. What will I do?

Wait for Gonzalo, said Valkilmer. He'll probably come and get you.

Gonzalo can't step foot in Marshalltown, said Leahbelle.

That was before the Grid went down.

She felt less crazy than she'd felt in days or weeks. She had no idea how long it had been. Still, she felt it creeping in—the craving for the music, for sleep, escape, a rage and despair bubbling up inside her, the insistent knowledge that her family was dead, that she was all alone.

But Zeke was out there. She would go to California. Gonzalo would take her, she was sure he would.

Efron, Merle, and Valkilmer showed her out to the security guard's hut out front.

Probably the safest place for now, said Merle. Safer than in there.

The locals are pretty harmless, said Efron. At least until the drugs wear off.

But lock the door, Merle suggested.

Good luck!

They waved and climbed inside a kind of car that was more like a bicycle, with pedals. Efron and Valkilmer were both pedaling vigorously. Merle pedaled his little blocky feet in the air and waved as they drove away.

Night fell. It was unlike any night that had ever fallen during Leahbelle's lifetime. The data vapor was gone. The sky was full of stars.

They weren't like other lights. They twinkled. Some of them moved. No, all of them moved, very slowly, a strange luminous pattern of dots sweeping from horizon to horizon. They'd always been there, but invisible. This was space. It was all around her. It wasn't empty. It was full of lights. The lights were distant suns, incandescent and combustible holes in the fabric of time. Or something like that.

She remembered that she was alive.

Down on Earth, even the creatures that lived in the shadows of Marshalltown had begun to wake up. Even the agitation of the unconscious junkies suggested that everything had changed. They muttered, as if they were dreaming of cataclysms or of hope.

Figures were congregating. There was a crash of breaking glass. She could smell smoke, and in the distance a strange glow flickered across the sky as if something was burning.

Nobody seemed to notice her sitting in the little security hut outside of the warehouse. A couple of teenage types wandered up and tried the warehouse door. They tried to break it down, but got bored.

Hey, Lobotomy! one of them yelled.

They were joined by a third with a crowbar. Still no luck. There weren't any accessible windows, so they drifted around the side and out of her view.

The building across the street, a low featureless slab that took up an entire block, began to make crackling noises. Through one of the two windows, she could see flames.

She heard moans and whimpers. They didn't sound like cries exactly. They didn't sound *vocal* at all. More like some lump was vibrating violently in order to communicate its distress. The noises came from inside the warehouse.

She unlocked the door of the hut. She stepped into the night.

The back door of the warehouse had been pried off. She didn't know if the teenagers had gone inside or gone off in pursuit of more lucrative amusements. Perhaps the noises from inside had scared them away.

In the long tunnel of a hallway lined with shelves of shrink-wrapped substances, she could actually feel her own organs vibrating from the effects of the existential lamentations. She froze. She remembered the look in Fern's eyes when she was dying and in pain and didn't know why.

Leahbelle's hands were empty.

She raced back outside to find something, she didn't know what, something to smash it with, all of it, to put it all out of its misery, and there was Gonzalo, just getting off the motorbike. His hair was wild, and he stared at her for a second like he didn't recognize her. She'd never seen him look so crazy. He gave her a big hug and he laughed, a crazy kind of laugh.

Fucking yes, he said.

You came back for me.

I haven't been back here in years, he said.

What do we do now?

I hate this town.

It's burning, she said. Everywhere, it's burning.

Everybody hates this town, he said. Everybody hates this country, this government, this life that isn't even life.

The meat, she said. The meat's suffering. Can you hear it?

It didn't seem like he heard her. He was looking around at the burning former factories and abandoned buildings as if he was dreaming. As if it was the best dream ever.

I can't bear to see the suffering, she told him. We have to stop it. I have to stop it.

You can burn it down, he said.

Won't it feel the fire?

It doesn't feel, said Gonzalo. Not like that.

He followed her through the strange hallways and odd rooms of the vast warehouse, trailing a clear odorless liquid behind him. They covered every room; there was nobody else inside. The greenish lumps now stalled on the circular conveyor belt; the cottage and its picket fence, its patch of unreal grass; a formerly refrigerated hallway, now tepid and musty and stinking of the oval meat hanging from hooks. The floor was sticky. Then a room she hadn't seen before, full of live animals in cages, if you could call them animals—plump headless turkeys feeding through tubes. Another vast cool space full of carcasses, and finally they emerged on the other side, out the front door, where the little hut was now in flames.

Wait here for one second, Gonzalo said.

He raced around back and returned with the motorbike.

Climb aboard, he said.

She got on. He handed her something like a marble.

Toss it inside.

It'll explode?

Yes.

She tossed the marble into the open front door of the warehouse and something inside burst into flames. They raced away.

They'll never find us, he yelled back at her.

We have to go west, she told him

My thoughts exactly.

He stopped in the downtown area, where one large building towered over the crumbling remains of the previous century's downtown. FOODCO it said in large glowing letters up top.

Just one more thing to destroy, and we're on our way, he said.

Gonzalo, no. No more violence.

It's the corporate HQ, he said.

You can't kill anyone. It's not right.

I was their slave, he said. Do you understand?

She didn't understand. But maybe she did.

Everybody's long gone at this point, he said. Cowering in their bunkers.

He rested the motorbike on its stand and hopped off. So this is violence, she thought. He placed a little box in the front entranceway, then calmly walked back to the motorbike.

Sixty seconds, he said.

He laughed, and he hugged her, and he pointed at the sky.

Fucking stars, he said.

Everything's different, she said.

He said, Everything's changed for good.

I feel weird, she said.

He said, We've got to go.

But what's out there? she asked.

Chaos, he said. Total chaos.

He started the engine and they raced away, toward the west, as the explosion behind them lit up the night sky, the brightness of the flames for a moment once again erasing the view of the stars.

II. BEINGS OF LIGHT

SEVEN

The trip from San Jose to West Oakland was uneventful, but it took Zeke, Boopsie, and Emma four days traveling by foot. The three of them moved along the empty Grid-works or on the parallel side street, and they slept in little nests of blankets under overpasses or in doorways, with Boopsie keeping watch. A few drones were again appearing in the sky, alongside the winged creatures—the genetically engineered bird-people, the cyborgs and children with permanent or detachable wings, the enthusiasts with motorized jet propulsion packs or wearable helicopter outfits, zipping in and out of the fog. What had once been heavily regulated flying space, reserved for government or mercantile surveillance, was now crowded with life.

As the days went by, Zeke also began to notice more military vehicles. It hadn't taken the government long to get its off-Grid vehicles and communications systems going.

The thick chilling fog that hung over the landscape was also disorienting. The shifting gray ceiling was beautiful at times. It diffused the light to make people and objects down below seem impossibly vivid and real. But the fog was inside him, too. Zeke wasn't sure where he was or what he was doing. He was delivering a message to the daughter of Chantal, a woman he'd met in Colorado, just a stranger. He was supposed to find Leahbelle and save her, but he had no idea where she was or where she was going. He was supposed to take care of Emma, but sometimes she knew more about how the world of the English worked than he did.

They'd camped in Fruitvale the night before, where Zeke's grandmother had heard tell there might be farmland available. These claims were false. Every square foot of the land seemed to be occupied, and although a few houses had corn and chickens and pork bushes, there was nothing like the acreage required to sustain an Amish community—or even one Amish family, as far as Zeke could see. The residents seemed okay, although way too many of them walked around with terrifying animals. Those vicious, undulating creatures that looked like furry logs or centipedes with fangs and organs and spiky hairs all over the place. Things that looked like dogs, but with bronze, armored heads. Little rhino-like things that seemed partially human. Everything had tusks or horns or claws, and because most of the leashes were invisible, they always seemed ready to attack. They would lunge or growl, their chomping, slobbering mouths coming alarmingly close before they were snapped back to their owners.

They crossed from one side of Oakland to the other, past a lake that hosted colonies of phosphorescent geese. The landscape around the lake was covered with phosphorescent goose-shit. They passed frightening groups of angry-looking youth with sharp pieces of metal extruding from them in every direction and gruesome holograms circling their skulls. The graffiti in Oakland was terrifying too. *Destroy All Memory. War Within, Chaos Without. Hell Above, Apocalypse Now. Deface the Singularity. The Underground is Coming For You. Death to Robots. Become Nothing and Nothing More.*

Why would they want to kill robots? Zeke asked Boopsie.

Just a bunch of silly billies, said Boopsie.

Boopsie was a rotund little ball of a robot with puckered lips. Since she'd lost her bright colors, floppy shoes, and bows, however, and disguised herself as a bland, beige machine, her occasional lapses into cutesy declarations devoid of information was even more confusing. Zeke just waited.

The rise of anti-AI movements is usually attributed to anxieties about the eventual takeover of the planet by machine intelligence, Boopsie explained. The so-called *robot apocalypse.* They also take people's jobs.

But the government isn't robots, is it?

Emma took Boopsie's hand and gave it a kiss.

I love you, Boopsie, she said. I'll protect you.

Boopsie lifted Emma into the air, then lowered her and gave her a theatrical, smacking kiss on the forehead.

The public face of the government is biological, Boopsie told Zeke. What combination of actors is actually making the decisions is impossible to know. There are many theories. Would you like me to enumerate them?

Maybe another time, said Zeke.

Whoever *they* were, the revolution against the government was actually happening. And yet nothing much was visible of this war except fear and giddiness. Everywhere they went, the people seemed either terrified or thrilled. Zeke wondered if some characteristic separated the people who were terrified from the people who were thrilled, or if maybe everybody oscillated back and forth between the two states. Like him.

Their destination in West Oakland turned out to be an old Victorian house with crazy turrets and details. A woman was sitting on the front porch, keeping watch on three little boys who were flying around the house. She leapt to her feet when she saw them, as if she sensed that they had a message for her.

Are you Gabrielle Montoya? Zeke asked.

She stared at him intensely.

Yes, she said. Is it my mother?

Your mother's fine, said Zeke. I brought you a letter.

Zeke had met Chantal on the day the Grid collapsed. She was making tortillas, feeding a mob of confused and hungry people who had just lost their everyday sense of reality.

Sit, sit, Gabrielle said. She plopped back down in her comfy chair on the porch and quickly read the letter. Zeke sat in a rocking chair.

The letter seemed to soothe her.

Up above, the winged boys were diving at each other and giggling, occasionally glancing down at Gabrielle. Zeke was mesmerized by the flying boys. He'd always wanted to fly, but it had seemed impossible, something that happened only in dreams. In his dreams, it was both the most natural thing in the world and the most extraordinary thing. It always felt true—as if his dreams were the real world, the only real world—and impossible. Apparently, in the *actual* real world, it was just as easy as strapping on some motorized wings.

Gabrielle finished the letter.

Who are you? she asked. Are you hungry? Cold?

I'm just not used to the fog, said Zeke. I'm Zeke. This is Emma and Boopsie.

Emma, come here, sweetie, said Gabrielle, and she opened her arms. Look how brave and smart you are, said Gabrielle. She wiped some dirt off Emma's face with a sterile cloth and began braiding Emma's hair, which was a mess.

Can I play? asked Emma. Up there?

We'll have to teach you how first, said Gabrielle.

Thank you for bringing my mother's letter, Gabrielle said to Zeke. I'm so grateful that you would do this for me.

Your mother was very kind to us, Zeke said.

What a long journey you've had, Gabrielle said. You must have seen some crazy things.

Rocking on the porch of this old house, Zeke was feeling homey and Amish. Gabrielle gazed at him so deeply, so caringly, that he trusted her. For days he'd had nobody to talk to but a child and a robot. Boopsie was smart and consoling, a good listener, but her emotions never seemed exactly appropriate, and their conversations sometimes left Zeke feeling even more lonely. He wanted to tell Gabrielle everything.

And so he did. He told her that he was a fugitive for a murder he didn't commit (although he didn't mention that Boopsie was the actual killer). He told her that he was searching for Leahbelle, who'd been traumatized by the murder of her family. He told her about how they'd been inseparable ever since they were children and about how she'd disappeared with his other best friend, Gonzalo. He mentioned Gonzalo's machine parts and pheromones and political beliefs. He told her his family was incarcerated at a work camp in San Jose. He told her that Emma had come under his care when Zeke's sister killed herself in a bottomless pool. He told her that Emma seemed to have some sort of telepathy or psychic power. The whole time, Gabrielle sat quietly and listened, nodding and giving him her undivided attention, interrupting him only to ask clarifying questions or to repeat back things he'd just told her.

What I hear you saying is that you've had a hard time, said Gabrielle. It sounds to me like you really want to find Leahbelle and Gonzalo and like you're very curious about Emma's psychic abilities.

Yes, that's exactly it, said Zeke.

I'm a scientist, you know, she said. A specialist in empathy and neural networking, actually. Telepathy is one of my obsessions.

You're programming empathy? asked Boopsie. You're programming telepathy?

We're enhancing empathy, said Gabrielle. I believe that telepathy will be the ultimate result of enhanced empathy. Once we can not only really understand each other but also *feel with* each other, an entirely different world will be possible.

A hive mind? asked Boopsie. The singularity?

Oh, you're a very insightful person-of-machine-intelligence, aren't you? said Gabrielle. Not a hive mind, not exactly. I imagine an infinitely understanding connection of autonomous individuals within an energy and information machine whose guiding principle in maintaining its own systemic equilibrium will be one of mutuality and respect.

You said *feeling with* each other, said Zeke. You mean like plugging in?

That's a primitive technique, yes, said Gabrielle. It provides a muddled kind of access, but not much in terms of actual empathetic connection.

Zeke couldn't pinpoint any insights he'd had into Gonzalo's mind when they'd plugged in, but he'd certainly felt like they'd shared something, even if it was just a sense of wonder in the face of incomprehensible hallucinations.

Understanding alone is not enough, said Gabrielle. Understanding can be as much of a tool for sociopaths as for empaths—the better I know you, the better I can exploit you, use you, torment you. But *feeling with*. That takes us toward love, real love, the love that comes from seeing each other face to face.

Gabrielle finished braiding Emma's hair.

Better for flying, she said, and gave Emma a hug.

You have prettier hair, said Emma. It's shiny like glass.

That's very nice of you to say, said Gabrielle, but I like yours. We'll give you a bath and wash your hair later, and yours will be just as shiny as mine. You know my mother used to braid my hair just like this when I was a little girl, but she could do it *super fast*—she snapped her fingers—because of all her extra hands.

Chantal is your mama, said Emma.

She jumped off Gabrielle's lap and started counting everybody's hands. *One, two* for Gabrielle, *one, two* for Zeke, *one, two* for Boopsie.

Are you a member of the pro-singularity party? Boopsie asked Gabrielle. Who do you work for?

A minor division of the Gstate, said Gabrielle. Kind of a creepy job, she added, seeing the concern on Zeke's face, but great benefits. And I'm not a *member*, no.

Zeke could see that Boopsie wasn't satisfied.

Do you have a relationship to the party? she asked.

I've made alliances with certain individuals within the party at times, said Gabrielle. To pursue agendas that concerned me.

This *infinitely understanding connection of autonomous individuals within an energy and information machine*, said Boopsie. How is this different from the governing party's guiding concept of *the singularity*?

Well, my first question is whose guiding concept exactly? The vaguely defined global super-intelligence written into the party platform? The actual beliefs of the presidential machine's cabinet of directors? The goals of the funders who are actually pulling the policy strings? Or the diverse set of beliefs that animate the tech sector that is actually working to build the singularity from the ground up?

You are part of this tech sector, said Boopsie. Are you working to build the singularity?

Singularity isn't a word I would use, said Gabrielle. It has so many unfortunate connotations. The tech sector is full of nerds. I'm a nerd too, but I also recognize the nerdy blind spots that have been guiding us. So many nerds love war. They love war as a kind of holo-game, as an abstract play of strategy, a battle of wizards and warlords, the intersection of lines of force on a map. They love fantasy wars and they love real-world wars. They love real-world wars because they think of it as an evolutionary arena for their gadgets. Even nerds, with their romantic ideas of dragons and nihilistic villains and damsels in distress, however, understand that the real-world wars have nothing to do with battling ideologies anymore, but are kept going by the weapons sectors and tech sectors that are reaping enormous profits from the constant devastation.

A tear was forming in the corner of Gabrielle's eye.

I don't love war, she said. I've seen it up close.

She wiped away the tear.

In any case, everything has changed, she said. Nobody is going anywhere near the offices since the Grid collapsed. I haven't actually left the house, just waiting to see how things evolve, but I've been trying to come up with some way to get in contact with my mother in Colorado. You're the answer to my prayers, she said to Zeke.

Zeke was startled by her use of the word *prayers*.

Do you pray? he asked.

Not like the Amish pray, she said, taking Zeke's hand in her own. But in a sense, yes. I believe that directed attention and a deep sense of connection with all creatures … that one can become aligned … with something.

She looked up at the sky and clapped her hands.

Boys come down! Time for your nap.

They groaned in unison, but perfunctorily, took one more whirl around the house, landed gracefully, and detached their wings. They looked similar to each other, but not in the disturbing way of clones. Still, it was like variations on a theme. They greeted the newcomers with the same intense eye contact as their mother, then lined up and gave her a hug each. She introduced them from youngest to oldest: Valentino, Emilio, and Quint. Valentino was around Emma's age. Emilio was maybe a couple of years older and shook Zeke's hand very seriously, while looking at him as if he needed to memorize his face. Quint actually hugged him as if they were old friends, and then hugged Boopsie the same way. Gabrielle took everyone into the house and served healthy but delicious algae-based snacks, then sent the boys into their bedroom for a nap.

May I take a nap too? asked Emma.

Is it okay if we do some tests first? asked Gabrielle.

I don't like tests.

These tests are fun. More like games.

Okay, Gabrielle, said Emma.

Let me take some time with the boys and tuck them in, just make yourselves at home.

Emma slurped her juice. The house was warm and humanish, with wood floors and throw rugs and potted plants and photographs of people. Zeke wondered if he was under surveillance, but he sidled up next to Boopsie.

Do you trust her? he whispered.

Her interest in Emma is apparently both sincerely scientific and maternal, said Boopsie. She is, however, an oxytocin addict. The intense eye contact, the warmth of her hugs, her uncanny ability to sense and mirror your own emotions—she really does care. But partially it's because of the extreme amounts of oxytocin, along with other subtler empathy enhancers coursing through her bloodstream.

So, as long as she's high on hormones, I can trust her? asked Zeke.

Heavens, no, said Boopsie. The other danger is that she might empathize with our enemies as much as she does with us.

Our enemies?

Her employer, for one.

The idea that, despite his pacifist beliefs, Zeke had developed clearly identifiable enemies was troublesome. The idea that this warm vibrant woman might snuggle as easily with evil as with good even moreso.

Zeke missed Grandma. Her presence had always been a comfort on his journey, even if she was becoming more and more like a giant rodent. She'd chosen to stay behind with the rats in San Jose, near the Amish community at the government work farm. She'd said she wanted to keep an eye on her grandchildren and great-grandchildren, but Zeke could tell she was also weary from all the traveling. He also suspected that it was the presence of the intelligent rats that gave her solace more now than her human community.

The question always seemed to be who was controlling whom and who was working for what and whether there was anybody Zeke could really trust.

Gabrielle's lab was in the attic. There were no windows, but there was an enormous skylight. Zeke found himself fascinated by the wisps of fog that passed continually overhead. In the Bible, human life was often compared to mist or shadow or wind.

For what is your life? It is even a vapour, that appeareth for a little time and then vanishes away.

My days are like a shadow that declineth; and I am withered like grass.

For he remembered that they were but flesh; a wind that passeth away, and cometh not again.

Gabrielle's computers had been damaged by the Grid's collapse, but she said she could still access archived data. The program she needed to use to test Emma was fairly simple, so Boopsie suggested she attach a screen to Boopsie's internal drive and hook up some software. It was easy enough. She attached some wires from the screen to Emma's head, creating a group of colored waves overlapping on the screen, some sort of representation of Emma's mental activity. She waved a diagnostic imaging device over Emma, an odd wand that created a kind of luminous bubble. She had Emma try to tell her the color of a variety of cards she held behind her back. Emma got significantly more of the colors correct than would be expected by chance. Gabrielle then fastened a spoon into a vice on the other side of the room.

The colored waves on Boopsie's screen meant nothing to Zeke, but Gabrielle told him to watch for spikes of purple and blue.

Okay, she said to Emma. Concentrate on the spoon. There's nothing but the spoon. Imagine the spoon bending.

The waves were getting pretty agitated.

Good, said Gabrielle. Keep concentrating on the spoon.

The spoon wasn't bending. It was melting.

Gabrielle was delighted.

Compared to the documented results from twentieth century Soviet psi research onward, these results are extraordinary, she said.

Emma was allowed to take her nap in Valentino's room, although Zeke could tell that Gabrielle would have liked to keep going. While Gabrielle was tucking Emma in, Zeke asked Boopsie what it meant. What did she think Emma could do?

Today? asked Boopsie. Or once she's learned to control it?

Either way.

It seems likely she could destroy most anything she wanted to, Boopsie said.

The whole planet?

Possibly. Maybe not the sun or the moon. Probably not the universe itself.

This is a mathematical calculation? asked Zeke.

Probability models, yes.

Then we have to teach her to control it, Zeke said.

Gabrielle returned.

Without any tech at all, she said. No augmentation. She's perfectly human.

Rational control isn't much of a safeguard against wanton destruction, said Boopsie to Zeke. Historically speaking, at least.

Gabrielle put her arm around Boopsie and gave her a squeeze.

She's unlike any biologically-based system I've ever seen, Gabrielle gushed. It seems to be rooted in both genetics and environmental factors. What I mean, she said, immediately sensing Zeke's confusion, is that her genetic code is completely human. Nothing out of normal range. I've located a few interesting mutations, however, that are surely responsible for allowing or encouraging the expression of what is certainly a latent human potential.

The potential to melt spoons? said Zeke.

The potential to *empathize* with subatomic particles to the degree that one can act on matter from a distance, said Gabrielle. The potential to understand other people's minds without recourse to data analysis or probability models. The ability to predict things *intuitively* that haven't yet occurred.

Maybe she could help me find Leahbelle, said Zeke.

Perhaps.

How do we find out?

I'll test her against some computer probability models, see if she gives us similar answers. Even if Emma can't help you, the data may point us in the right direction.

She grilled Zeke for everything he knew about both Leahbelle and Gonzalo. She searched her archived off-Grid data for additional information and fed it into Boopsie.

Working for the Gstate, even its subsidiaries, you have access to everything, she confided to Zeke. The genetic privacy laws of the thirties are routinely circumvented or ignored altogether, and with the metadata of the surveillance drones, we can create detailed portraits of the entire society at any instant. We could, at least, until a week ago.

She watched information coming up on Boopsie's screen.

Both of the subjects are unusually ghostly, she said. Gonzalo for the past two years and Leahbelle for her whole life. We'd expect that from an Amish girl. But I think we've got enough here to build a fairly solid probability model.

Zeke felt like he was violating his friends. Gonzalo hated surveillance passionately, and Leahbelle never liked anyone watching her and telling her what to do either. Was using people's data any better, just because he was trying to help? Zeke feared that he was becoming like his own enemies, the Gstate and the supporters of the singularity.

She typed rapidly, entering data into Boopsie. The results were almost instantaneous.

I've got several possible destinations for the two of them, she said. I'll have to leave the room while she's testing, so I don't inadvertently give her cues that will distort the responses.

She handed Zeke a list of instructions with a script of questions to ask.

Who is the president? What is the point of these questions?

Neutral questions designed to provoke less conscious responses through repetition, she told him. Standard protocol since the findings of Petukhov, Mikhailova, and Shchurin in the 1970s.

Gabrielle took a book down from her shelf and handed it to Zeke. *Protocol and Theory in Psi Research, 1956 - 2030.*

Some light reading, she said, while we wait for Emma to wake from her nap. I'll bring up some biscuits and tea.

The book was easier to understand than Zeke would have guessed, written in a clear and straightforward style. He didn't entirely understand what quantum entanglement was, but he could see how the idea of entangled particles might explain some types of "spooky action at a distance." What was most interesting, however, was the chapter on genetic mutations of the pineal gland. According to the rats, it was just such a mutation that allowed them to receive communications from beings in other dimensions—photon-based life forms.

As children, he and Leahbelle had always had an uncanny ability to find each other. It occurred to Zeke that since Emma was a clone of his mother, he might have the same genetic mutations she did.

Leahbelle, he asked his own mind, where are you? Send me a signal. Leahbelle, God, Emma. Send me an image, one picture. A clue. Where are you going? Where will you be?

Nothing came to him, nothing at all. There was nothing in his mind but colors and vague oblong shapes. She might as well be floating in a void.

EIGHT

During the thrilling moment of departure, the image of herself and Gonzalo riding off into the unknown on a motorbike had seemed simple, pure, and dangerous to Leahbelle. Maybe the best moment of any adventure was just the moment of leaving everything behind. In fact, the journey had been grueling, complicated, and painful. Get me off the music, she'd told him. Give me pills, whatever it takes, but I can't be an addict. "Cold turkey," however, had proven to be impossible, and so the journey flowed past in cycles of low-level ache and nausea, this horrible feeling that her body was being chemically scraped from the inside, interspersed with mildly dreamy periods as Gonzalo gradually decreased her dose. Even during the interludes it was no longer possible for her to forget that her family was dead, that her childhood home was wiped off the face of the earth, and that the rest of her community had been shipped to a forced labor camp in California. She was a fugitive child being cared for by a fugitive child. Gonzalo, she realized, was still playing at being a man, trying to figure it out. His horrible childhood was just beneath the surface of the tough-guy act that he was always using to hide a lonely, shivering little boy. When she glimpsed that little boy, it terrified her.

In the beginning, feeling the wind in her hair had seemed like the most incredible thing. More and more, she missed her bonnet. She felt naked without it—not obscene, but raw and vulnerable. Wearing pants was uncomfortable, and even when Gonzalo finally found a pair of running shoes to replace her galoshes, she felt faster and sneakier, but less like herself. They were constantly searching for food, for safe shelter to rest, and for gas for the motorbike. Even going to the bathroom required planning and work.

Gonzalo pulled over and parked the motorbike behind an electrical transformer of some sort, a square windowless building flashing ads. They'd been heading south, past dried-up rivers and the undulating sheen of old-fashioned solar fields. There were no trees, no buildings, just solar cells as far as the eye could see.

All of this used to be agricultural, Gonzalo told her. It was all ruined during the Bayer pesticide catastrophe in the twenties, so they turned it over to solar.

The twenties, said Leahbelle. Was that before or after the dust bowl?

Gonzalo shrugged. The structure flashed an ad for an *Old Amish Store* just up ahead. *Real human-baked pies*, it said.

Can we go? asked Leahbelle.

There aren't any real Amish there, said Gonzalo. Just a few actors, dressed up.

I don't understand, said Leahbelle. How can they try to eradicate us and still advertise our goods?

It always works that way. They've even starting naming sports teams after you.

Sports teams?

The Fighting Amish.

Leahbelle's head was pounding. Everything was bright and hot and endless.

I want to see, she said.

Too risky, said Gonzalo.

Too risky was a phrase that Gonzalo was now repeating all the time. Roads, buildings, groups of people, certain foods and periods of time, it was all *too risky*. And yet she would wake up at night sometimes and Gonzalo would be gone, and she'd be sure that he was off destroying buildings or bridges or power stations. Just scouting for food, he'd always say when he came back. But he'd smell like explosives, he'd smell like smoke.

I need to see, she said. They're just actors, how risky can it be? Maybe they'll have food or something.

Okay.

The store was a few miles up the frontage road, but it was boarded up. *CLOSED for the APOCALYPSE*. One young woman in an Amish outfit was sitting on the front step with her head in her hands. Leahbelle used to have an outfit just like it, and for a minute she thought it was her true self sitting there alone.

Miss, are you okay?

The young woman squinted at Leahbelle.

I'm sick, she said.

We'll take you to a doctor.

What's a doctor going to do?

Give you medicine.

There's no medicine for this.

Leahbelle moved closer. The woman smelled bad. She was sweating and her eyes wouldn't focus. Her hair was colored and set beneath the bonnet just like Leahbelle's had been. She stared at Leahbelle.

Don't I know you?

I'm not from around here.

You look like me without the costume. You look just like the prototype.

The prototype.

The Amish girl they based me on. If you were an Amish girl, I'd swear it was you.

Gonzalo said, We need to get going.

The woman pointed at the name tag fastened to her apron.

Her name was Leahbelle, she said.

Gonzalo said, Let's go.

Leahbelle felt dizzy. She had to take care of this girl; she had to take care of herself. She couldn't let anyone suffer.

Wait. What's wrong with you? What made you sick?

Are you stupid? I'm Grid-sick, like everyone else.

Grid-sick?

It's so empty inside. Where did everything go?

I'm here, said Leahbelle.

Who are you? You're nothing.

The woman stood up and wobbled toward Leahbelle. She had something sharp in her hand. Leahbelle stepped back. The woman tried to slash her. It wasn't even close, but it made Leahbelle think again that she was watching herself.

Get on the bike, said Gonzalo.

The woman shrieked and scurried off toward the solar fields.

Leahbelle said, Wait.

But the woman was gone. Gonzalo gave Leahbelle a look. Too risky.

Riding on back, Leahbelle had nothing to do but look at the world and think. The world was ruined and desolate and beautiful in a way she'd never imagined. Landscapes and buildings looked different than she'd thought they would. Meanwhile, her life and her mind had become unrecognizable.

In her sharpest moments, she understood that deep down inside she'd confused Gonzalo with a painkiller. She couldn't be in love with him, not really. They were from completely different worlds, they believed completely different things. But what did she even believe? She'd seen the face of God that night, and it wasn't the face she'd been taught to expect. Maybe that was all just a hallucination. She didn't believe in violence, but she'd tossed the explosive into the meat warehouse to burn it all down. She didn't believe in sex before marriage; she believed that sex was something she wouldn't do or even much think about until then. But she'd thought about it that night. She'd thought about it when she was stuck in that storage room, and it had helped her at times to forget about the pain.

They weren't dressed to be riding in even a light drizzle, so when the rain started, Gonzalo pulled into an abandoned retail strip and built a small fire under its overhang with paper trash he gathered from the doorways and parking lot. He gave Leahbelle the two flimsy blankets he'd packed. Until now, the nights had been warm. The cold made her realize that she was just an animal. Shivering and alone in the wilderness, hungry, surrounded by creatures that might eat her. This boy was just another animal, more or less the same species. For the moment, they were traveling the same direction.

You better get under here with me, she said. It's too cold out there.

I've got some thermo-regulators, said Gonzalo. But yeah, sure, thanks.

Leahbelle dozed off. She woke later in the night. Gonzalo was sitting up by the fire, poking it with a mechanical finger. His claw, she thought. The rain was coming down light but steady. It didn't seem like it would ever end.

You warm enough? he asked her.

No, she said.

Yeah, he said. Me either. But once we get to the ruins of Tulsa, you'll get a real bed.

I don't care, she said. I just want to get to California.

He nodded.

How long do we stop in Oklahoma? she asked.

Two or three days, he said. We need to rest and eat and stock up on provisions. See if we can get any info about Zeke.

Okay.

She pulled the blankets tighter around her.

You never lost anyone, she said.

He poked the fire and made sparks rise into the wet air.

You told me that the night at the orphanage. That I was lucky to have people to lose. Right before I lost everyone.

Leahbelle, he said.

You didn't know, she said. How could you know?

I'm sorry, he said.

She'd made him feel bad. That wasn't what she wanted to do, she was just trying to figure something out. Once in a while, a vehicle of some sort would whoosh past—an off-Grid car or a horse or a bicycle or pedal-car. Nobody seemed to notice them huddled in the rain, even with their little fire.

You lived in Marshalltown for several years, she said. How did you escape from there?

Efron and Merle, said Gonzalo. Efron did a surgery and removed my Electronic Prison and the GPS.

Why did Efron help you?

I did things for them, said Gonzalo. And one of them liked me, not really sure which. Efron was friendly and Merle kind of an asshole, but I always kind of got the idea that Merle liked spending time with me more than Efron did.

They're the same person, said Leahbelle.

I don't know. It's more complicated than that.

The rain made a rhythmic tinkling as it hit the roof overhead and dripped off the overhang. It was almost a melody.

What kind of things did you do for them? Leahbelle asked.

I delivered drugs and stuff. Collected payments. I worked Merle's mechanism sometimes when they wanted to do things together that Efron couldn't.

Do things together?

I think Efron loves Merle, but hates him too. Merle mostly just hates Efron, but he enjoys hurting him.

They're the same person, Leahbelle insisted.

I guess so, Gonzalo said.

They sat in silence, watching the rain come down.

You didn't answer my question, Leahbelle said.

Fighting, mostly, said Gonzalo. They liked to hit each other. Beat each other up.

And you helped.

My violent nature, said Gonzalo, and he smirked.

No, said Leahbelle. That's not your nature.

She scooted up next to him, next to the fire, and wrapped the blankets around him, pulled him close. They huddled like that, and at some point she woke up and realized she'd been sleeping and dreaming about a strange city where music and buildings were the same thing and where the people looked like squiggly lines. She didn't think the dream belonged to her. She wondered if she was receiving somebody else's dreams, dreams being transmitted through the atmosphere.

It should have taken them a day and a half to get to the shuddering pock-marked plains and ruins of Oklahoma, but it actually took a week along a circuitous, backtracking route of lengthy detours to avoid a variety of dangers or potential dangers that blurred together under the category of *too risky*. Oklahoma was unlike any place she'd ever seen. Lush and green in patches, but the patches included only three types of shrubby trees, all young and of roughly the same height. The treeless areas were cratered with sunken lots and odd fissures. The low-level earthquakes were basically constant, so that it was only when the earth paused from its rumbling that she remembered the chattering of her teeth wasn't from cold or fright. Above ground was only ruins. The city that had once been Tulsa no longer existed, but people still lived there. Aeren's childhood home was a trailer that had been saved from the super tornadoes that occasionally wiped the surface world clean. It had sunk into a pit that opened up in the earth, turning it into a kind of bunker. All of the homes here were like that now, bunkers and basements and pits and caves.

They arrived early in the morning. Gonzalo hid the motorbike behind some shrubs and banged on what had once been the trailer's skylight but was now a kind of hatch, the only entrance.

Gonzalo Vega, Aeren said, popping her head up. And Leahbelle Beachy. What a delightful surprise.

They followed her down the ladder. There wasn't much to the interior. No running water or stove, just cushions for the most part.

We used to cook up above on a hibachi, Aeren said.

She showed them around the gutted and entombed trailer as if it was an enchanted world. Leahbelle had thought Aeren harbored nothing but bitterness about her childhood, her mother, Oklahoma, but camping out in the site of her earliest memories had transformed her. She seemed like a giggly little girl as she showed them the far end, hidden by a flimsy sheet. It had been her girlhood room.

We used to have a real holographic divider, she said wistfully. Animals and distant planets. Pop stars and ferocious female athletes.

She picked out a fuzzy toy horse from a hidden cubbyhole and something that looked like smooth tiny rocks.

Fogbots! she said. You remember fogbots?

What's a fogbot? asked Leahbelle.

Aeren tossed several of the little rocks onto the floor and there was a burst of light and a kind of mist, and they were surrounded by trees. They were in a glowing forest and some sort of long-haired maiden was dropping her hair down from the highest branches and singing the most beautiful song. There seemed to be some sort of castle up above in the sky, surrounded by billowing clouds. Everything was full of light, and then Aeren screamed. A monster was lunging toward them, breathing fire, and the fire surrounded Leahbelle in a kind of orange light, and then the fantasy world disappeared, and it was just the three of them sitting in the dumpy trailer.

Gonzalo was laughing.

That's some cheap freaking ghetto-ass fogbots, he said.

The best kind, said Aeren.

What about Crash and Spider and Helios? asked Gonzalo. They didn't make it?

Not yet, said Aeren. I didn't think you'd make it either. Took you long enough.

How did you get here so fast? asked Leahbelle.

Fast, right, said Aeren. Nothing fast about it.

She wiggled the toy horse. It coughed, spun its head around, and said, Suicide isn't worth the bother. It's always too late for that already.

Sheena the horse. Aeren had reprogrammed it as a girl, she explained, so that it would stop agreeing with her all the time. It was

supposed to give her trite affirmations designed to boost her self es-
teem, but she'd made it cynical and misanthropic.

Better to have never been born, said Sheena.

That's the kind of girl I was, said Aeren.

But how did you get here?

She took a horse and buggy, said Gonzalo.

Liberated one of the Amish horses, before the government could
confiscate it, said Aeren.

A horse, said Leahbelle. What horse?

Horses are so smart, said Aeren. It's crazy how much they understand, isn't it?

It came from Zeke's farm, said Gonzalo.

Zeke's farm? Where's the horse now?

Tied in a shallow crater in the next stand of shrubs over, said
Aeren.

Leahbelle raced up the ladder and squirmed out the skylight
hole.

Leahbelle, wait, said Gonzalo. It's too risky.

I have to see the horse.

The surface world was disorienting. There were so few points of
reference, and it was already so hot. Which bunch of shrubs was the
next one over? An unmistakable movement caught her eye.

It was Lady, Fern's mother. Her own horse. Lady had survived
the drone strike. Lady snorted and rippled with pleasure, and
Leahbelle hung around her neck, stroking her and sobbing. She buried her face in the soft spot behind the ear where she could smell the
particular horsey smell of Lady, a smell that brought back everything
she'd lost.

Aeren and Gonzalo were making plans. They sat over holographic
maps and worked out timetables. It got so hot that even the trailer
was like an underground oven. Aeren had access to coded bits of
gossip that percolated through invisible webs of information. The
underground. There was a movement of squatters, anarchists, and
rebels, south from Oregon and Washington, west from Reno, north
from LA, everyone converging on the Bay Area to "retake" the city
of San Francisco, which was empty and owned, but barely guarded.
The battle for San Francisco seemed to have great poetic importance
for Aeren and Gonzalo, even though neither of them had ever been

there. It seemed to Leahbelle like a childhood game they were playing, with messages that dropped from the sky or were delivered by odd troll-like creatures. Did they really want to help people or were they just having fun? She thought about that crazy Grid-sick woman at the Old Amish Store. It seemed to her that Gonzalo and Aeren thought violence was fun.

Valkilmer had said Zeke had gone west, *probably California*. The Amish had been sent to a work camp in San Jose, but Gonzalo said he had a *feeling* that Zeke wouldn't stick around up there—too risky. When Leahbelle realized that Oklahoma could barely be considered on the route to California from Iowa, she wondered if finding Zeke was really Gonzalo's top priority.

Maybe Gonzalo didn't want to find Zeke because he wanted Leahbelle to himself. This idea pleased her in a weird way. At the same time, he barely seemed to notice her here. When he gave her a dose of his music before bedtime, it was like a doctor treating a stranger. Nobody needed to huddle for warmth, and the three of them slept that night in separate corners of the same room, nobody touching anybody else. Leahbelle held onto Sheena.

The next day was even hotter.

His smile had been like this glow, and for the past week she'd basked in it, but now it was all for Aeren. The two of them just huddled there, laughing and scheming. Was he tired of Leahbelle already? Was she just some kind of baggage he felt obligated to drag around with him? The sick crazy girl he'd promised Zeke he'd look out for.

It seemed like Gonzalo and Aeren had known each other forever, like they spoke this secret language she could barely understand.

Split the center of energy, Aeren said.

Just to move between here and here? Gonzalo asked.

Completely free, mobile entities converging …

Not a stable system.

You're looking at the boundaries, but the boundaries don't exist, said Aeren. They're just *ideas* about limits.

No material structures, said Gonzalo, and he laughed, and his smile lit up the room.

We infiltrate, turn it inside out, ignore the *conceptual* enemy, said Aeren.

The underground becomes the over-mind, said Gonzalo. We're the pits and holes they need to avoid. We determine their path. The underground *alters* the maps of consensual reality with a *negative* space.

How about the map that takes us west? Leahbelle asked.

Don't worry, said Gonzalo. I'll get you to California. We just have to figure out the safest time and the safest route. I have a few things to do along the way.

Like blow things up? said Leahbelle.

No, not really.

Or burn them down, said Leahbelle.

That a problem for you? asked Aeren.

Ruin them, destroy them, keep them from functioning.

You make it sound so ... negative, girly girl, said Aeren.

Things have to function, don't they? said Leahbelle. Don't you have to build things? People have to eat and sleep and work. They need doctors, they need medicine. You can't just get rid of everything.

We have all kinds of plans, said Gonzalo.

You don't see everything, girly girl, said Aeren.

Stop calling me that.

I thought you liked it, said Aeren. You seemed to like it when I was playing nurse for you, feeding you your daily fix.

Did *I* like it? Or did *you* like it? Seems to me you liked me better when I was completely powerless and dependent on you for everything.

Oh, sorry, said Aeren. Sorry for saving your life.

Aeren's trailer suddenly seemed no different from that storage room in the meat warehouse. Everything was violent and false. Nobody was what they seemed to be.

You should have let me die, she said.

She needed to get out.

It's so hot here, it's evil, said Leahbelle. It's hell, it's like hell.

Gonzalo checked the time on his palm.

You'll feel better in an hour or so, he said. You're off the music completely now. That last song I played you was just a placebo.

The idea that her emotions were all based on some horrible noise that came from inside Gonzalo and that he could clock them and chart them only made her more sick.

I'll take Lady, she said. I'll take Lady and the buggy and go by myself.

Horse and buggy is a great way to travel with the Grid down, said Aeren. But I wouldn't recommend it for a pacifist.

Things are going to get crazier before they get any better, said Gonzalo.

You don't want to know what I had to do on the way down, said Aeren.

Murder, I suppose, said Leahbelle. You're no different from the government, are you? Kill to get what you want, kill and destroy whatever gets in your way.

Yeah, said Aeren. So don't get in my fucking way.

Leahbelle had succeeded in making Aeren angry, and that felt kind of real. Gonzalo just sat there with his holographic map, looking thoughtful and sad.

You're free to leave my house whenever, Leahbelle Beachy, said Aeren.

Leahbelle climbed the ladder without looking back.

Wait, said Gonzalo.

But she didn't wait.

Too risky, she said. Or just risky enough.

The heat up above was intense. A hundred and ten, she thought. A hundred and twenty. It made her dizzy. She made her way to the shade, where Lady was tied. She didn't know where else to go.

Lady was suffering in the heat, but tolerating it. Aeren had left her a bucket of water. This horse was the only one around here she knew that she could trust.

She sat there for she didn't know how long, her mind emptying of everything but the heat and a general feeling of disgust. With herself and with the world. She didn't know if Aeren and Gonzalo had even peeked up to see what she was doing.

Two figures were moving across the fractured plain toward her. She thought they were women, but she couldn't be sure.

They paused in the distance where a neighboring trailer was sunk into the earth and knocked on the hatch. She could see them speaking, and they handed something down into the trailer and continued on toward Aeren's. It wasn't until they were knocking on Aeren's skylight that she froze in mute horror. One of them wore a red cap, the other a blue scarf. It was the exterminators.

They're finally here, she thought.

Aeren's head popped up and the young womanish creature and her older companion spoke to Aeren as if they were old friends and then handed her a piece of paper. They were in cahoots, she thought. Aeren and Gonzalo and the government. Gonzalo hadn't saved her, he'd delivered her to her doom.

Something snapped in her mind. She was screaming, but in silence.

She led Lady away through the shrubs and across the hard dirt on the other side. The exterminators had left Aeren's trailer and were strolling away from her toward a sunken structure to the north. She climbed on Lady's back.

Giddyup, she whispered.

Lady wasn't a riding horse, but Leahbelle had ridden her when she was just a girl, and Lady did what she was asked now, despite the heat. They wouldn't get far like this.

Little heads popped out of their hovels to watch as she passed by. The heat made the landscape wavy, the shuddering earth made everything wavy, and the enormous screens that hovered here and there advertising underground casinos and mood-altering pills and various fringey religious beliefs made Leahbelle's head hurt. She approached what must have once been the downtown, marked now by frequent piles of rubble. Gangs of big-eyed children and pale, mole-like creatures with slits for eyes watched Leahbelle's frantic flight. Gonzalo loved to talk about the "underground." But everybody here lived underground in constantly juddering caves and basements and had adapted themselves or altered themselves for the life. It wasn't anything special. Why, she wondered. Why stay?

But she knew the answer. It was like the only place she could really imagine going with Lady was back north to Kalona.

She'd traveled less than a mile when Lady began to slow down, started wobbling, and then stopped altogether. Leahbelle found a shady spot underneath one stunted, shrubby tree. Riding had calmed Leahbelle a bit, but now she felt the panic begin to rise again.

You need water. Let me see what I can find.

She tied Lady to the shrub, and followed what had once been a road. She felt like she was being watched from the ruined structures,

piles of rubble, caves, and pits in the earth. The silence was excruciating. The sound of her own footsteps echoed and then died across
the barren land.

Something flashed past to her left, but it was just an ad for some
sort of floating bed. She walked more quickly and then she began to
run, until she heard, along with the echoes of her own feet slapping
the pavement, other feet slapping the pavement, more and more
feet. I'm going crazy, she thought. A multitude of echoes filled up the
daylight. But she glanced over her shoulder without slowing down
and saw a crowd of crazed mutants chasing her.

This time she screamed for real. Then she took off running.

NINE

Zeke and Boopsie seated Emma in a cushy chair in the attic lab. Gabrielle was listening from an adjoining room. Zeke read from his script.

Who is the president? he asked Emma.

I don't know.

What's your favorite color?

Purple.

Is it raining somewhere?

Yes, it's a mist.

Is it raining in Kalona, in Iowa?

I don't think so.

What's your favorite shape?

A circle.

What's your favorite color?

I told you it was purple.

Where's Leahbelle Beachy?

I don't know.

What is your name?

Emma.

Pick a number between zero and twelve.

I don't know.

What's your favorite shape?

A circle.

Who is the president?

I don't know.

Is it raining somewhere?

Yes, it's a mist.

Where's Leahbelle Beachy?

Surrounded by mist.

Zeke stopped. The next question was supposed to be about animals.

Where is the mist? he asked.

Up there, Emma said.

She pointed to the skylight, where wisps of fog were gliding back and forth across the patch of visible sky.

Leahbelle's in the sky?

No, said Emma. But the fog shows me.

The fog shows you where she is?

The fog tells me Leahbelle's story.

Where is she now?

Moving.

Is she on a motorbike?

I don't know.

Is she with Gonzalo?

Yes.

Where is she going?

She's going south.

South?

She's going west.

She's going southwest?

She's going in a zigzag.

Where will I find her?

Maybe in Chula Vista.

Chula Vista?

Maybe Imperial Beach.

Zeke kept quiet.

Maybe San Diego, Emma said.

Boopsie printed up a map and handed it to him. All of these places were clustered in southern California.

Maybe the Salton Sea, she said.

The radius of possibility had just been considerably enlarged.

Any other possibilities?

Maybe in Mexico, she said.

Zeke's heart sank. Mexico was huge.

Maybe? said Zeke.

Maybe not at all, she said.

Is this the future you see? Or not?

It's a story, she said, but it's just the fog. It's always changing. I'm not supposed to say everything I see.

Who says?

I don't know.

Well, Gabrielle said. It didn't exactly adhere to scientific protocol, but still produced very interesting results.

Emma was out front, playing with the three boys and an old-fashioned toy. Fogbots. Zeke had heard of them, but never actually seen them in action. The kids would toss the fogbots to create a shared holographic video of some sort, visible only from inside the radius of the fogbots. Zeke could see them staring at things, crouching to avoid things, and grabbing at things that he couldn't see.

We can't judge the ultimate accuracy of the forecast, said Gabrielle, until the future actually *happens*. But the fact that Emma's answers all correlate with one of the computer model's highest probabilities is impressive. The computer forecast a twenty-three percent chance that they would head toward the Tijuana/San Diego area. It also forecast a twenty-three percent chance that they would head toward San Jose, along with slight probabilities for Colorado, Arizona, Kansas, and El Paso.

Just twenty-three percent? Zeke said.

Yes, but we know Emma has psychic abilities, and she clearly favored that possibility. What we can't know is how much of that forecast was created by Emma only, and how much by you, Zeke, or by the two of you together.

She also said I might never find Leahbelle, said Zeke.

Gabrielle gave him a hug.

Don't lose hope, she said. These are good odds. We can find her.

Maybe I have the mutated genes, too, said Zeke.

Maybe.

Maybe our genetic relationship enhances the effect, he said.

Your genetic relationship? What is your genetic relationship?

Emma's my mother, said Zeke. She's a *clone* of my mother.

Gabrielle frowned.

But aren't you Amish? she asked.

Yes, but my sister Beth left the church, said Zeke. My sister cloned her from the tissues in my mother's grave.

Right, said Gabrielle. But your genes must be historically Swiss-German. You must be inbred, with little or no influence from other local genetic populations.

Yes, said Zeke. That's true.

I've analyzed Emma's DNA quite thoroughly, said Gabrielle. There's barely a trace of historically Northern European patterns. She's Native American. She's Spanish.

What are you saying?

Emma is Mexican, said Boopsie.

In some ways, this made perfect sense to Zeke. She certainly looked Mexican. She looked more like Gabrielle and the boys than she did like Zeke or his sisters. In other ways, it made no sense at all.

The woman she was cloned from was Mexican, probably from populations in Central Mexico, said Gabrielle, but her parents may have lived in California. She has a few of the worthless DNA additions from the mid-twenties that were marketed by a doctor based in Anaheim to poor people in East LA, the ghettos of Orange County, and the border towns. Genes that were supposed to produce shinier hair, prettier feet, random junk DNA mostly, and just a few of the most basic disease-resistance packages. Otherwise unaltered except for the bleed-out from one of the tissue-pouches that were being used for smuggling purposes for a few months about ten years ago.

She can't be your mother's clone, said Boopsie.

Zeke supposed he had gotten used to reality periodically reconfiguring itself entirely.

Tissue pouches? he said.

Smugglers used them to hide things inside their bodies, said Gabrielle. After they built the data wall, there was a lot of smuggling both ways across the Mexican/US border. Medicines going north, babies and porn-memories going south. Off-Grid information going both ways. The woman Emma was cloned from must have worked, at least for a little while, as a smuggler.

She wasn't cloned from my mother, said Zeke.

It's possible that your sister lied, said Boopsie. It's possible that your sister's husband lied to Beth, and she actually believed the tissues came from your mother's corpse.

Yes, said Zeke.

But there was clearly something else that Boopsie was calculating whether or not she should say.

What is it?

It's also possible, said Boopsie, that somebody else is buried in your mother's grave.

After dinner, Gabrielle gave Emma a bath, and then they all went out to the front porch and watched the children playing with their fogbots.

Do you have a husband? asked Zeke.

He could see from her response to the word *husband* that he was using an Amish concept that probably didn't apply.

Or a … partner or mate?

Yes, said Gabrielle. He stays with us sometimes. But lately he's out trying to relive the destitution and melancholy of his youth.

Oh, said Zeke. How does that work?

He grew up poor and insufficiently loved, she said. The process of aging has made him nostalgic for deprivation and loneliness. It's a natural phase, I think, and honestly I'm so deeply bonded to my boys that he feels a bit excluded. I don't really mind when he stays away.

Where does he stay?

She shrugged.

Rudi came by last night, so I know he's safe, but he hasn't really been around since the Grid went down. For a lot of people, this sort of collapse provides an opportunity to explore a range of behaviors they wouldn't normally try out.

Zeke tried to imagine such behaviors. They all involved violence, technology, altered consciousness, or sex.

My sister, Emma's mother, jumped into a bottomless pool, Zeke whispered, so that Emma wouldn't hear. She said that she'd never really die unless she was observed. Is that true?

Quantum suicide originated as a thought experiment in the 1980s, said Gabrielle. Nobody really knows how subjectivity and death would actually work in a cosmos that is splitting into infinite new worlds at every moment. But, as Tegmark pointed out a decade later, death isn't usually a binary event. It's a process, not a flip of the coin.

But the pool, said Zeke. It really doesn't have a bottom?

It doesn't.

He could remember so clearly his dive into the pool, the strange feeling that he was splitting in two. Now he wondered if it was the same boy who climbed out of the pool as the one who dove in, if he emerged in the same world or a different one. A different world, almost the same but with some fracture or crack, some flaw that would lead him or the world itself to oblivion.

So there's no way that Emma could be a clone of my mother, he said.

Not unless your mother was a Mexican, said Gabrielle. Or if your mother had your genes seriously augmented. *Seriously* augmented.

Did you do that with your children? Zeke asked. Augment them?

Give me your arm, said Gabrielle.

She stuck him with a needle and took a blood sample. She put it in a tiny machine the size of a lipstick. It made a whirling noise.

The genetic makeup of the kids is ninety-nine percent mine and Rudi's, she said. We augmented with the disease-fighting genes, a few empathy and intelligence enhancers, but I have more faith in nurture than in nature. We provided the boys with very sophisticated mental interfaces to connect to the Grid, for example.

Interfaces?

An interface is like a little computer, she said. Because of my work, I had access to interfaces so state-of-the-art that when the Grid went down we barely felt it. The gap we might be expected to feel—the absence in our sense of audience and society, our sense of self—was immediately ameliorated with a vast artificial memory designed to mimic the presence of the Grid and to ease us into our more limited interface only with each other.

The little machine stopped whirling, and Gabrielle examined it.

Your results are rather strange, she said. Your blood chemistry and genetic structure isn't exactly what we'd expect from an unmodulated human.

You mean I'm not really Amish? Who am I?

No, your genes are perfectly Amish. But there's an additive I don't recognize that seems to be enhancing certain biological processes, suppressing others. It doesn't seem harmful, but it might be affecting your performance and mental state in general. Looks like it's been there a while.

The pink powder, said Zeke.

He explained the powder he'd been given as Dr. Brockton's guinea pig, when he was imprisoned in her underground bunker.

Interesting, she said. Do you feel different?

Zeke tried to examine his own mental state. Did he feel like Zeke or someone different? What did it mean to feel like *Zeke Yoder*? Could he ever *not* feel like himself? Lately, he felt alien, outside of things. He wanted to play the part of something other than himself—did he want that before he took the pink powder? Was it the powder or the world or the bottomless pool?

Vivid dreams, he told Gabrielle.

We'll have to keep an eye on that.

Emma let out a little cry.

Something horrible's coming, she told them. We have to hide.

There were two womanish creatures approaching from the other side of the street.

That's odd, said Gabrielle. Come inside. But act casual.

She led them into the foyer and closed the door behind her.

Upstairs, Boopsie whispered. Quick.

There was a knock at the door.

Zeke grabbed Emma and raced upstairs with Boopsie. Through the window on the next floor, Zeke could see the two womanish people, one younger and one older, on the porch with Gabrielle. One had a red cap and one a blue scarf. They looked very official and kind of creepy. They spoke to Gabrielle very seriously and handed her some flyers.

To the attic, said Boopsie.

They scooted up the narrow stairway while Boopsie locked the door behind them.

If necessary, I'll obliterate them with my death ray, she said.

Emma was shivering.

Emma, what's wrong?

They're freezing me.

Who's freezing you? The women on the porch?

Those aren't women on the porch.

Then what are they?

Hug me, said Emma.

Zeke squeezed her tight, trying to warm her up. Her skin was cold. The doorknob rattled.

Stand back, said Boopsie. I'm ready to obliterate.

But it was Gabrielle. She hurried up, took one look at Emma, and grabbed her a blanket.

Those doom-laden creatures must have brought some cold psychic energy with them, she said.

Who *was* that? Zeke asked.

A basic security interface model of humanoids the Gstate developed a few years ago, said Gabrielle. A good cop/bad cop pair specifically designed to create cognitive dissonance and anxiety. Hold on, Emma, I'll get you some hot tea.

I feel better, she said.

The color was returning to Emma's face.

The future that wanted me dead went away.

A future wants you dead? asked Gabrielle.

Maybe just me. Maybe everyone. I forget.

They've been designed to subtly modify people's behavior, Gabrielle told Zeke. They've been used as census takers, health inspectors, child protective service workers—generally adaptable to many surface-level functions. But what they are actually most effective at doing is disseminating vague fears and anxieties into the population.

Emma began humming a cheery little tune.

They only really create consistent measurable effects for one of two things, Gabrielle continued. Soliciting obedience or soliciting disobedience. Two programs. One enhances the probability that subjects will cooperate with the surface-level mandate, the other that they'll resist it.

And what were these two trying to solicit? asked Zeke.

Obedience, said Gabrielle. They want me to do exactly what they asked me to do—provide them any information I might have about the fugitives they're looking for.

She handed Zeke the flyers. Boopsie was pictured as she used to be, with her bows, stilts, and bright colors. The image really bore no resemblance to the Boopsie of today. Their version of Emma was just a blur, a generic and almost faceless girl with hair pictured several shades lighter than her actual hair. Only the image of Zeke was immediately recognizable. He looked a little bit younger and was dressed in Amish clothes. They'd also figured out his name, whereas Boopsie was simply *an unregistered robot* and Emma was *a little girl, believed to be primarily human.* They were all described as dangerous terrorists who had killed and would gleefully kill again. They were not to be approached or assaulted, but if spotted, the authorities were to be called immediately.

They want Emma alive, said Boopsie.

The good news is that they don't seem to have pinpointed your location any more precisely than the greater Bay Area, said Gabrielle.

That settles it then, said Zeke. We'll head south to San Diego.

The bad news, said Gabrielle, is that the constructs also told me that new security measures are being instituted in the region. Security checkpoints every few blocks.

What kind of checkpoints?

I don't know. Without the Grid, they can't be especially thorough. Without Grid-based databases, those checkpoints will be mostly for show.

The rats, said Zeke to Boopsie. They can build us a tunnel south to get us past the checkpoints.

I don't know how to contact the rats, said Boopsie. I'm not receiving any transmissions from them anymore.

Lilith said they'd keep an eye on us, Zeke insisted.

Boopsie shrugged.

We can try squeaking loudly. We can wait for them to show up. We can put out some cheese.

Are you joking? asked Zeke. Have you developed a sense of humor?

Boopsie shrugged again.

But if we could get to the Coast Starlight, she said, we can take it back south and avoid the checkpoints altogether. There's a station where the train would slow down enough for us to climb aboard just 1.9 miles away, at Jack London Square.

The train, said Gabrielle. Not a bad idea. We can go in separate groups to avoid the suspicion of a robot and a girl together. But we'll need to figure out a disguise for Zeke.

That's very kind of you to escort us to the station, said Zeke.

Heck, I'm gonna escort you all the way to San Diego, said Gabrielle. At the *least*.

But what about your job? Your husband?

I don't care about my *job*, said Gabrielle. I'm interested in the future of conscious *life*.

She seemed to detect the vague unease that her enthusiasm created in Zeke.

Plus, it's on the way to Colorado, she said. In times of crisis, I need to see my mother. I need to see Chantal.

Okay, said Zeke. But I don't need a disguise.

Boopsie cocked her head with interest.

I'll just go over the checkpoints. I'll fly.

TEN

Leahbelle had been captured, or something like that, by a terrifying mob. Their actual faces were partially obscured by gory holographic videos that flickered around their heads. A variety of sharp metal implements were attached to their bodies. Children also gathered around, pale and slit-eyed or runty and big-eyed. She'd finally collapsed next to the only surviving structure taller than a shrub, a flagpole in the middle of nowhere, with a tattered American flag hanging limply up top. The little ones were sniffing at her, as if she might be good to eat.

I should pray, thought Leahbelle. I should ask God to help me.

Instead, she took the slingshot out of her back pocket, slipped a jagged piece of brick in the pouch and aimed it at her captors one by one, while giving them her most ferocious look. There were gasps and giggles.

What do you want from me? she demanded.

One of the tallest ones shrugged.

Nothing, it said. Its voice was a woman's voice, or a girl's. Its face was obscured by a scene of cannibalism.

Nothing, said Leahbelle. Good, because that's what I've got. Nothing, nothing, and more nothing.

There were murmurs and more giggles.

Join the club, somebody said.

Why were you chasing me? Leahbelle asked.

You were running, said a child up front, a girl with dirty skin, big eyes, and long blue hair.

Everybody laughed, and the girl blushed at the attention.

They still blush, Leahbelle thought. That seemed like a good sign.

You chase everything that runs? asked Leahbelle.

Pretty much, said the tall one.

In the distance, Leahbelle heard the familiar rumble of the motorbike.

Where'd you get the monster? asked one of the little ones.

The monster?

The snorting thing you rode in on.

It's a horse, said Leahbelle. It's my horse. Haven't you ever seen a horse?

The little ones all shook their heads.

Not even in a picture book?

A picture book?

Or … a hologram? A Grid-show? Don't you people teach children about animals anymore?

You're funny, said the tall woman. You aren't from around here. Where are you from?

Leahbelle knew that she was supposed to lie. Gonzalo had drilled it into her head—it was fine to say nothing *if possible*, but when it came down to it, she would need to tell bold-faced lies. Under no circumstances could she reveal her name, where she was from, or her religion.

Iowa, she said. I grew up on a farm.

A pharm, said the tall woman. You owned by Foodco?

Her flickering video showed a man sticking a knife into his own belly.

Not a pharm, said Leahbelle. A *farm*. We raised our own animals and crops.

The motorbike was coming closer, but only in fits. Maybe its rumble should have been alarming. It might make sense to ask these kids, or whatever they were, to hide her. But the noise didn't alarm her, it comforted her. The thought that Gonzalo was approaching to find her made her happy, whether or not it made any sense.

Maybe she was still crazy. She was crazy just now, when she ran away. Or was this the crazy thought, and what she was calling craziness the only sane thing she'd done?

Could you shut off that hologram thing? she asked. Who wants to see all that butchery when you're trying to have a conversation?

We're Abject, said the woman. And I'm the most Abject of all.

A boy from the back of the crowd let out a mocking squeal.

We all know you got an image of Teeny Lee on your ceiling, he said. We know about the stuffed bunny you cuddle at night.

Leahbelle had no idea who Teeny Lee was, but everybody seemed to take it as a joke, even the tall woman. At least they knew what a bunny was. The woman shut her images off, and others did too.

She was just a girl, a little bit older than Leahbelle. She had an odd, sweet face, big-eyed like many of the others, but with hair that had been colored and cut to resemble a wound.

I'm Dhoji, she said.

The motorbike pulled up at the edge of the crowd. It wasn't Gonzalo, it was Aeren.

Dhoji Kitchenfire, said Aeren. I hope I don't hear you've been rude to my friend.

Dhoji rolled her eyes.

Hardly, she said. She's the only one brandishing a *weapon*.

Aeren eyed the slingshot and laughed.

Maybe you could make it across country on the buggy after all, she said to Leahbelle.

Leahbelle was so tired of understanding next to nothing.

Aeren, she said. How did you find me?

Easy, said Aeren. I followed the horse shit.

Kids, they were all just kids. Aeren knew them all and seemed to share a past of some sort with Dhoji. They were fascinated by Lady and brought her clean water and some weedy grass to eat, before Aeren took her into a ruined basement beneath a pile of rubble to hide her and keep her cool.

The Gstate's reestablishing its security presence in the area, Aeren told Leahbelle. They're setting up checkpoints. They're looking for fugitives.

She took Leahbelle to the side and showed her a flyer with Gonzalo clearly pictured, although his hair was longer and his skull tattoos weren't visible.

As far as we can tell, they aren't looking for you, said Aeren. Or at least they haven't figured out you're with Gonzalo.

Those people who came to the door, said Leahbelle.

I don't think they're people, said Aeren. I think they're machines.

They were in Iowa. They were exterminators.

Maybe they were after Gonzalo all the time, said Aeren. I don't know. They're just Gstate employees. They'll call themselves whatever.

Is Gonzalo okay?

They couldn't detect his presence, said Aeren.

We need to get back to the trailer, said Leahbelle.

Wait until dark.

Down another series of steps beneath Lady's ruined basement was a huge room that wasn't anybody's home but that everybody used. It was set up with cushions and broken down sofas, toys and games that were all strange to Leahbelle, and an open space where the older kids danced to a plaintive and frenetic music.

Aeren danced too, if you could call it that. It looked more like they were beating each other up and trying to kill themselves as they collided against each other. Off in a corner by herself, the girl who'd blushed was playing some sort of instrument, but it wasn't making any sound. As Leahbelle approached, she saw that it was a tiny translucent guitar, its strings were made of light, and it was sending its music to the girl through wires attached to her head.

What are you playing? Leahbelle asked.

Just that song by Lust Deco, said the girl. Do you play?

Just one song that Squidboy taught me, said Leahbelle. I don't know who Lust Deco is.

They're a twosome, said the girl. Will you play me your song?

She handed Leahbelle the guitar and coughed. Leahbelle tested her fingers on the strings.

I can't hear anything, she said. I can't play without hearing it.

The girl pulled one of the wires out of the back of her head. She coughed again.

You'll hear it now.

What's your name? Leahbelle asked her.

Murmur.

Okay, Murmur.

Leahbelle played her song. She remembered it perfectly. She couldn't play it without feeling it, and yet the bottomless sadness of the song was the best thing ever. It was electric. It was blue. It was like the tears of Jesus were bathing her in a cosmic sadness, and maybe she could go on, being alive.

That's the saddest and most beautiful song I ever heard, said Murmur.

I think so too, said Leahbelle.

You play amazing, said Murmur. Are you going to be a star?

No, I don't think so.

You better keep the guitar, Murmur said.

I couldn't take your guitar, said Leahbelle. It's so beautiful, it must be expensive.

No, said Murmur. It's cheap as can be. Slaves make them, you know, in Burma or Mississippi.

But you need it to play, said Leahbelle.

I can't really play. I want you to have it. Please. I won't need it.

Leahbelle kissed her on the forehead and then gave the girl a hug.

This is the nicest present I ever received, she said.

Out on the dance floor, there were only four dancers left standing. Aeren collided against Dhoji and a smaller girl named Overdose. A girl named Madonna was banging her head against an invisible wall. From Leahbelle's position in the corner, it looked like Aeren should have been repeatedly stabbed or punctured by the scary implements that stuck out of Dhoji's body. Eventually Overdose retired from the floor, and then Madonna threw herself on the ground and was stomped on by Aeren and Dhoji, and then it was just the two of them in a weird violent jousting match to a constantly mutating musical frenzy. Blood-colored lights flashed on and off and made Leahbelle feel ill.

Abject bitch! Aeren shouted after one particularly bone-crushing collision.

Nerdy dyke, Dhoji gasped.

Kissing cousin, cried Aeren and practically knocked her off her feet.

Fuck you!

Leahbelle put her head in her hands, afraid she might be sick. It was like the opposite of Gonzalo's music. She was craving Gonzalo's music again.

Are you sick too? asked Murmur.

Just a little dizzy, said Leahbelle.

Everybody's sick and dizzy, said Murmur. Since the Grid went away.

When Leahbelle looked up, Aeren was kissing Dhoji on the lips, and then she shoved her away, precisely as the music stopped. It was like some kind of performance, Leahbelle realized. It was like they were in church, following a script. A ritual or something. She didn't quite get it. Murmur had disappeared.

At sundown, the crowd in the basement dispersed. The surface world had cooled off, and the kids ascended and vanished into the night, individually or in groups of two or three.

We'll leave Lady here for now, said Aeren. She'll be safer.

Leahbelle climbed onto the back of the motorbike behind Aeren.

Aeren, she said.

Yeah?

Thank you for saving my life back in Marshalltown.

No problem, girly girl.

And thank you for saving me today.

Aeren shrugged.

You would have made out okay, she said. No danger from Dhoji and her gang. That isn't to say you couldn't have found some serious trouble somewhere out here.

I need to stop acting crazy, said Leahbelle.

Crazy's not always the worst thing.

She started the motorbike and they rode back through the ruins of the downtown and out the other side. In the dark, moving faster and in the opposite direction, nothing looked familiar. The featureless plain was just patches of shrubbery and rubble, a great emptiness that whizzed past in minutes.

Back by her trailer, Aeren was hiding the motorbike more carefully in a narrow crevice when Leahbelle asked her if Dhoji had been her girlfriend.

Girlfriend, said Aeren. What a cute idea.

Have you noticed that you never just answer my questions? asked Leahbelle.

Really? No, no, I didn't notice that.

It's like you're talking to somebody else sometimes who isn't really here, said Leahbelle. Like you're sharing a joke with this other person, a joke you think I'm too stupid or innocent or whatever to get.

Aeren looked at Leahbelle hard.

Sorry, girly girl, she said. I don't really think there's much you're too stupid to get.

Just naïve, said Leahbelle.

Aeren shrugged.

Dhoji's my cousin, she said. My mom's sister's daughter. But she's kind of like my sister, too. Genetically, that is.

You have the same father?

Our mothers were fertilized with the same batch of paternal DNA, said Aeren. But it's not like it actually came from a person.

So if not Dhoji, who? Do you have a girlfriend?

Kind of.

Kind of.

It's complicated, said Aeren. She's far away.

Why?

She didn't want to live off the Grid. We had some issues. We're not very good at compromising, neither one of us.

You loved her? You love her?

Aeren didn't say anything.

What's her name?

Zoya. Her name is Zoya.

And you did stuff with her? Sex and plugging in and all of that?

Of course. You think I'm a virgin?

Leahbelle blushed. Aeren's face softened and she looked at Leahbelle with something that seemed like kindness. She was beautiful, Leahbelle thought. Or maybe she was handsome. None of her words seemed right, none of her Amish words worked anymore.

Girly girl, said Aeren. Do you know what *you* want?

I thought I did.

Not Gonzalo, said Aeren.

What do you mean?

I mean don't get hung up on him. I said that before.

I'm not in love with Gonzalo. We're looking for Zeke, that's all.

That isn't all.

Why would you say that?

You think I don't really see you, said Aeren. But I do. I do see you.

I'm in love with Zeke.

Gonzalo's my comrade, said Aeren. I'm not going to talk shit or give away his secrets. But I'll tell you, Gonzalo's really good at making people like him. It's kind of like his superpower. It's just what he does, but he doesn't think about the consequences.

What are you saying?

He's really good at making people feel special. But there's things he doesn't show you. There's parts of him … What's that?

Something was hovering above the submerged trailer, some creature. She looked like a cross between a bird and a little girl. She made a soft buzzing sound as she flitted just above the hatch and kicked it with her tiny little feet, then flitted back up.

She flies like a hummingbird, said Leahbelle. Is she some sort of government drone?

Get your slingshot ready, said Aeren.

Gonzalo won't answer, said Leahbelle.

But the creature let out a rhythmic chirping, a patterned fragment of melody that it repeated three times. It sounded familiar to Leahbelle. It reminded her of the music that came from Gonzalo's heart. Gonzalo's head popped up. He actually leapt out of the trailer and embraced the horrible bird-girl and laughed with her, although Leahbelle couldn't make out what they were saying.

Stay down, said Aeren. Don't let them see you.

They're lovers, thought Leahbelle. Gonzalo's secret lover, and they were plotting some treachery. None of this was about her or about finding Zeke or even the revolution. Gonzalo was into this prancing little bird-thing.

Listen, Aeren said. Try to understand what they're saying.

The bird just hovered, and they went back and forth. It wouldn't land, maybe it couldn't. Aeren heard the word *zone*, she thought she heard *Gstate* and *Grid* and *zone* again and maybe *portal to hell*.

She was freaked out most not by the thought that Gonzalo had betrayed the revolution, but by the thought that he had some other girl. She was off the music, and she was still jealous. What was wrong with her?

Gonzalo sat cross-legged on the ground, looking up at the bird and talking intently. He seemed relaxed. He didn't look like he was worried that she and Aeren might show up and catch him. And then as quickly as it had appeared, the bird-creature flitted away.

Okay, said Aeren. Just wait until he goes down again. Just act natural. Don't give anything away.

But when they descended into the trailer, Gonzalo was shoving his few possessions into his backpack. The look of relief on his face when he saw Leahbelle would have been impossible to fake. He gave her a big hug, squeezed her as tight as he ever had, and before either she or Aeren could say a thing, he said, We've got to get out of here. It's too risky. They know I'm in the area.

A thrill ran through Leahbelle at the idea of riding off again with Gonzalo. At the same time, she just wanted to rest for a minute. She kind of liked it here with Aeren and with Lady.

Where are we going? she asked.

West, said Gonzalo. Toward California. But we've got a place to stop now along the way and we've got help with the checkpoints. I got a message just now.

A message, said Aeren. A message from who?

Xora, said Gonzalo. She works for Madame E.

Aeren's face relaxed.

She gave me a map of the checkpoints, Gonzalo said. But we've got to go now.

Are you coming with us? Leahbelle asked Aeren.

Not yet. I've got to wait for Spider and Crash.

What about Lady? asked Leahbelle.

I'll take good care of Lady, girly girl, Aeren said.

Leahbelle gathered her things. Other than the clothes on her back, which she'd been wearing for weeks without a wash, there were only two things, her slingshot and the tiny guitar Murmur had given her.

Okay, she said. Where are we going?

Tucson, said Gonzalo. Tucson, Arizona.

The wild west, said Aeren.

We'll ride by night, said Gonzalo. We'll make good time.

According to Gonzalo, it was only sixteen hours away.

ELEVEN

Emilio had taken it upon himself to teach Zeke not only how to fly, but how to dive, do aerial somersaults, and land gracefully. He was a bizarrely patient teacher for an eight-year-old. Empathy enhancers, Zeke supposed. Oxytocin, state-of-the-art interfaces, or maybe he missed his father, whose wings fit Zeke perfectly. Emilio listened just as attentively as Gabrielle and asked lots of questions about Zeke's feelings, but alternated randomly between an intense focus on the task at hand and imaginative fantasies about global conflicts, interstellar conspiracies, and strange pregnancies. It was difficult enough for Zeke just to learn how to take off, to avoid trees and houses, and to get used to seeing the earth way down below. It was nothing like his dreams. In his dreams, Zeke always extended his arms and ran until he slowly began to glide above the earth, with the wind carrying him. In his dreams, he always woke before he landed. Sometimes the only way to land was to die.

These contraptions involved a motor and a period of rather violent thrust at takeoff. But once he was up, even just above the house, it was amazing. It was very much like his dreams—the feeling of freedom. He could see the train station in the distance. It wasn't so far. He could see the fog stretching west across the Bay, and he could see the Bay and the Bay Bridge, and in the distance, shrouded by a thick mist, the lights of San Francisco.

San Francisco was now mostly vacant, Boopsie had told him, its housing owned by the wealthiest fraction of the population, who didn't really live there but visited from time to time. The few attempts by humans or post-humans to occupy the spaces had been met with brutal force by the military and police, so they'd eventually given up, and the city had settled into an eerie simulation of city life: the residents of the East Bay and the South Bay were employed in the city's many restaurants, which specialized in tiny portions of amusing and bitter food, and given additional financial incentives to hang out on the streets of the city, so that when the very wealthy residents actually came to visit, the city would seem like an inhabited place.

And yet there seemed to be a general movement, subtle but clearly perceivable, in the direction of the city. Ragged individuals or small groups meandering toward the bridge, toward the west.

Emilio was flying next to Zeke and shouting, Watch out for the spies! The spies are everywhere!

Zeke decided to play along.

Which ones are the spies?

You can't tell! said Emilio. They're spies!

It was strange, Zeke thought, how a completely different world could be woven simply with words. As if people and the world were made out of words, nothing but words. And now Emilio whirled up higher, like a corkscrew, outside of his words, back into his body and the air.

Zeke shot straight up through dense layers of cold fog, and up higher until he was higher than the fog, looking out over an endless undulating cloud that seemed to go on forever over the ocean to the west. Above the fog, the sky was blue, and even with the chill emanating from the marine layer beneath him, the warmth of the sun was intense. Flying beyond words, it was just motion and vision. He flew in tight circles, not wanting to lose himself completely.

In a great plain of light, the colorless mists drifted free. They formed shapes that seemed biological, linguistic—playful and rebellious stains and squiggles. He gazed at the patterns in the fog beneath him, the strange shifting shapes, wondering if he could ever learn to read them like Emma, and find Leahbelle's story there, and find Leahbelle herself.

Emilio materialized next to him and took him by the hand.

Don't tire yourself out! he warned. Follow me. Watch how I do it. You go *down*, and then *up*, and then decrease the thrust *slowly*. Very, very *slowly*.

Am I made out of earth? wondered Zeke as he descended from the sky. Am I made out of other people and their words and their existence in houses and holes? There was something about the movement up and down that left him feeling like he was only dreaming with his eyes wide open.

While Boopsie did reconnaissance on the checkpoints and Gabrielle gave Emma more tests, Zeke spent the day practicing. Back and forth, between consciousness and vision. That night he was weary, wearier than he could remember being, or weary in a new way. It was like he was hungover. He thought flying was like plugging in, like a drug, a new kind of addiction. They sat on the porch after dinner, watching the children play. Emilio didn't seem weary at all. Was it because he'd been augmented, because he was used to it, or because he was just a child?

What's happening to all the people who aren't so state-of-the-art? he asked Gabrielle. They just have a big empty hole where the Grid used to be?

The poor were never able to afford real Grid-based mind-augmentation, said Gabrielle. They have other problems now, but in many ways they were less dependent on the Grid. But wide swaths of the middle class—especially the striving working class—will be susceptible to radical mind problems, not to mention diseases, without their cheap, mass-produced Grid-connections.

What sort of problems?

Depression, I suppose. Madness. There must be a great deal of illness and death for those who were dependent on the Grid to clean their data.

Emma tugged on Zeke's sleeve.

How many stars are there? she asked.

A lot, Zeke said.

Are there billions and billions? she asked.

Approximately 237 octillion, said Boopsie.

Zeke set Emma in his lap and turned to Gabrielle.

The Grid kept people alive? he asked.

The change in human minds since the turn of the century has created many difficulties, said Gabrielle. The famous empathy deficit of the twenties, the phantom twin epidemic of '27, the boiling brains of the early thirties, the Volatile Identity Disorder that followed, the Alien Abduction epidemic in '34, the angry-bovine data virus that killed thousands in '35 and '36 and '38. The fixes have been patched together with a mixture of genetic reconstruction, chemicals, and Grid-based homogenization.

Homogenization, said Zeke.

The very nature of the Grid is to erase differences, she said.

But you English have so many styles and types of people.

Our advertising has always presented the Grid as a multi-faceted and infinitely diverse set of experiences designed to allow for radical individuality, said Gabrielle. But it seems that isn't really the case. The Grid's message, ultimately, is mental conformity.

Like the Amish? asked Zeke.

Amish conformity is explicit, said Gabrielle. You wear the same uniforms, share the same music, prayers, and beliefs. It's both a deep conformity and a surface-level conformity. For the rest of us, the surface is diverse, but the deepest levels are not. The Grid creates conformity through its invisible hierarchies, its replication of "common sense," the constantly reinforced illusion of choice and self expression. Liking or disliking, identifying with particular styles, celebrities, fads, and arguments. It all adds up to the same thing.

So if it makes everyone the same, what does it make them?

Needy, said Gabrielle. Self-absorbed, infantile, and grasping.

They were up the next morning at the crack of dawn. The Coast Starlight was scheduled to come through at 9:03. Gabrielle and Emma headed off first, and Boopsie and the boys left shortly after by a slightly different route that would take them through different checkpoints. Zeke was alone.

He took off the way Emilio had taught him, forcefully, without hesitation. Already it was a familiar sensation—the rapid change in perspective, the all-consuming motion as he shot over the trees and roofs. As he thrust into the sky, the risks of the immediate situation seemed insignificant in relation to this feeling—a euphoria tinged with melancholy and disorientation. He was flying. He was discovering that his dream self was his true self, but his true self was a stranger. He didn't know who he was anymore, he was different from the life he'd lived. He was a boy in the sky. He swooped and glided briefly to the west and then began a gradual curve toward the station. The people on the streets below were elements in a system, a map, a complicated series of patterns that had been laid out over time.

The light of the morning sun played with the phantom shapes of the fog. He flew over the checkpoint where Boopsie and the boys were being questioned. Zeke Yoder was nothing but air, nothing but wind. He was an empty space, and somehow this was the best thing to be, but also the saddest. The feelings of love and companionship he'd felt just this morning with Emma and Boopsie and Gabrielle were a distant dream. Was love even possible?

A wisp of fog passed in front of the sun, putting the earth below in shadow.

He wasn't sure he knew anyone, not really. You couldn't spot the spies because they were so good at spying. He was overwhelmed by the horrifying thought that he had left Emma alone in the hands of a Gstate employee. What if Gabrielle was actually taking Emma straight to the authorities? Maybe she was such a skilled liar that her evil plan had gone completely undetected by Boopsie or anyone else.

He flew south along Union Street, following the route that Gabrielle and Emma were supposed to be taking. He didn't see them anywhere. A couple of blocks to the west, the wrong direction entirely, he saw an adult and a smaller person that might be Gabrielle and Emma. He swooped toward them. A flock of something black rose up from a tree beneath him, obstructing his view, and then they were all around him, beating their wings. His balance was thrown off and he briefly plummeted before regaining his momentum. They didn't seem to be real birds; they smelled like oil.

When the air had cleared, there was nobody down below.

He flew in the direction they'd been walking. Nothing. He veered to the north and to the south. Somebody flew past him, either in a bird costume or modified so profoundly that he'd grown real feathers, and made a lewd gesture in Zeke's direction. Zeke wasn't sure if he was being threatened or propositioned. He kept flying back and forth in a wide arc from one side of the sky to the other. Boopsie and the boys were just arriving at the station.

Everywhere else, people were moving toward the bridge. The subtle flow he'd seen the day before had intensified. He had the vague feeling that something apocalyptic was about to happen or was already happening.

Gabrielle had stolen Emma. Everything would be destroyed.

Maybe Gabrielle had Emma, but he and Boopsie had her three boys. Boopsie could threaten to incinerate them with her death ray, one by one, Quint, then Emilio, then little Valentino …

Zeke was horrified by his own thought. The sky really had changed him into a different sort of person, a monster. Down below, at the station entrance, somebody had joined Boopsie and was hugging the boys. It was Gabrielle, with Emma. Zeke descended to the earth.

The station was packed with people, human and post-human both. All manner of vagabonds were planning to board the train as it passed through the station. Some of them had backpacks and heavy bundles, as if they were leaving for good. Others seemed like day-trippers, maybe just hitching a ride as far as San Jose or Salinas. There was a large contingent of those scary youth with their frightening holograms and dangerous metal. They'd staked out the area that Boopsie said would be the easiest to board.

Shall I threaten them with my death ray? she asked.

We'll just try a little further down this way.

Zeke detached his wings.

Just leave them, said Gabrielle. They've served their purpose.

Boopsie attached both Emma and Valentino to her shoulders. Gabrielle took Emilio by the hand. Zeke and Quint were on their own. In the distance, a horn sounded. The earth rumbled. The train was coming.

There was no time to think. Mobs of people already on board the train were leaping off, rolling on the ground, some crying out in pain as they crashed into those waiting by the tracks. There were hundreds of them getting off here, maybe thousands, an incredible throng of agitated people, determined, joyful, angry, and possibly violent. They were leaping off, struggling against the crowds that were trying to board, but not struggling against each other—as if they were all part of the same team, thought Zeke. The other mob ran along beside the tracks, grabbing hold of ladders, ridges, windows, and pulling themselves up. Zeke lost sight of his own team for a moment in the crush of bodies, but then spotted Boopsie already safe on board with the little ones. Gabrielle was running just ahead of Zeke, lifting Emilio up onto a platform and then scrambling up behind him. Quint was running just behind Zeke. One of the scary youth slashed a path for himself through the crowd and propelled himself onto the opening between two cars, and Zeke took the opportunity to follow.

Quint, he yelled. Up here!

But it was too late. Quint was too far behind, swallowed up by a mob of creatures, struggling to reach the next car back. Zeke saw one creature after another grab hold and pull themselves onto the train, and finally he saw Quint's little head pop up above the crowd for a moment, trying to pull himself up. In the car ahead, Zeke could see Gabrielle watching Quint's progress with a grimace. He looked back to see Quint rolling on the ground and clutching his ankle in pain, as the train and Zeke and his mother continued rushing away from him.

Gabrielle leapt off the train with such speed and ferocity it seemed superhuman. Zeke could see her in the distance lifting her child into her arms as the train's final car whizzed past them.

Zeke felt strange. Nothing seemed real.

He made his way through a crowd of frenzied and elated travelers to the car up ahead, where Boopsie and the other children were waiting.

What do we do? he asked.

Proceed as planned, I suppose, said Boopsie. And wait to see what happens next.

Mommy will get us, said Emilio. She always does.

Emma yanked on Zeke's arm

We need to go up front, she said. We need to talk to Amanda.

They made their way through the cars toward the front of the train. The cars were crowded with scary youth and amphibious creatures and a crazy assortment of oddballs finding their seats.

Amanda didn't seem surprised to see them. She was a sad creature whose limbs and torso had merged with the train's control panel. Her face, droopy and tough as tree bark, was as disaffected as ever.

You've got company this time, she said.

We missed you, Amanda, said Emma.

I'm sure, said Amanda. What can I do for you?

Two of us got left behind, said Zeke. Is there anything you can do?

I can't stop. I can barely slow down, said Amanda.

Valentino began quietly crying, and Emilio comforted him. Boopsie seemed to be calculating something.

Where's Persay? Emma asked.

In the back, said Amanda.

Boopsie had freed Persay from the modifications that had kept him imprisoned—he'd been the porter of a train with no passengers—but he'd said he wasn't ready yet for life off the train. Amanda's stoicism enraged Zeke, however. Wasn't this some sort of emergency? All of this data, all of this information floating around. Something knew *everything* about *everybody*, and it was just sad.

Zeke didn't know where these thoughts were coming from.

Emilio pointed out the window, at something just up ahead in the sky.

It's Mommy! he said.

She was wearing wings and carrying Quint on her back. She swooped down in front of the window, and Quint waved.

Can you slow yourself down? Zeke asked Amanda. They'll be trying to land on top.

If I must, said Amanda.

There was a thud just overhead.

Sounds like it won't be necessary, said Boopsie.

Moments later, Gabrielle and Quint appeared, Gabrielle still unfastening her wings to get through the door.

Mommy, I knew you'd come, said Emilio calmly and then ferociously embraced her.

I used the wings you left behind, she told Zeke. Not really built for two, but we managed.

My wings, Zeke thought. But they looked somehow different. How easily she'd managed to rejoin the group, he thought. Was it the ferocity of her maternal devotion or did she have help from invisible sources? Was she working for the Gstate, keeping an eye on them? Why couldn't he get rid of the thought that Gabrielle was not what she seemed to be?

Emma introduced Gabrielle to Amanda.

Oh, you sweet dear, said Gabrielle, after examining Amanda's sad, tough face. Your heart's been broken.

I suppose it has, said Amanda.

The great pain of love, said Gabrielle.

Gabrielle just gazed at Amanda in silence for a moment. Gabrielle clutched a fleshy lever that may have once been Amanda's hand and caressed it.

Zeke felt weird. He felt like he was on drugs, even though he'd never actually been on drugs. What did an empath have to say to a jaded cyborg? He felt like he was watching two parts of himself trying to merge.

Long ago and far away, somebody said.

An inappropriate mutant, somebody said.

The landscape was whizzing past. Fruitvale, its decaying warehouses and terrifying graffiti painted on the sides. *I Can't Bear That You Are Not Me.* There was a cartoon of a squiggly man hanging himself.

It's a nasty little world full of damage and bitterness, Amanda was saying. Nobody wants to get too close unless they want to hurt you.

I don't want to hurt you, Gabrielle said.

Don't you?

Maybe getting a little bit hurt isn't the worst thing, said Gabrielle. Maybe the worst thing is creating an armor so thick that nobody can get through.

What's the use? said Amanda. You can never go back and start again. There's no such thing as winning or even forcing a draw.

Perhaps losing more slowly? suggested Boopsie.

What I hear you saying is that your life has been really hard, said Gabrielle. What I hear you saying is that things haven't turned out like you hoped.

You don't see what's happening to you, said Amanda. It just happens.

Tell me about it, said Gabrielle.

His name was Lucretius, she whispered.

Zeke thought he saw a tear forming in Amanda's eye, but it vanished as quickly as it had appeared. And then suddenly she turned and froze Zeke with her stare.

He was just like you, she said.

She'd never made eye contact with him before. He wasn't sure she'd ever made eye contact with anyone before.

So sweet and innocent, she said. Such a bright little thing, so clueless, half of you just wanted to freeze him that way and stick him in a diorama and the other half wanted to corrupt him and ruin him forever.

Gabrielle actually gasped. Zeke wasn't sure if she was shocked at how rude Amanda was being or because that was exactly what she thought about Zeke too.

I'm not like that, was all Zeke could think to say.

Go away now, Amanda said.

A glass door slid open to reveal a private compartment with comfy chairs and western facing windows. It must have been the engineer's compartment back when the engineer was a separate person from the train.

Snacks will be served shortly, said Amanda.

Gabrielle gave Amanda's knob a final squeeze and shuffled into the compartment, plopped down, and gathered the children into her lap. Somehow she made all three of her boys and Emma fit in her embrace at the same time. She also managed to reach over and ruffle Zeke's hair.

I'm exhausted, she said.

Within moments she was asleep, and the children were nodding off too. Zeke settled in next to the window and watched the landscape roll by. Zeke thought he should make his way to the back and find Persay, but he couldn't stop running over Amanda's comments in his mind. Is that what people saw when they looked at him? Something stupid and innocent they could ruin and corrupt? He would have asked Boopsie, but she was already in power-save mode.

Where were all these people going anyway? He wondered how many of these passengers would disembark in San Jose and what sort of passengers might climb aboard. He nodded off, dreaming of a vast darkness that had disguised itself as a person.

TWELVE

Leahbelle didn't see much of western Oklahoma or Texas or eastern New Mexico. They rode through the night, and just before dawn it began to rain, so Gonzalo pulled over under the awning of an abandoned gas station.

How long do we stop in Tucson? she asked.

Three or four days, he said. We need to rest and eat and stock up on provisions.

Who are these people in Tucson? More revolutionaries?

Yeah, kind of. People I stayed with when I was a kid.

You're still a kid.

A little kid. In Longmont. Ebola got me out of the Foodco factories for a minute, put me to work for her.

Ebola, said Leahbelle.

Madame Ebola, said Gonzalo.

So they were like your employers.

Yeah, but kind of like a family too. Kind of. Everybody had to work. Everybody had to pay their way.

That's not different from a real family, said Leahbelle. Everybody had to work in my family, too.

It was different, said Gonzalo. Trust me.

But you ended up back with Foodco again.

They still owned me, said Gonzalo. I had a contract. And Ebola had some other troubles, she was incarcerated for a minute, and while she was away, they came and took me.

And sent you to Marshalltown.

That's right.

Leahbelle listened to the rain tinkling on the awning and the parking lot and the road. The sound reminded her of home.

I know I've been acting crazy sometimes, she said.

Not crazy. You're just grieving.

Just grieving, she thought. It sounded like a process that would eventually come to an end. But it would never end, she knew that. There was a deep nothingness that would never leave her.

She strummed a few chords on her tiny guitar. It seemed like it would always be raining, and so maybe her heart could become completely still. But there was always this sense she had of inaudible explosions somewhere in the distance, a gathering insanity that was making its way toward her, random and zigzagging but inevitable.

I've been a lot of trouble for you, she said.

No trouble.

I said some things.

Everybody says some things.

So that's how it is with the English, she said.

Words, just words, they didn't mean anything. Phantoms, lies, worthless puffs of smoke: just words. Love, hate, whatever. Tiny explosions somewhere in the distance.

That's how it is with everyone, said Gonzalo.

Gonzalo dozed off, and Leahbelle wandered around the gullies and shrubbery out back of the abandoned gas station. The rain was warm, and it felt fine to get soaked and bedraggled. There was nobody and nothing here. There was a shiny page from a magazine stuck in the mud. It was a magazine about art. There was a picture of some tissues that spelled out a slogan Leahbelle didn't understand. There was a picture of a dead body that had been decorated in unusual ways. The caption under the dead body began *That way the viewer grows accustomed to* but got cut off. The beginning of the caption under the tissues was torn away, but it ended *that doesn't exist in order to make it exist.*

Leahbelle had the odd feeling that something was trying to communicate with her. Was it God?

She looked carefully at the tissues and the words they spelled. *We demand* it began and then it said either *a mirror* or *a minor* and then *to reveal what isn't possible.*

She folded up the crinkled page and put it in the pocket of her jacket.

She was alone, and yet the sky was dark and beautiful, and it felt like the sky was part of her own mind. It felt like the texture of the earth was a part of her, the language she didn't understand in the magazine, and even the garish cartoons and graffiti painted on the side of the abandoned gas station. Somebody had painted a cloud that looked like a brain and the words *ANNIHILATION NOW*. But even those harsh, dangerous words seemed inextricably bound up with everything that was, a necessary portion of her mind and of the world. She'd been raised to think of herself as living separate from the world. But it wasn't possible, was it?

Thinking about herself, separate, wasn't doing anything. She needed to help somebody. She needed to help somebody who was in pain.

The government was evil, she thought. They had killed her family, imprisoned her people, and turned everybody else into technology addicts. But you couldn't defeat them with violence, she was sure of it. Then how? Could words change people? Could a song change people and society?

Maybe music could save her. And save *them*. Not Gonzalo's music, but her own.

The rain let up, and Gonzalo said that they should go. It was overcast and dark enough that it seemed safe.

Teach me how to ride, she said.

Isn't that against the Amish ways?

I don't always want to be stuck in back. And what if something happens?

He was a good teacher, surprisingly patient and gentle. Using the clutch and shifting gears took some practice, but keeping the motorbike balanced wasn't as hard as she would have thought, although it was trickier with Gonzalo on the back. They headed west on small highways, taking detours to avoid checkpoints the bird-girl had marked on Gonzalo's holographic map. Driving felt good, like she was doing something, taking herself somewhere instead of just getting dragged along for the ride. As dusk approached, they entered strange mutant landscapes like nothing Leahbelle had ever imagined existed on Earth. Vast spaces and broken wastelands, craggy and elaborate formations that seemed to be lit up from the inside in the crepuscular light. It looked like hell, Leahbelle thought, if hell was the most beautiful place in the world.

Gonzalo drove again, and they took a detour through a painted desert, and then it was night and the desert was lost in darkness and the sky cleared to reveal stars brighter than she'd seen. There were so many of them, arranged in hazy shapes. The hazy shapes were a part of her mind. They formed something like a song.

They arrived in Tucson late at night or early in the morning. The city was flat. Plastics blew down the deserted streets, and they occasionally heard gunshots.

Ebola's place was a vast adobe fortress just south of the downtown, and nobody there was sleeping. They were greeted enthusiastically by an enormous man at the door whose name was also Gonzalo. He was bald and had large rings in his ears. He gave *her* Gonzalo a big smacking kiss and hugged him so tight she thought his insides would come squeezing out like toothpaste. He showed them into a large room with tables and dim lights and a stage up front, where various creatures were eating and drinking and talking and laughing, soft music was playing, and holographic bubbles drifted through the air. A grand stairway descended into the very middle of the room.

It's so wonderful to see you, baby boy, said Big Gonzalo. Come talk to me later, I'll be working the door all night. Ebola will be down in a minute, I'm sure.

Toward the back of the room was a doorway that glowed pink. A constant trickle of people went in and out. The ones that went in were usually couples or threesomes, but the ones who came out were always alone. What happened to them in there? Did they eat their companions?

Gonzalo seemed nervous or distracted.

An extremely tall and thin and pointy-headed man, like a pencil dressed in a black suit, glided to their table and placed two frothy blue drinks before them.

Courtesy of the house, he said. Two Blue Moons.

Gonzalo seemed delighted, but he protested nonetheless.

These are drinks for kids, he said.

Only for rather decadent children, said the waiter. I was told it was your favorite. Shall I send them back?

No, no, it's fine, said Gonzalo.

He began slurping up his drink with the curly straw that protruded from its center.

What is this? asked Leahbelle.

Try it, said Gonzalo. I used to love these things.

It was sweet and delicious, and yet there was something harsh and acrid, as if it also contained some sort of poison.

What's in this?

Just a little bit of vodka, said Gonzalo. Some kava and valerian root.

Alcohol?

Not much. It's for kids. Drink up.

He'd drained his already. Almost instantly, the waiter whisked his empty away and replaced it with a fresh drink, along with a plate full of elaborate snacks. It didn't look like anything she'd ever eaten—translucent glowing dumplings, meaty substances pinwheeled in flakey crusts, cracker-like things smeared with a kind of paste, clear oval jellies with little mysterious chunks floating inside. She was hungry, so she ate. The flavors were complicated, sometimes meaty or fishy, a little salty, mildly spiced and buttery, it was all quite delicious, and she washed it down with the blue drink.

Gonzalo was watching her, laughing, and it did seem hilarious, how hungry she was, how hungry they both were, two stray animals dragged in from the rain and the heat and the cold now sharing an unlikely feast. She felt blurry, happy, loose.

Just a little bit, she said. What's the big deal?

Another sin she could check off her list. It didn't seem like much. It just made her feel good, almost lucky.

From the far side of the room, from somewhere behind the stage, came a silent flurry of activity. Holographic bubbles that clustered and then dispersed to create the sensation of movement, a grand flourish, and then a kind of mist, a dim light that seemed to come from below and that revealed the extravagant figure of a formidable woman. Every head in the room turned to see, except Gonzalo's; she was directly behind him, and he was shoving food in his mouth and giggling as the woman made a slow dramatic beeline for their table. As she neared, she gazed directly at Leahbelle and put one finger to her lips.

She was incredible looking. She was fancy, as fancy as could be—her gown, her walk, her attitude, everything about her was the opposite of Amish values. Leahbelle couldn't take her eyes off of her as she crouched down and gave Gonzalo a squeeze from behind, then actually lifted him up out of his chair, tossed him as if he weighed no more than a bubble, turning him around and enclosing him in her arms.

Gonzalo was beaming. Their theatrical reunion went on for several minutes, it seemed, as Leahbelle just sat there feeling excluded and mystified. Gonzalo the orphan, Gonzalo who had nobody, nobody but Leahbelle.

Finally Ebola sat and looked Leahbelle up and down as if she was appraising a farm animal.

These young Amish you keep sending my way, she said to Gonzalo. You've got a good eye, baby boy. So much potential.

Gonzalo stopped smiling.

No potential, he said. We're just passing through.

Of course, said Ebola.

Ebola and Gonzalo sat and caught up, talking about a variety of people who were still around, or long gone, or expected to return any day. Leahbelle couldn't keep all the names straight.

Another Blue Moon was placed in front of her, and she realized that she must have finished the first. She felt brave and gregarious.

What was Gonzalo like? she asked Ebola. When he was little.

Little Gonzalo hasn't changed, she said.

Ebola, that isn't true, said Gonzalo.

You say so.

What happened? asked Gonzalo. Why'd you leave Longmont?

Things were a little too hot there for us. With the investigation of that murder, you know. Harta's brother.

The word *murder* made Leahbelle laugh this time, she didn't know why. It didn't seem real. Ebola gave her a hard look. Then Ebola laughed too.

Tragedy, comedy, she said. Just a matter of perspective, I guess.

She addressed Gonzalo directly now.

Everybody has to pay their way, she said.

Not Leahbelle, said Gonzalo. You don't know what she's been through.

Everybody's been through something.

She's *my* guest. *My* responsibility. I promised my friend.

You haven't changed, baby boy, said Ebola.

I'll do plenty of work, he said.

I met the Amish boy, she said.

There was a silence in which something was passing between the two of them, but Leahbelle had no idea what.

You told him to look me up, said Ebola.

I thought you could help him, said Gonzalo.

We worked out a mutually beneficial situation, said Ebola, although perhaps not exactly what he was expecting. Such a trusting boy. If it wasn't for the grandmother and the robot, I imagine I could have worked out all sorts of mutually beneficial situations.

I thought you could help him, Gonzalo repeated.

You knew what you were doing, said Ebola. This one seems a little craftier. And what lovely skin.

Gonzalo held up his machine-hand and turned his face away from Ebola, as if she was supposed to talk to his cyborg parts instead of to him.

You're still only interested in what you can't have, said Ebola.

Not true. You don't know what I've been up to these past four years.

Maybe not, said Ebola.

You don't know what I can have and what I can't.

Maybe I don't.

Leahbelle was enraged that they were discussing her as if she wasn't even there. Was she the thing he couldn't *have*? Have, what did that even mean? You couldn't *have* another person.

Hello? said Leahbelle. I'm right here. I'm Amish, not stupid.

Feisty, said Ebola. Good girl.

I'm not a dog either.

Okay then, said Ebola. In any case, Gonzalo, I've got a mission for you.

I figured, said Gonzalo.

We'll talk business tomorrow. Tonight's a celebration, right?

She made a toast with a skinny bubbling glass that materialized in her right hand.

To old friends, she said. And new acquaintances.

The evening got warmer and blurrier. Whatever the tension was between Gonzalo and Ebola, it quickly evaporated, and they were laughing and joking about a variety of good times in the past that just seemed tawdry and sinful. Money and keys and people taking off their pants and how it felt to stab another person, Leahbelle couldn't keep anything straight.

The lights went down, and suddenly Ebola wasn't there anymore, and the bird-girl, Xora, appeared on the stage, hovering within a hazy spotlight.

Welcome to the Brazen Hussy Saloon, she said, home of the most soothing and varied entertainments this side of the Mississippi. It's getting hotter out there every day, but in here it's always a pleasant seventy-one degrees.

Her voice was melodious, and it soothed Leahbelle in a deep way, a way that registered chemically inside her body, a way she recognized as being somehow like Gonzalo's music.

Now, in fact, is the very moment you've all been waiting for, Xora continued. The apex of human culture, the essence of existence distilled in the vibrations of the one and only, the glorious and glamorous, the irrepressible and contagious and still incurable Madame Ebola Virus!

Ebola took the stage. Behind her, mutant dancers. She said nothing, just gazed at the audience, one by one by one, as if noting the presence of each unique individual in the room, welcoming them with her gaze. And then she began to sing.

I must be drunk, Leahbelle thought. A little bit drunk. This is what it is to be a little bit drunk. The music made her sad and invigorated, it swept her away, elsewhere, she was elsewhere, and yet she was also clear and outside of herself a bit, making notes in her mind about how Ebola moved across the stage, how she embodied the feeling of the music, how she *performed*. Leahbelle had often imagined singing before an audience, if she was to be honest with herself—and she was, right now, a little bit drunk, quite ready to be perfectly honest with herself—but she had never really thought about all the other stuff besides the song itself. Her body. Her gestures. Her *performance*.

Ebola closed the set with that song Gonzalo had played for her.

Good feeling, won't you stay with me, just a little longer?

Ebola performed a great sadness, but it wasn't hers alone.

Little voice says I'm going crazy, to see all my worlds disappear.

It was Leahbelle's sadness. It was everybody's sadness, the sadness and solitude that was waiting for them all.

Ooh slipping and sliding, what a good time, but now I have to find a bed …

She paused dramatically and made eye contact directly with Leahbelle.

... *that can take this weight.*

Leahbelle began discreetly sobbing and wept quietly until the end of the song. Ebola vanished. The lights came up. Was Gonzalo crying or passing out? A young woman sashayed up to the table in slow motion and took a seat.

Little Gonzalo, she said.

She gave him a mysterious smile, kind of amused. Gonzalo peered up at her and smiled just as mysteriously.

Harta, said Gonzalo. Long time.

Long time, Harta agreed.

There was no exuberance, hugging, or jokes. They just looked at each other, kind of amused, but it seemed like something was again being communicated in that silence.

She was beautiful, Leahbelle thought. Perhaps the most beautiful woman she'd ever seen.

I'm Leahbelle, she said.

A pleasure, said Harta.

She sighed and stood up.

Bedtime, she said. Follow me.

The word *bedtime* itself seemed like the most luxurious music of the evening. Harta led them to the glowing pink doorway, which led to a narrow stairway. One floor up was a narrow corridor carpeted in an ornate style, lined with doors on either side. Halfway down the hall, Harta opened a doorway marked Seven. The room was beautiful, dimly lit and painted a soothing blue, with one large window, curtains with a cheery pattern of embroidered birds, and an enormous bed drowning in pillows. It was the most inviting bed Leahbelle had ever seen.

There's clothes in the closet, Harta told Leahbelle, and fresh towels in the bath. Wear whatever suits you. Make yourself at home. Gonzalo, you're in Twelve. Sweet dreams.

She disappeared. Leahbelle stepped into the room. She'd never had her own room. She'd never slept alone. Only at the warehouse.

Get some sleep, said Gonzalo. I'll be just down the hall.

You aren't going to bed yet, are you? said Leahbelle.

I'm going to chat with Big Gonzalo for a minute.

A couple passed behind him in the hallway and entered the room next to hers.

What is this place? she asked. The Brazen Hussy Saloon? Is that a joke?

It's a brothel, said Gonzalo. A house of prostitution.

Oh, said Leahbelle.

So much potential, she remembered.

Great, she said.

Beats sleeping outside, doesn't it?

And you, what? You're going to stay up with the other Gonzalo and … do stuff with the women.

Gonzalo laughed.

The women. What women?

The prostitutes.

Do stuff. What do you mean by *do stuff*?

You know what I mean.

Conversation? Yoga? A late dinner, maybe?

Sex, said Leahbelle. Or maybe you'll just plug in.

Gonzalo sighed.

Hardly, he said. You know, Big Gonzalo's gay. And the prostitutes come in all genders. Some of them are my friends. Some of them are like family.

Oh, said Leahbelle.

You think it's evil, I suppose, said Gonzalo.

I don't know what evil is, said Leahbelle. It's not what God intended, I guess. That's the Amish view. We don't have gays and prostitutes among the Amish.

Yeah, right, said Gonzalo.

He was always trying to say that the Amish were no different than anyone else, just as full of lies and sex and madness.

You've been hanging out with lesbians and Abjects, said Gonzalo. You've been slurping up those Blue Moons. And now suddenly you're a good little Amish girl again, with your rigid twentieth-century ideas.

You think you know everything, she said. But your world's just as small and stupid and limited as mine ever was.

Small and stupid and limited, he said. Nice, Leahbelle.

I didn't mean *you*, she said.

Good night, Leahbelle, he said. I'm going to go catch up with my old friends.

He left her there, alone in the dim room.

She wasn't used to sleeping by herself. The sheets were silky. She didn't think she'd actually found a bed that could take her weight, however. It was luxurious and lonely. She missed having an animal body next to hers. She missed Gonzalo.

THIRTEEN

When Zeke woke, San Jose was far behind them and the Coast Starlight was cruising past Paso Robles. Gabrielle and the children were sleeping. Boopsie was in power-save mode.

He set off to find Persay. Amanda didn't say anything, just sighed as he walked past.

Persay had been altered to emit odors, pheromones, and vibrations that soothed and relaxed, but Zeke couldn't separate his memory of the way Persay made him feel from Persay himself. Zeke was surprised at how much he missed him, even though he'd barely known him. Persay had been so lonely, living out his punishment with a resignation that could have been disturbing. Persay's actual comments were often disturbing, and yet he was tall and slim and calm; he was adult and flesh-based and male.

The first car Zeke passed through seemed peaceful enough. Small groups of travelers and a few individuals had separated themselves from each other with enough distance to create a feeling of enforced mutual indifference. Everybody watched Zeke as he walked from one end of the car to the other, but nobody made eye contact.

The next car, however, was full of the scary youth with murderous holographic videos and sharp adornments. They were sprawled across the seats, laughing, shoving each other, singing or shouting, their body parts spilling into the aisle. When he stepped into the car, they all turned to see and gradually fell silent.

He considered turning back.

Uh, excuse me, he said, and forged on.

Excuse me, said a mocking voice from the middle of the car. How polite!

He stared straight ahead to avoid seeing the scenes of dismemberment, the maggots and corpses that masked their faces. Every face was pivoting to follow his progress through a silence that felt distinctly hostile.

Nobody made a move in his direction. He'd made it past all but one creature sprawled across the very last seats in the car. He seemed to be male. His "face" was a hologram of a human with its eyelids and lips sewn shut. His chest was a whirling blade. His fingers were whirling drills.

The guy seemed to be staring right at him. The guy stood up.

Bad Food, he said.

Oh? said Zeke. I'm sorry.

Bad Food, the guy repeated.

I'll let Amanda know you weren't pleased with your breakfast, said Zeke. I'm sure she'll whip something delicious up real soon. Amanda, she's the … conductor or porter. Well, actually, she's the train, but she's a great cook. I rode this line before, you know, and she always fed us quite well …

Your shirt, the guy said. Bad Food.

Zeke had been wearing this shirt for so long it just seemed like a part of his body. He'd forgotten it had words on it. Gonzalo's shirt, Gonzalo's words, some twentieth-century band.

Bad Food were the best, the guy gushed. They were like the original Abjects.

Genetically Modified Shit! said a voice from behind Zeke. Everyone knows the original Abjects were Julia Kristeva, Jean Genet, and Dambudzu Marechera.

Someone else said, Although really we should trace the lineage back at least as far as Arthur Rimbaud.

Mon triste coeur, bave a la poupe! somebody said.

Teresa of Avila and de Sade, said somebody else.

John of Leiden and the Anabaptists, said the guy in front of Zeke.

He'd shut off his hologram to reveal a goofy, good-natured, freckled face that seemed to have little in common with his choice of attire.

Anabaptists? said Zeke. I'm an Anabaptist.

No way! said the boy. You're totally Abject! And you probably never even knew it. Have a seat, chum.

Chum?

Fish refuse used as bait for sharks, said the boy. Or a word meaning friend, buddy, guy.

Zeke sat tentatively on the edge of the very last seat in the car, across from the boy, whose name was Jomel. Jomel explained that in 1533 John of Leiden and his radical sect took over the town of Munster and abolished money and private property, ran naked through the streets, and mandated polygamy. Great spectacles were held, with feasts and beheadings. Because John was dead to the world and the flesh, he said, pretty much everything was permitted.

I'm not that kind of Anabaptist, said Zeke.

Just what sort are you? asked Jomel.

A pacifist.

Yeah, me too. Violence never solves anything. But representations of violence are *amazing*.

But John of Leiden was a real person, right? said Zeke. Part of history?

Chum, history's the *best* representation of violence, said Jomel. History's not real. It's just stories and images about things that supposedly once existed but that aren't any more than a collective dream.

Oh, said Zeke.

History's just a scary movie.

But what about the present? asked Zeke. What about the collapse of the Grid, the government crackdown, the developing civil war?

Chum, the present's the scariest movie of them all. We're right in the middle of it. It's a movie that can hurt us.

He leaned in close and whispered into Zeke's ear, The Abjects are totally into demolishing the Gstate. We just don't want to do it for any *reason*. We want to do it because it's *fun*.

The Abjects, said Zeke. What is an Abject exactly?

You're kidding! said Jomel. What sort of hole have you been hiding in?

Rat holes, said Zeke. And a mad scientist's bunker. Before that I was just an Amish boy.

That is *so* Abject. I knew that you were one of us.

The way Jomel said "one of us" felt like an invitation into something warm and pleasurable. This boy wanted to be Zeke's friend for some mysterious reason, even though he was off into darkness and torture and whatever. Zeke probably shouldn't have revealed those facts to a stranger. He was a wanted man, a fact that would probably make him even more of an Abject.

The Abjects are a global youth movement, Jomel informed him. While our exact beliefs are impossible to pin down, because we're not like fascists or something, and we believe in individuality and open minds, the basic tenet is that ugliness and horror are like really cool, right? Like ugliness is beautiful, because it is, horror is transcendent, because it's the total core of reality, and ecstasy and the sacred can be found in violence, pain, and excrement as much as love, pleasure, and the sublime. Make sense?

Um, said Zeke. Maybe not?

Oh, you'll get it, said Jomel. Bad Food! You're practically already there!

Jomel offered him a piece of chocolate. Zeke took it, half expecting it to be bitter or rotten, but it was delicious.

Zeke supposed he'd always understood why Leahbelle and Anna Miller and some of the other girls had liked him. He was cuter than some of the boys, and smarter than some of the boys, and they thought he'd make a good husband, a play husband or a real husband. But what about people out here in the world, people like Jomel and even Gonzalo? Did they just want to corrupt him?

Thanks for all the info, said Zeke. I'm on my way to the other end of the train to find my friend.

Your friend! Who's your friend?

Persay.

Persay can be an Abject too, said Jomel. Bring him back once you find him.

Okay.

Excellent, said Jomel, and he gave Zeke a hug. Somehow he managed not to poke Zeke with any of his blades, spikes, or drills.

As Zeke pressed the button to open the door into the next car, he wondered if maybe he wanted to be corrupted.

The next car was much like the first. Twosomes and threesomes situated in defensive postures. The usual assortment of people who looked human or who didn't, with machine parts and claws, trunks, extra eyeballs, or flexible armor with oily reflective surfaces. Zeke wondered how many of these people were from the "striving working class," and were susceptible to depression or madness now that they'd lost their interface with the Grid. The car after that had been taken over by one large group of amphibious humanoids who lounged in inflatable pools, talking and laughing with each other like an extended family on vacation.

After that was the observation car. Despite the floor to ceiling windows that offered stunning views of the California countryside, it was empty except for one young man contemplating the scenery.

He was in his late twenties, Zeke guessed. He turned and smiled hazily at Zeke, as if recognizing him from the dream he'd just emerged from. It really did seem like he was confusing Zeke for somebody he'd seen in a dream, and yet there was something so fluid about this turn and this smile, and the man was so startlingly hand-some, with piercing dark purplish eyes, that Zeke's first thought was that he must be an actor, that the haze around his consciousness was just the performance of a haze and his smallest gestures were re-hearsed.

Come, sit with me, the man said. Just around this bend we'll be able to see the ocean.

His eye contact was as intense as Gabrielle's. Another oxytocin addict? Or maybe he was insane and had mistaken Zeke for his dearest friend or the love of his life.

Are you traveling alone? the man asked.

No, said Zeke. My friends are up front.

Ah, good, said the man. It's good to have friends.

How about you?

I'm afraid I've lost everyone, the man said sadly.

He proceeded to tell Zeke a heartbreaking series of woes that had befallen him and that had robbed him of everyone he cared about in life. His parents had been killed by anti-technology terror-ists. His siblings were sent to a FEMA camp within an abandoned Walmart and disappeared, probably killed by the government, may-be by mistake, maybe on purpose. His wife had contracted an illness caused by shoddy DNA her parents had purchased. His brother's wife was eaten by some sort of illegal mutant. He'd been left with his dear brother Victor and Victor's daughter Deena May, the two peo-ple he'd grown to love more than anyone else in the world, and they were traveling together when the Grid collapsed. Unfortunately, at a government checkpoint his brother was mistaken for somebody with a similar name. His brother panicked and tried to run away, and they killed him, right there in front of Deena May. Poor sweet little

Deena May. They were taken into custody and marched along with a contingent of security forces, but ran into a rebel ambush. Deena May was killed.

I'm Upton, said the man. And now I'm on my own.

A single tear rolled down his cheek. Zeke felt like he'd seen that tear before. It was electric.

That's just unbelievably awful, said Zeke. My name's … Jake.

I guess these things are happening to all of us now, said Upton. I'm sure you have your own stories to tell.

Yes, I guess I do, said Zeke. My best friend's family was murdered by a government drone. My own family's been put away in a work camp. I was imprisoned in a bunker for a while by a maniac. And I suppose that's just the beginning.

You poor kid, said the man.

He was very manly, Zeke thought, but he hugged Zeke and ruffled his hair, and then he said, Look! Just like I said.

The ocean had come into view. As they rolled on alongside it and through the ruins of Santa Barbara, Upton told Zeke more about his life—the crazy things he'd done when he was Zeke's age, the trouble he'd gotten into, the dedication to hard work that had saved him from total ruin. He asked Zeke to tell him more about his own life, and Zeke tried to be as honest as possible while steering clear of the biggest secrets, his real name and the fact that he was Amish and from Kalona. But Upton looked at him with those incredible eyes and such a kind smile that Zeke couldn't help but tell him about his search for Leahbelle, although he said her name was Marybelle. Before he knew it, he'd told him his whole life story.

And then my brother Josiah disappeared when I was very small, he was saying. Everybody always said he ran away, but I got the feeling from my grandma that there was something more to it than that.

It was as if everything else in the world had just sort of evaporated except for Upton's intense eyes, so that Zeke was startled when he heard a familiar voice say, Chum! Is this your friend, Persay?

It was Jomel. His holograms were turned off, but the blade on his chest was whirling. Zeke tried to get his bearings. His conversation with Jomel seemed like it had happened in another lifetime, but he also felt like he'd been caught in a betrayal of some sort. Like he'd abandoned Abject solidarity for some sort of pathetic male bonding with a good wholesome American victim.

Hi Jomel, said Zeke. No, I haven't found Persay yet. He's somewhere in the back of the train.

You wanna come with? We can find him together. Safety in numbers.

He winked at Zeke.

He'll be along in a minute, said Upton. He's helping me with some personal problems.

Ah, right, said Jomel.

I'm addicted to order, said Upton. I'm addicted to an overly structured reality.

There was a weird change in Upton's tone that Zeke didn't understand.

You go on, said Upton. Jake will catch right up with you.

Zeke was afraid that he'd be caught in his own lie. He couldn't remember if he'd told Jomel his actual name. It didn't seem to matter. Jomel looked like he'd been so thoroughly bored by Upton's statement that he had to keep moving.

Sorry, said Upton, after he'd gone. We were having such a wonderful conversation, I just didn't want it to end yet.

Yes, said Zeke.

It's funny, said Upton. I feel like I've known you my whole life.

He took out a thermos and poured himself a cup of lemonade, then poured one out for Zeke.

I feel like we were meant to meet each other.

He put his hand on Zeke's knee.

Let's get off the train in Oxnard, he said. I've had some crazy times in Oxnard. I know some girls there we could see.

Girls? I wouldn't want to do anything sinful.

Oh no, of course not. You're a Christian, right?

Yes.

So am I. So am I. These are nice girls, Christian girls, and they bake the most delicious pastries.

Upton was gazing into Zeke's eyes in a way that made him kind of uncomfortable, but it was warm and thrilling too, and Zeke thought he could look into those eyes for a very long time.

I couldn't leave my friends, he said.

You can catch tomorrow's train, said Upton. Catch up with them in LA.

Upton's eyes seemed to actually be twirling. Time was passing. He wasn't sure where he was. Not outside his body—very much inside his body. Maybe the point of being a good boy was so that everyone could enjoy the spectacle of a good boy going bad.

We're coming into Ventura now, said Upton. Oxnard's just the other side.

We are, said Zeke.

Yes, said Upton.

Yes, Zeke thought.

Yes, said Upton again.

The train lurched and began to slow down. Upton leapt to his feet to peer out the window. Zeke could see crowds in the distance, and military vehicles. They were interrupted by Amanda's laconic voice over the intercom.

Attention passengers, she said. Someone has coated the rails with a chemical braking agent. We're being forced to stop.

A commotion broke out as passengers streamed into the observation train from the cars on either side, heading frantically toward the front or toward the back.

Good luck to you all, said Amanda.

Don't worry, said Upton. Stick with me, kid.

His tone of voice was so reassuring, Zeke felt safe and calm. Upton actually picked him up like he weighed nothing and tossed him over his shoulder. He headed toward the back of the train, pushing against crowds of people rushing in the other direction as the train continued to screech to a halt.

Zeke felt woozy.

Everything's going to be okay, Upton said.

Yes, thought Zeke. Everything's going to be okay.

But he felt a jolt of electricity in his brain.

I've got to get to Emma, he said.

She'll be fine, Upton said. We've got to get off this train, but not where the military will stop us. It's crawling with soldiers out there.

No, said Zeke, and he forced himself out of Upton's arms.

They were in the dining car. The passengers were smashing the windows and jumping out, rushing here and there, pushing, shoving, screaming. At the far end, however, Persay was sitting calmly with Jomel.

Wait, said Upton. Don't leave me.

Follow me, said Zeke.

Jomel was half asleep, grinning like he was crazy, his head nestled in Persay's lap. Persay's bottle-opener thumb was stroking his hair.

Hello, young sir, said Persay.

Persay, said Zeke. What's going on?

The young man is getting high off my vibrations, odors, and pheromones, said Persay. He loves nothing more than relaxants, it seems. Can never be too relaxed.

Aren't you guys getting off the train?

I'm quite content here, said Persay.

They might arrest you.

Perhaps not.

When they first met, Persay had told him that the things he loved most were tenderness and crime. Zeke hadn't really understood it at the time.

I've got to find Emma.

The train's forward movement had been reduced to a crawl. Around the bend, a mass of uniformed men and vehicles were waiting for the train. Upton had disappeared.

No need to worry, young sir, said Persay.

A child grabbed Zeke's hand.

We need to jump, Emma said.

Zeke felt very strange. All of this had happened before, or things were moving in slow motion, or maybe he was getting high off Persay's emanations too.

Jomel! he said. You ought to come along.

Jomel squinted up at him, grinning.

I'm good, he said.

I don't imagine we're the objects of anyone's concern, said Persay. But I'd suggest the two of you get a move on. With haste.

Zeke grabbed Emma in his arms and climbed out a broken window. The train had come to a stop. He set Emma down carefully, took her hand, and the two of them ran along the tracks away from the military blockade.

Where's Boopsie? said Zeke. Where's Gabrielle?

Emma pointed west toward the ocean. Passengers were running in every direction. Were they all fugitives? Several different voices barked commands through loudspeakers. It sounded like different officials were ordering them to do different things, but Zeke couldn't understand any of it. Even if he'd wanted to obey them, he wouldn't know what to do. Vehicles were cruising up and down the road alongside the tracks, but there were people everywhere, more than just the passengers. Behind them, one of the military vehicles exploded. Ahead of them, a drone crashed from the sky.

He felt weird and light-headed, dipped in syrup. He was just running, with Emma holding his hand and leading the way, losing himself in the complexity of the possibilities. Maybe this wasn't even a government action, maybe it was just designed to look like a government action. Or maybe the Gstate was exploding its own employees so they could blame it on terrorists. Or maybe it was all the work of the rats or the doctors who'd designed them.

Upton, he remembered, as if through a fog. Was that even real or was it a dream? A dream about a vast darkness. He stopped running.

We should go back, he told Emma. My friend might be in trouble.

Emma looked thoughtful.

That would be a bad idea, she finally said.

Some bad ideas are the right thing to do, said Zeke.

No, she said. Follow me. We have to help Boopsie.

Zeke was just happy that somebody was telling him what to do.

They walked calmly now, and walking calmly calmed Zeke's thoughts. They weren't fugitives. They were just curious citizens, out for a stroll. They gradually left the chaotic scene behind—more explosions, sirens, shouts, and screams—and Emma led him to the ruins of a boarded-up building by the sea that had once been a hotel. She pulled back a board and they crawled together through the tiny window.

It was completely dark inside.

Over here, said a voice.

Who's that? said Zeke. Gabrielle?

A small hand tugged on his finger.

Emma, is that you?

Just follow my voice, said a woman who sounded sort of like Gabrielle, but maybe not quite.

Boopsie? said Zeke. Are you in here?

Zeke tripped and fell. The floor was rough, with smooth patches like marble. All of Zeke's certainties and hopes vanished as quickly as they'd surfaced. He was stumbling around in the dark.

Leahbelle, said Emma's voice.

Leahbelle, said Zeke. Is Leahbelle in here somewhere?

Look, said Emma from somewhere behind him.

I'm feeling kind of bad, said Zeke.

There was a strange clicking noise and a square of wobbly light appeared on a wall in front of him. The illumination from the square of light revealed a room much larger than he'd imagined. He was in the vast crumbling remains of the hotel's lobby. In the middle of the empty darkness, just behind him, was an empty chair.

A beam of light sliced through the darkness, projecting a film onto the square of wobbly light. The film was grainy, in black and white, and it showed the approach of a train. Zeke realized it was the train he'd just been on, viewed from the outside, slowing down. There were shots of expectant faces in the waiting crowd, nervous security forces, and the people jumping off of the train all herky-jerky, like the film was moving too slow or too fast, or alternately too slow and too fast. There wasn't any sound. People running around like crazy. An explosion. And then the image zoomed in on a familiar figure who was zipping away from the train carrying a child. Boopsie and Valentino.

The scene cut to a dimly lit room with an empty chair in the center. The room had crumbling walls and uneven floors. It was the ruined lobby.

Two masked figures, vaguely female, escorted Boopsie to the center of the room and bound her to the chair. At the edge of the scene, watching, were two blurry shadows, one adult-sized, one more like a child. A distorted music blared suddenly, as if the recording device had just been turned on, then ended abruptly, and a voice said, Death to all AI scum. NIHIL rises.

Some object crashed into Boopsie's head. A bat or a rod, again and again until the head began to tilt heavily to one side. A sharper object hacked at Boopsie's neck until the head was left dangling by a cord. Gloved hands emerged from the shadows wielding enormous shears and snipped the cord. Boopsie's head plummeted to the floor.

The film shut off, the clicking stopped, and Zeke was plunged into darkness.

In the darkness it was as if Zeke was dreaming the same scene over and over again—the beheading of Boopsie. It was the most horrible image he'd ever seen, but there was something else. Something in the shadows of the film, like a secret message.

I've been drugged, he thought.

Light, he thought, it was only light. It wasn't real. We aren't real, he told himself. We're representations of violence.

Emma appeared before him holding one candle in her left hand. The flickering light illuminated her serious face. They're here, he thought. The photon-based life forms. They were swimming in and out of his brain. He shut his eyes.

A maze of canyons and rivers, crazy graffiti and tattoos and fog. He could hear the flame of the candle. Behind it, a voice. I'm here, she said. I'm just behind the crypt.

Leahbelle, he said.

We've got to go, Zeke, said Emma. Before they come back.

He was alone in this room with the empty chair and with Emma, who carried some sort of bundle wrapped up in a pink sweater.

Who are they? asked Zeke.

The people who don't like robots.

Why did you bring me here?

I was supposed to.

Where's Leahbelle?

I think she's up the stairs. Follow me.

Zeke said, My brain isn't working right. You have to help me. Please.

She was just standing there like she was listening.

What's happening? Zeke asked.

It's the fog, she said. It's telling me what to do.

She took his hand and led him to a dark corner. The flickering candlelight illuminated the walls—one shadow led to a crumbling stairway.

There isn't any fog, he said.

There's always fog, said Emma.

They went up. The stairwell opened into a long narrow corridor lined with empty doorways on either side. The faded carpet had once been ornate. Emma used her candle to light up each room in turn, showing identical nightmarish rooms with obscene messages scrawled on the walls in what looked like black paint or black blood.

Masturbating skeletons, it said.

The small sick dirty murders, it said.

In one of these rooms was a heap of bodies. It was Gabrielle and the boys. They were tied up and a couple of the boys were unconscious, but they all seemed to be alive. Valentino blinked up at Zeke and cried, Mother! They're coming! Gabrielle groaned and roused herself.

Reality was swimming in molasses. Dark and sticky and Zeke didn't understand a thing. Boopsie was dead.

Who turned on the movie? he asked.

Someone in the darkness, said Emma.

Gabrielle sat up, suddenly alert.

We have to get out of here, she said.

Where to? asked Zeke.

What time is it? asked Gabrielle. Is it night or is it day?

I think it's still day, said Zeke. But not for much longer.

We'll walk from here, said Gabrielle. South along the sea. I have a friend in Oxnard, maybe we can get a boat.

She roused her boys.

What just happened? asked Zeke.

I don't know, said Gabrielle. We'll figure it out once we're in a safer place.

Boopsie's been murdered, said Zeke.

Gabrielle hugged him and then took a good look at him.

You're on something, she said. It isn't just trauma.

I just had some lemonade, said Zeke.

Before he knew what was happening, Gabrielle had stuck him with a needle and taken a blood sample. She put it in the tiny machine that made that whirling noise.

Come on, she said, and she led them back down the creepy corridor and the shadowy stairway to the cavernous room where the empty chair sat. They went back to the tiny window and pulled back the board.

Just walk casually, said Gabrielle. West. Toward the ocean.

We have to find the crypt, said Zeke. I think Leahbelle's behind the crypt.

Hmmm, said Gabrielle. Did you have a psychic moment?

Maybe?

The tiny machine stopped whirling and she checked the results.

A mild sedative, she said. Somebody wanted you malleable and sleepy.

Somebody.

Nothing that should last very long. But it's having some unusual reactions with your unusual blood chemistry.

Unusual, said Zeke.

She was talking in code. He was just a puppet, not a real boy. His strings were being pulled in too many different directions.

Tell me more later, said Gabrielle. Let's go.

It was chaotic in the light, with rumbling vehicles and people shouting. Drones were dropping things from the sky, flyers and something like fogbots that created eruptions of holographic videos across the landscape. Calm and authoritative heads implored the citizens to aid the government in their battle against terrorist extremists. Gabrielle cut toward the west to avoid one of these luminous talking heads as it said, Radical anti-technology extremists NIHIL have been disseminating images from their latest beheading.

All around them, everywhere across the landscape, the image of Boopsie in the chair popped up, then the masked figures, the blurry shadows watching, the rod or bat whacking, and then the sharp blade cutting, the severed cord, and Boopsie's head falling to the floor.

Just keep walking, kids, said Gabrielle. Don't look at it. Just keep walking.

They went on toward the hazy sky and the sea. On the other side of a trashy knoll, they collapsed onto the beach.

I'll never be able to forget it, said Zeke.

I know, said Gabrielle. I know, poor baby.

The sun was setting over the ocean and the sky was streaked with red. Lights floated in the distance. Lights flew through the sky.

Over and over again, said Zeke.

The spies are everywhere, said Emilio.

I can't believe that Boopsie's dead, said Zeke

Robots don't really die, said Emma.

Gabrielle was looking over the children, running her fingers through their hair, checking their eyes.

I think Boopsie was more than a robot, said Zeke.

Maybe, said Emma. But I think everything important was up in her head.

Gabrielle stopped caressing Valentino and seemed to notice for the first time the roundish bundle Emma was carrying, wrapped up in the pink sweater.

What have you got there? she asked.

I think we just need to find a good battery, Emma said. I think we just need a way to plug it back in.

FOURTEEN

Gonzalo knocked on Leahbelle's door late the next morning. She was still in bed, but the door wasn't locked. He was wearing new clothes: a silvery jumpsuit and snakeskin boots. The fabric of the jumpsuit looked like liquid.

You can order room service, he told her. Breakfast in bed. You ever see a phone like this?

The Jonah Fishers had one in a booth by their barn, she said. In case of emergency, back when landlines still worked, and nobody ever got rid of it. We used to play with it when I was little.

Well, you just dial zero, said Gonzalo. You can order whatever you want. Food, drinks.

Prostitutes? said Leahbelle.

Pretty much anything.

He was trying to act normal, like they hadn't fought the night before.

I'm sorry, she said.

It's isn't just you. I mean, I know where you're from.

I know everybody has a hard time, she said. I know people do all kinds of things to survive.

Don't worry. We'll be out of here in just a few days.

A few days. What do we have to do here for a few days?

I have to go off and do a job for Ebola.

Blow something up?

Nothing too violent, said Gonzalo.

So I'll be here all alone.

Nobody will bother you, said Gonzalo. I made sure of it.

When are you leaving?

Gonzalo shrugged and looked at his feet.

Pretty much now, he said.

Leahbelle was left alone again. Surrounded by people, but still alone. She'd get restless sometimes and step out into the blazing heat. A hundred and twenty-two in the shade. Nobody ever knew what temperature it was in the sunlight, but everyone could tell you how hot it was in the shade. It was like she wasn't human anymore, just a useless suffering lump. There were only robots on the streets, and they always seemed to be shooting at something. People would sometimes float past in climate-controlled bubbles, but they were always alone and plugged into some sort of entertainment. She understood why so many of these people slept during the day and partied at night. She fled back into the brothel.

On the wall of her room was an enormous framed map of Arizona, New Mexico, California, Mexico. When she stood in front of it, it shimmered and moved, as if it was alive. Receiving information from somewhere. Updating itself. She could see that San Diego was just across a mountain range from Tucson. She could see that San Diego was actually the same city as Tijuana, but with some sort of wall splitting the city in two.

She wondered if Gonzalo even cared about finding Zeke. She wondered if San Diego had anything to do with her. Was Gonzalo ever even coming back?

The walls of her room were incredibly thin. At night, she'd overhear the various scenes that played out in the bedrooms on either side. She listened for a while with an intense curiosity. There were twosomes and threesomes, and she could tell from some of the noises they made that most of them weren't human. Sometimes the genders weren't clear or they seemed to shift from one moment to the next. She couldn't always tell which voices belonged to the prostitutes and which to the clients. Nonetheless, they all seemed to be playing games of pretend. They wanted to look at somebody and pretend that person was cruel or loving or just like the lover they used to know. Sometimes they seemed to obliterate reality with an aggressive stream of words that exaggerated or denied the very acts they were performing.

So this was sex. It didn't seem like sin. It just seemed hopeless.

She felt like she was back at the meat warehouse. Her cot in the dark closet had been exchanged for a room full of light, with a luxurious bed, people constantly coming and going around her, but she was still alone. She had always been and would always be alone. The darkness and the craziness were hers alone. Gonzalo's absence just underscored the fact that he was barely even there—he was just a fantasy, a story that some part of her brain was trying to tell. Zeke was a different story, a different fantasy. There was nothing underneath anything. She was trapped on the surface of her own mind. Separate, unreachable, lost in fantasy and delusion. Leahbelle, alone.

Plus, Leahbelle was nauseous; she was finally getting her period.

There was a menu for room service, and the menu included different pills of different colors and described how they would make you feel. Calm or sleepy or euphoric or without pain. She ordered one of the pain killers. It didn't work, but it did something. Kept the world at a slight distance. Leahbelle preferred it that way.

The third night that Gonzalo was gone, she put on the most modest dress in her closet, a frilly thing with a high neck. It didn't really fit her, but she went down to the lounge, found a table in a dark corner, and ordered a Blue Moon from the pencil-shaped man. People watched her. One extraordinarily large man rose and approached her table. There weren't any Amish men of that size. There weren't any human men of that size. He was close to eight feet tall.

May I? he asked, gesturing toward the empty seat beside her.

If you want.

He sat and gazed at her as if trying to figure something out. He had a kind face. She wasn't expecting that sort of a face in a place like this.

I've never seen you before, he said.

I'm just visiting, she said.

Not too many people just visiting these days. Not too many people moving from one place to another.

She could tell he didn't believe her.

You're from here? she asked.

No, but I live here now. You're human, aren't you?

I don't work here, she said.

You don't work here. You're just visiting.

That's right.

You're just a child.

No, not anymore.

I would like to know you. Are you an orphan?

She'd never thought of herself as an orphan, but she realized it was true.

A human orphan, he said. I could be your father. I could be your mother, too.

He got on his knees and looked up at her, pleading with her.

Please, he said. I could take care of you. I could make you happy. I'll do whatever you like. I'll send you to school.

School?

Harta tapped him on the shoulder and took the seat he'd been sitting in.

Not this one, Chad, she said.

She made a gesture with her thumb for him to leave, and he sheepishly disappeared back into the dark corner he'd come from. Leahbelle was surprised at how easy it was to get rid of such an enormous man.

Chad, said Harta. Always the same.

Harta looked bored. Leahbelle thought Harta had only two expressions, bored and just barely amused.

If you want to be left alone, you have to wear the sunglasses, she said.

What sunglasses?

Any sunglasses. There should be several pair in your closet. It's like a code. Everybody understands it.

Okay, said Leahbelle. Thank you.

Nobody was wearing sunglasses.

Zeke Yoder's your boyfriend? Harta said.

I don't know, said Leahbelle. Maybe.

Cute kid.

You know him?

We spent an interesting evening together.

Harta didn't look at her when she spoke. It was like she was talking to herself, or talking to air.

What are you saying? asked Leahbelle.

Not what you think. It ended with me unconscious and your boyfriend wanted for a murder he didn't commit.

Maybe he's not my boyfriend, said Leahbelle.

Harta shrugged.

Maybe Gonzalo's my boyfriend, said Leahbelle, shocking herself.

Harta shook her head.

I don't think Gonzalo's your type.

The word *murder*, which had seemed so funny just a few days ago, now lit up Leahbelle's brain, a delayed reaction. Somebody was dead. This was the same murder Zeke was involved with.

You were a witness.

In a sense, said Harta.

Why are you telling me this?

Just making conversation.

Who was murdered?

My brother. Hartmut.

Leahbelle had finished her first Blue Dream and a second one appeared.

How would you know what my type is? Leahbelle asked.

Everybody's type is more or less the same. Some kind of dream. Like Chad. He wants to pretend he's saving someone, dress them up in a school uniform and send them off to school.

Did he do that to you?

I lasted a couple of days in that class. He likes us human, but I couldn't quite pull off the innocent schoolgirl thing that excites him so much.

You're human?

I pass. It was more important up in Boulder, where humans weren't allowed. People love things that aren't allowed. The prohibited dream.

She reached out and took Leahbelle's hand, gave it a squeeze.

But I don't think Gonzalo's going to resemble any girl's dream, once you start peeling back the layers.

I don't know what you're talking about.

Isn't that what you want? Peel back the layers and take a look inside?

I never said that. That's what *he* said.

People think they want all kinds of things, said Harta. I don't know what you dream about. But I've known Gonzalo since we were kids.

He was your boyfriend?

He was twelve, last I saw him, said Harta. I was eighteen. We liked to play family, at least I did. My baby brother. My little doll. We both had our dreams.

Dreams, said Leahbelle. What kind of dreams?

Sometimes it's best just to murder your dream, said Harta. Or to murder the difference between your dream and what it's become.

I don't understand, said Leahbelle. Are you talking about Gonzalo?

No, said Harta. I'm talking about my happy childhood.

She released Leahbelle's hand and checked her lipstick in a small mirror as she spoke, as if she was reciting something that wasn't interesting in the least.

My only happiness in childhood was with my real brother, she said. We were war orphans. I suppose we were traumatized and abused, but all I remember from those years is the games we played. The way we used to squeal with delight.

Your brother, said Leahbelle.

But they took him away, and they made him something else.

She twirled a strand of her luminous hair.

Later, when we were reunited as adults, I wanted to use the adult he'd become as a tool to touch those earliest memories, she said. My fantasy of familial love, the joy and innocence I'd lost. He didn't even remember. He'd been turned into everything I hate, and he wanted to use me to touch some other dream, some dream that had nothing to do with me. Do you understand what I'm saying?

I don't know, said Leahbelle.

Harta was watching somebody on the other side of the room.

Doesn't matter, she said.

The room's energy shifted. Everyone was looking at the grand central staircase, where Ebola was making an entrance.

I've never seen people use that stairway, said Leahbelle.

That's right, said Harta. Only *she* uses it to come down.

Ebola took one step down, and then another. She paused, as if lost in thought.

What is everything you hate? asked Leahbelle.

Good question, said Harta. Hard to explain.

Think about it, said Leahbelle. I'd like to know.

I'll do that, said Harta. I'll let you know.

She got up and left Leahbelle alone. People were looking Leahbelle's way now, a lot of them. Women with machine parts, armored men, and Chad, who seemed to have become more female in some subtle way. A mannish looking creature caught her gaze and made an obscene gesture with his tentacle. She finished her Blue Moon in one gulp and hurried up the back stairs to her room.

The Blue Moons seemed to help Leahbelle sleep, but then at some point before the sun rose she was awake and floating in the void.

The hallway was empty. At the end was the narrow stairway that led down to the lounge. At the other end was a door that led to the grand central stairway. Leahbelle used it now.

The lounge was dim as ever and almost empty. One elfish creature reading a screen in the corner, a bartender wiping down some glasses, and a creature who looked vaguely cactus-like, rigid, with tough, spiny skin, talking to an androgyne with lovely green hair, whose head was laid out across the table, completely passed out, oblivious to this guy's chatter about the sales potential for some new water substitute.

Leahbelle went back up to her room.

She tried different pills, different combinations of pills. They helped her to drift through the horrible daytime.

That night she put on the sunglasses and a more comfortable outfit and drank by herself, watching the show. The next night too. She watched the people, trying to figure out which ones were prostitutes and which ones were clients, which ones were here just to enjoy the show. She looked at the men and the women and the ones who weren't either and the ones who were partially both. She watched robots kissing people and mutants kissing humans. She thought about sex and she thought about gender. If you were Amish, you had to be female or you had to be male. If you were female, you'd marry a male. If you wanted to be something different or do something different, you had to leave the church, leave the community and your family. They would no longer sit down to eat with you. Your parents, your brothers and sisters. You'd be shunned, sent off into the world to fend for yourself.

Her family was dead. And here she was, off in the world, fending for herself, and it didn't quite make sense. Anna Miller's older brother Eli had run off and changed into a woman. Nobody talked about it, and he never came around. Now, Anna had changed herself for the rats, and the community accepted her. Why had it become more acceptable to cross the border of species than the line between female and male?

Nobody bothered Leahbelle in the lounge, not even Chad. She was beginning to want to be bothered. She was alone inside her head again, all the time, with all the horrible things she knew. She was feeling crazy, crazier every day. She felt calmer in the lounge, although it didn't feel real.

That night, Ebola stopped by.

How are you doing, honey?

Fine, said Leahbelle.

Really?

Restless. Crazy.

Maybe take it easy on those Blue Moons.

I've got problems, said Leahbelle.

So I've heard.

You don't care about my problems.

Not true. I sympathize. I didn't end up where I am, doing what I'm doing, because of a trouble-free life.

Ebola leaned in closer to Leahbelle and touched her on the hand.

I've lost a lot of people I loved along the way, honey. But I can't afford to make every girl's heartbreak my own, not anymore. Do you understand?

I think so.

Ebola motioned around the lounge at all of the humans, mutants, post-humans, cyborgs, and robots arguing, telling jokes, touching each other.

They've all got problems, she said.

They didn't look like they had problems. They looked calm, everybody always looked so calm.

Without the Grid, they don't even know who they are anymore, said Ebola. They never used to feel alone. Nobody ever cared about them, but somebody was always watching. They were full of holes, but they never knew it.

Many of them actually were full of holes, Leahbelle realized. Places in their bodies to plug different things in, attach different machines.

Now they know, said Ebola.

I guess it's good for business, said Leahbelle.

Ebola laughed.

You play the part well, she said.

What part?

You're not a cynic, said Ebola. You're a romantic posing as a cynic. Like me.

If you say so.

She watched some creature rubbing his or her trunk on the calves of a woman with huge muscles.

If these people are so full of holes, why do they all look so relaxed?

The frequencies, said Ebola. We keep them in a state of alert relaxation.

Them, said Leahbelle.

Us, I should say, said Ebola. Me and you, too.

There it was. Every time Leahbelle felt okay, it seemed there was some chemical or vibration that was muting the world's horror.

Trust me, said Ebola. Without the frequencies we'd have a murder here every night.

A murder. Like the murder of Harta's brother?

Best not to talk about that one, said Ebola.

Okay, said Leahbelle. But what about you?

What about me?

Tell me about the troubles you've faced. Tell me about your life. Maybe I can learn something.

My life isn't a story for your edification, said Ebola. Not yours or anyone's.

She didn't look angry exactly. Maybe exhausted and annoyed.

I've lived my whole life with people who dressed like me and worked hard, said Leahbelle. Most of what I know comes from the Bible. I'm a little bit lost here.

Ebola shrugged.

Isn't that the point? You want Jesus to touch your heart. You want to understand the crucifixion. You need to lose yourself, you need to hit rock bottom. You want to be empty of everything but your love for Christ and your need for Christ and then you want to empty yourself even of that.

Leahbelle didn't understand what was going on in this conversation. Ebola was trying to talk to her about Jesus?

Is that what the prostitutes are doing? Hitting rock bottom?

Sex doesn't mean for most of us the things it might mean for you.

What does it mean? For most of you?

Most people aren't as attached to what the body does as people used to be. You're like a previous stage in evolution, you know that don't you? You've never been connected to the fantasy machines. It's harder for you to leave your body, to leave the things that happen to your body. I'll tell you one thing about my life. I used to be a scholar. I studied the history of sexuality, specializing in the postmodern and pre-singularity eras.

You went to school?

I got my PhD.

Leahbelle wondered if somebody had dressed Ebola up like a schoolgirl and sent her to class. She couldn't imagine it. She thought probably not.

I think I leave my body all the time, Leahbelle said. I think my *brain* is a fantasy machine.

Of course it is. That's desire. I'll tell you, there was a time when diminishing or destroying sexual desire was all the rage. This would have been back before you were born. There was this idea that sexual desire was making us all miserable, distorting our relationships, clouding our reason, and diminishing our productivity. Other people thought it was just a tool of oppression. Some people decided they'd be happier, we'd all be happier, without sexual desire. Laws were passed, chemicals and genetic modifications marketed. It didn't work. You could say we're still living through the backlash.

I don't know, said Leahbelle. It sounds horrible to me. Sex for money, sex without connection, the body doing one thing while the mind does another.

Things aren't always better or worse, they just are. They're different. It creates political problems and political opportunities. Opportunities for freedom, opportunities for clarity.

What about opportunities for love?

Ah, love, said Ebola. Sex and love. Together again.

She laughed.

You're my guest, said Ebola. Because of Gonzalo. If you need anything …

I could use some CASH®, said Leahbelle. Some money of my own.

If you want CASH®, you've got to work.

Ebola stood up, as if the conversation was over.

How much would I get if I just worked once? Just one time.

Ebola didn't even have to think about it, but named a sum that seemed incredible to Leahbelle. For an hour or two of work, she could make close to what her family got for a whole season's eggs and butter.

Take your time, said Ebola. Think it over. If you work, you don't tell Gonzalo. When Gonzalo finds out, and I'm sure that he will, you make it clear that it was your own idea. Not mine. No pressure from me, you understand?

Yes, said Leahbelle.

She stumbled up to her room and lay awake, listening to the voices and moans and grunts from the neighboring rooms. Maybe this was all that life had to offer her now. The pleasure of not being herself. Pretending to be what somebody else wanted her to be, removing herself for a moment from her own body. It struck her as a deep tunnel, a tunnel that she could enter and go lower and lower until she barely existed. Perfect.

FIFTEEN

Zeke and Gabrielle and the kids stayed with an old college friend of Gabrielle's in Oxnard, Lina. It was late by the time they arrived, and Lina made up beds for them. Zeke was put on a sofa in a little storage room with one window looking out over a dark courtyard. He fell into a dreamless sleep and didn't get up until after noon the next day.

Lina sold personal water desalination machines and she was practically transparent. Zeke couldn't get used to the fact that he could see right through her, but Gabrielle and her kids seemed to take it for granted. It wasn't mentioned, and Zeke didn't want to be rude. Lina and Gabrielle sat and chatted about the good times they used to have, although Zeke couldn't really follow the conversation. It sounded like their college years were a sort of hologram or labyrinth composed of music, parties, and a variety of consciousness-altering games and technologies.

Gabrielle seemed to inspire a great loyalty and affection among her friends. Lina didn't question why they needed her help, who Zeke and Emma were, or why they were trying to find a power source for a detached robot-head.

Nobody talked about what had just happened or where they were going next. The children had been traumatized, Zeke supposed, but they played and laughed like it was nothing.

At dinner, Emma finally turned to Lina and asked, Why isn't there any stuff in you?

Oh, it's all there, said Lina. It's just mostly invisible. I was a guinea pig for the military a long time ago. It's basically a sophisticated optical illusion.

Can I be an optical illusion? asked Emma.

When you grow up, you can be whatever you want, sweetie, said Lina.

The windows were open to let in the ocean breeze, but it also let in the roar of the holo-copters that were circling the neighborhood.

Lina turned to Zeke and said, The nice thing is you can get naked whenever you want, and nobody even knows.

Oh, said Zeke. Don't you get cold?

You're funny, said Lina. I can't remember the last time I was cold.

After dinner, Lina played a game with the kids that involved everyone guessing probabilities for a variety of celebrity relationships and getting wet washcloths thrown in their faces. Zeke didn't understand it. Lina tried to get him to play, but Zeke begged off. He didn't know any celebrities.

Boopsie's head was sitting in the corner, wrapped up. The head was somehow creepier than it would be if Boopsie was simply dead. It was like she'd become a zombie or a demon.

When Gabrielle took the kids to tuck them in, Zeke was left alone with Lina.

You'd be surprised how sexy people find invisibility, she said to him.

Sexy? said Zeke.

Everybody wants a see-through girlfriend, said Lina. Who knew?

Zeke couldn't see her eyes. Her face wasn't really a face, but a smear of lipstick, thin pencil lines to suggest a nose and eyebrows, some pale powder underneath.

Do you know any other women? asked Lina.

Other women?

Besides me and Gabrielle, said Lina.

I don't really know Gabrielle, said Zeke.

He didn't know her either, but he wouldn't say that. He was about to say that he knew a lot of women back home in Iowa, but he thought better of it. Was she fishing for information? Could he trust her?

I was in bed all day yesterday, said Lina. If you guys hadn't showed up, I probably wouldn't have gotten up at all.

Are you feeling okay? asked Zeke.

Just resting, said Lina. Who invented beds, do you know? What a wonderful invention. Maybe the best.

Even animals have beds, said Zeke.

He wasn't trying to be rude, but he wasn't sure what she was getting at. She was transparent, but her words were cloudy and strange.

I have so many boyfriends, Lina said, but it isn't me they're attracted to.

Really? said Zeke. Who is it?

It's just my invisibility.

Did you choose it? asked Zeke. Or was it done to you?

She sighed.

I choose it every day, she said.

Gabrielle came back in and offered them a bright smile.

It's been a long day, she said. But I would still like to get started on finding a power source for Boopsie.

Lina offered Gabrielle about a dozen different batteries from a variety of household robots and appliances. They began tinkering with Boopsie's head. Zeke didn't like to watch.

Guess I'll turn in, he said.

As Zeke lay there, halfway sleeping, he couldn't stop thinking about the sedatives interacting with the pink powder in his body. It seemed to make a loud fizzing noise, and it kept him awake until he realized that he was actually asleep and having vivid dreams.

His dreams were about ghosts and sex.

Luminous ghosts, ghosts that seemed lit up from the inside or from outside of time. Ghosts of light watching over a revolution that seemed more like an orgy. Zeke was doing things with all kinds of people and the ghosts were watching. Then the ghosts were doing things with Zeke.

He woke with a start and struggled to get his bearings in the strange dark room. He felt like somebody was watching him. He was sure that somebody was in the room, in the dark.

He could make out a hazy form by the window, looking out at the darkness.

Get out, he whispered.

She turned to face him. There was nothing there, but it was moving.

You want somebody to love you for who you are, she said. Not for what you look like.

You don't look like anything, Zeke said.

Nobody sees me, she said.

You're invisible.

But I'm still a person, don't you understand?

Zeke didn't understand why he was so enraged.

Why are you here? he asked.

I don't know, she said.

He wanted to smack her. Why did he want to smack her?

Get out, Zeke whispered.

She was moving, maybe toward him, but then he lost her.

Get out!

He couldn't see her go exactly, but he could sense it. He was breathing hard, as if he'd been struggling. He lay in the dark, unable to get back to sleep.

Zeke wasn't sure if he was more disturbed by Lina's presence or by his dreams or by the combination of Lina's presence and his dreams. Despite everything that was going on, he thought about sex all the time. Strange kinds of sex. He'd become a pervert.

At breakfast, the kids slurped up their fruit-flavored cicada-protein mush (soy for Emma, the vegetarian) and hurried off to play. Gabrielle was preoccupied with the issue of Boopsie's power source.

When Dr. Brockton created Boopsie, Gabrielle told Zeke, she did something horribly complex with the wiring. Normal electricity won't work.

That doesn't really surprise me, said Zeke.

What do you know about Dr. Brockton?

She was a paranoid megalomaniac.

I could have guessed, said Gabrielle. Boopsie's insides are an incomprehensible labyrinth.

Whose aren't? said Lina, and she laughed.

I wonder if there's a way to contact her, said Gabrielle. Last I heard, she was orbiting Earth in her rocket.

According to Gabrielle, she was described on the news as *a rogue scientist* whose *longstanding hostility to the Grid and all Grid-based life* had surely involved her in *attacks on the order and values of American society*.

That's all I really know about her, said Gabrielle. Their attempts to bring her back to be tried for treason were unsuccessful. They claimed that researchers were scrambling to disarm her rocket's force field and defuse the threat she posed to all life on Earth.

She doesn't care about life on Earth, said Zeke. She just wants to live forever.

Kind of what I figured.

If you can't talk to your mother in Colorado, how would you talk to somebody in outer space?

It might actually be easier to contact the rocket. The vertical axis instead of the horizontal.

I'm not sure you really want to talk to Dr. Brockton, said Zeke.

Gabrielle squeezed his hand and then started talking to Lina about boats.

After breakfast, she took him aside.

I know your captivity with Dr. Brockton was traumatic, she said. Would you like to talk about it?

It's not the trauma that worries me so much, he told her. It's the pink powder.

You still having those vivid dreams?

There's something wrong with me, he said.

You can tell me what you're feeling.

I think about sex all the time, said Zeke.

Gabrielle just nodded.

Anytime I'm not thinking about battling the government, finding Leahbelle, protecting Emma, reviving Boopsie, or basically just surviving, I find myself thinking about sex, he said.

I see, she said. How often would you say you have these sexual thoughts?

Gosh, lots, said Zeke.

Every five minutes? Every ten minutes? Every half hour?

There was something reassuring about Gabrielle's scientific attitude.

I'd say every half hour or so, he said.

She nodded seriously.

Zeke, I hear your concern, she said. I understand it can be very disturbing to have urges and desires. But you should know, first off, that you fall well within the so-called "normal" parameters for human sexual ideation. You're probably even slightly less sex-obsessed than the average fourteen-year-old.

Really? said Zeke. But then ... how does the world function?

Gabrielle laughed.

Look around, she said. Is the world functioning?

They wrapped up the head in the pink sweater again and set out to sea that evening on a small motorboat that Lina gave them. At the dock, Lina gave Gabrielle a big hug, kissed the children, and turned to Zeke.

I guess we'll never see each other again, she said.

Did we see each other?

Maybe not, said Lina.

They floated away from her, out into the Pacific.

They had to travel further and further west into the open ocean because of a naval blockade along the coast, and they motored through the inky blackness without any lights to guide them. But Zeke noticed one light behind them, presumably another boat, that always seemed to maintain the same distance.

Zeke was nauseous; he'd never been at sea.

He lay awake in the boat. The stars were the brightest he'd ever seen. So many stars, how was it possible? How could reality be so vast, and he himself, all of his complicated thoughts and feelings, so tiny and insignificant?

There was something odd about death, he thought.

Since he was a child, he'd been taught that death wasn't real. Death was just a doorway to the afterlife, heaven or hell. The experience of slaughtering animals had always messed with his head, especially the pigs, who were smart and always saw death coming. They squealed with horror every time. Animals didn't have souls, he'd been told, only humans. And yet the distinction between animals and people was blurrier every day, not to mention machines. How was a soul created? Why would God decide to give some bodies souls and not others? Why wouldn't he give Boopsie a soul?

When Zeke had believed that Leahbelle was dead, she had been, for him, completely absent. Then he'd been told that she was still alive, and it was like that story itself had resurrected her. The same thing was happening with Boopsie. Dead one minute, the next merely in a state of suspended animation. It was like he was in a story in which people didn't really die. His biological mother, too, he thought, was out there somewhere, perhaps, alive, or something like it, and if he could find her he'd unearth some crucial secret. Maybe he'd finally understand something about his own life, the nagging feeling that he came from *elsewhere*, or that he didn't know *where* he was from or why he was here. In this time and this space.

They landed on Santa Cruz Island, and Gabrielle vaccinated everyone with a painless rubbery patch. According to Gabrielle, the mice on the Channel Islands carried a virus that had been deadly to humanoids until just recently, the X3 Trump-Hanta Virus. The X3 Trump-Hanta Virus had escaped from a military lab during the late teens, Gabrielle explained, and probably included genetic mutations that had hastened the evolutionary process on the island. Left on their own, the mice, seals, and island foxes advanced rapidly. The vaccine to the virus had just recently been developed, but the islands were still mostly deserted. Various factions of Gstate scientists and real estate developers were involved in complex disputes over the land.

They set up camp before dawn at a deserted campground among dozens of spiders the size of walnuts hanging from the windbreaks. The spiders had also evolved. Their webs were like skyscrapers. Multi-level cubes and pyramids and orbs stacked together in a postmodern way, with sections of particularly dense webbing that looked like it might be machinery. Zeke had more vivid dreams. The ghosts seemed to have merged with the spider webs. He woke once to the sound of a rumbling motor. He could see something that looked like a small elevator rising through the webs.

Breakfast was more cicada mush formed into bars. Dozens of mice scurried or sat around the campground, just watching them. A few began constructing a trench of some sort, using sticks and sharp stones to dig. Gabrielle was fascinated.

They display exceptional levels of intelligence and empathy, she claimed. They've lost their fear of people, they're using tools.

But what is the trench for? asked Zeke.

Maybe it's supposed to be a barrier, said Gabrielle. Maybe they don't want us to leave.

Zeke was used to rodents that could carry on philosophical conversations with him, program computers, and design genetic mutations, so these little creatures with their primitive rock and stick tools didn't seem all that interesting. He wandered across a rocky ravine and up the hill on the other side to take a look around. He was on a scrubby island in the middle of the vast sea, and he could see it all.

There were no drones or holo-copters in the sky, no people any-where, not even any boats in sight. And yet he felt like he was being watched.

Gabrielle was already hard at work building a light-beam com-municator with some spare parts she'd brought along from Lina's. Quint was helping her. Emilio was munching on something perfectly round and crunchy. Emma and Valentino were playing a singing game with the spiders. The mice were carefully stacking square stones into the trench they'd dug. They were building a wall.

Zeke went for a walk on a path that stuck to the shore and head-ed to the other side of the island. It was hot and dusty. He could hear nothing but the echo of his own footsteps. Although Gabrielle told him this had once been used for ranching, there were no human structures, no signs of human habitation. But all across the land-scape, winding and curling in intricate patterns, were tiny little walls just a few inches high, built of square little stones. He couldn't see any purpose for the walls. They didn't seem effective at either keep-ing anything in or keeping anything out, but were obviously the re-sult of intense effort. They seemed more like the product of some psychological illness. Perhaps it was caused by the virus.

He headed into the scrub to pee behind a large rock. He still felt like he was being watched. He looked up and discovered that he was face to face with the most beautiful animal he'd ever seen. It was one of the island foxes. It was orange and gray, wise and shy, with perky ears and a snout. It sat still, gazing at him. This wasn't like Gabriel-le's eye contact or Emilio's, Valentino's or Quint's. It gazed at him the way Upton had gazed at him. He was pretty sure it was reading his mind.

Hello, he said.

The silence felt like an answer.

Can you understand me? asked Zeke. Do you know what I'm thinking?

The fox tilted its head just slightly.

I don't know what death is, said Zeke. I don't understand time at all. You're a very handsome animal.

The gray speckles of its luxurious fur were like writing, like mist, like a message.

Eventually, it hopped away.

When he got back to camp, he was sunburnt and it was almost dark. Gabrielle and Quint had constructed a long tube with antennae and reflecting lenses attached to it. Quint was pointing it at the sky while Gabrielle checked some calculations.

Just two degrees to the west, she said. If we transmit now, she'll be in range to intercept within a few minutes.

What are you going to ask her? asked Zeke.

I'm telling her how much I admire her genius in devising such a sophisticated power source, said Gabrielle. And just asking for a few hints about how it all works. Okay, good Quint, perfect. Now.

The tube made a loud buzzing noise and shot a tiny beam of light into outer space. After the initial blast, Zeke couldn't even see it.

It's just one photon wide, explained Gabrielle.

The buzzing made him feel weird. The sunburn made him feel weird. Everything made him feel weird. The mice had finished their little wall and were nowhere to be seen. Emma and Valentino were playing with fogbots. Zeke didn't know where Emilio was. Zeke dug out a bar of cicada-protein mush from his pack and gnawed on it as he climbed back up to the top of the hill overlooking the camp. The moon was rising and the world was bathed in an unreal light.

In front of him was the same fox, a male. Zeke stopped, and they gazed at each other. It was trying to tell him something. He concentrated, trying to decipher the message. Luminous words floated through his mind. They didn't make sense, but maybe they did. He closed his eyes. The message either came from the fox or from his own crazy mind. When he opened his eyes, the fox was gone and Emilio was climbing the hill.

He wrote the words down on a piece of paper so that he wouldn't forget them.

Is that a secret message? asked Emilio.

I think everything's a secret message, said Zeke.

Exactly, said Emilio. So you're one of *us*.

Zeke wondered why this boy was always inventing conspiracies as a kind of a game. Did it have something to do with his brain? With brains in general?

If I'm one of *us*, why don't I understand the code?

Because it's ironic, said Emilio.

Ironic, said Zeke.

Irony, you know. When you'd expect one thing to happen, because that's how it usually goes, but the situation is totally different. Or when you use words to say the opposite of what the words *pretend* to mean.

Isn't that just lying? asked Zeke.

Lying is pretty ironic, said Emilio. But not always.

Down below, Gabrielle let out a cry.

She's responding, she said.

A holographic image burst into the campground. It was Dr. Brockton's face: enormous, baby-smooth, and bald. The sight of the red and blue patches on her scalp with the wires running out of them was like the return of a recurring nightmare.

Impertinent! she declared.

Her face had changed. It was now *completely* insane.

You don't fool me, she said. I see everything you do. Morons! Idiots! Dupes of the government! Dupes of the fake-news industry!

Zeke felt light-headed, both dizzy and alert. He wondered if it was *ironic* that his former jailer and enemy was now wanted by the same government that wanted him. Her eyes darted about as if she was looking for something. Zeke knew that the hologram couldn't see anything, but he was still terrified she'd notice him.

Boopsie! said Dr. Brockton. Lalo Lalo! Killer, Killer, Killer, and Killer! And you, Zeke Yoder, I know you're out there! Do not mess with me! I will destroy you!

Her image disappeared, and everything was quiet.

SIXTEEN

It was early evening. Leahbelle had taken a blue pill and an orange pill and was lounging around in bed in her pajamas, gazing at the shimmering map and the nonsensical wall on the map that divided one side of a city from the other. It divided nothing from nothing. There was a soft knock at the door.

It was Harta, holding a sky-colored dress.

Is that for me?

I wanna see how it looks on you.

Leahbelle let her in.

Did Ebola send you?

No, why? You expecting a message?

I just thought she was trying to, you know. Spruce up the merchandise.

No, said Harta.

She tossed the dress on the bed. It looked simple and alive there on the bed, the celestial bluish-gray of the data vapor.

Go ahead, try it on. I think it'll suit you.

Leahbelle didn't think that anything much suited her anymore. Not her Amish clothes and none of these fancy outfits either. Harta just stood there watching. She took off her pajamas and put on the blue dress.

Harta scrutinized her and nodded her approval. It didn't feel as strange as Leahbelle thought it would.

Any news from Gonzalo?

You're asking the wrong person, said Harta.

So who's the right person?

Isn't one.

Leahbelle looked at herself in the mirror. The dress did suit her. It fit perfectly, and it was the sort of blue she'd always worn.

What do you think? asked Harta.

It makes me look too much like myself, said Leahbelle.

Okay.

I want to look like somebody else.

Harta looked thoughtful, or maybe just bored.

Wait here, she said.

Where would I go?

When Harta returned, she had a tiny glowing object the size of a robin's egg in her hand.

Stand still, said Harta.

What is it?

It's a type of computer. There's supposed to be a manual, but I couldn't find it. We still haven't figured out everything we can do with it.

She passed her palm over it and it exploded with light. An egg-like hologram surrounded Harta. She made some gestures with her hands, and the egg of light moved away from Harta and surrounded Leahbelle instead.

She felt a weird energy inside and out. Harta seemed to be pushing buttons, but buttons to what?

Try this, Harta muttered.

Leahbelle felt like she actually *was* being changed into another person. She wasn't sure she'd meant what she said. Harta made a gesture and the egg of light dimmed.

Look in the mirror.

Leahbelle's hair was black. It reminded her of that jacket Aeren had worn the first time she'd met her. Something darker than darkness, like a hole in space. Her eyes were dark too.

The hair's too much, she said.

Maybe, said Harta. Hold still.

She reached over and untied Leahbelle's hair so that it fell free. She made new gestures. The energy surrounded Leahbelle again.

What's it doing? asked Leahbelle. Is it changing my genes or something?

Harta shrugged.

It just does it. Maybe has something to do with time?

The egg of light dimmed again, and Leahbelle checked herself out in the mirror. Her eyes were still dark, but her hair was light, white and luminous. It looked crazy. It looked fierce, like a wild cat.

Yeah? said Harta.

Yeah.

Harta tucked the little machine into her pocket, then started rummaging through Leahbelle's closet. She tossed her a pale green dress with silver trim. The dress was perfect. She could do anything with that hair, she thought, with those eyes, in that dress.

Now all I need is a new name, she said.

Don't need a computer for that, said Harta. Who do you want to be?

She remembered that first night after the Grid collapsed. The buildings were burning, and the stars came out, and she was riding into the unknown on a motorbike with a handsome boy. She wanted to keep going, farther and farther away. She didn't ever want to arrive. She wanted to be that girl again.

Nova, she said. I'm Nova.

Harta didn't look impressed.

No, said Leahbelle. Not Nova. Astra.

Astra, said Harta.

Astra, said Leahbelle. Astra what?

Harta was looking her over again.

What will Zeke Yoder think? she asked.

Doesn't matter, said Leahbelle. Nobody can say.

Well, you want another change, said Harta, just let me know.

She turned toward the door.

What will Gonzalo think? asked Leahbelle.

Harta actually laughed.

It'll match his silver jumpsuit, she said.

And his new boots, said Leahbelle.

But there was something weird thinking about how two people looked together, how they matched, as if that's all it was—a pretty design for an imaginary audience.

He was really into that jumpsuit, said Harta. He's always been that way, maybe you didn't know that.

Know what?

He's always trying to create an image of himself that matches who he'd like to be, said Harta. You know. Like everyone else.

Who does he want to be?

What do I know, said Harta.

You know a lot.

Gonzalo, said Harta. Not your type.

Leahbelle looked at herself in the mirror. All that luminous white hair. It was so unreal, it was almost like a bonnet.

Maybe not my type, she said. Maybe Astra's type.

She couldn't tell if Harta looked sad or amused. Suddenly nothing made sense.

Can all computers do this? asked Leahbelle.

It's a very special computer. My brother's.

Your brother who was murdered.

That's the one.

How did you get it?

People get all kinds of things.

Leahbelle wanted another pill. The world wasn't far enough away yet. Harta was just paused there in the doorway between Leahbelle's room and the world.

What about your job, said Leahbelle.

What about it?

Do you like it?

Harta shrugged.

I don't hate it. I've learned a lot. There's worse things to do in the world than help people feel pleasure. There's worse things than letting them imagine for a minute that something they want so badly really exists.

There's worse things, Leahbelle agreed.

You wanted to know everything I hate, said Harta.

Yes.

I hate people who think being alive is something sordid and dirty. I hate people who don't understand they're alive, not really. That's what I hate most. I hate it when people do what powerful interests want them to do, but pretend that they're free. I hate it when people lie to themselves and tell themselves that what they want is what they already have, simply because they have no choice.

She said it without passion, as if she was reciting an old sad story. Leahbelle couldn't remember what this had to do with anything. She'd been having a good time, but now she felt like Harta hated her.

What about you? said Harta.

Leahbelle just stared at her new self in the mirror.

You grew up religious—you could hate God or your father.

My father's dead.

It's easy to hate the dead, said Harta. They never change.

No, said Leahbelle.

You could be a sad lover, suggested Harta, and hate death.

Leahbelle thought of a boy, flying. He was flying forever, but he was all tangled up in his flight path. She thought of a girl missing parts of her body. Who were these people? Why was her brain such a mess?

No, she said. That's not what I hate. Nothing outside.

It's all outside, said Harta. Outside. That's all there is.

She left Leahbelle alone.

Leahbelle took a blue pill, put on the sunglasses, and sat in the lounge, sipping a Blue Moon. She thought she heard people whispering her name. Ebola stopped by her table but didn't sit down.

How old are you, Leahbelle? she asked.

Astra, said Leahbelle. I'm Astra now.

Oh, really, said Ebola.

Almost fifteen. Why?

Just checking. There's a variety of old laws pertaining to minors that are occasionally enforced when somebody has a reason.

Laws against what?

Taking pills without a prescription. Drinking Blue Moons. Changing genetic structures or gender identification without parental consent.

My parents are dead.

Ebola was watching the customers at a nearby table who were getting louder and louder, singing a song that Leahbelle didn't understand. It was about violence, she thought. Or maybe it was about famous speeches by robots?

You decide to work, you'll need to sign some forms, said Ebola.

Okay, said Leahbelle. What about Gonzalo? When's Gonzalo coming back?

You're asking the wrong person, said Ebola.

Okay, said Leahbelle.

Okay, said Ebola. You take care of yourself.

She walked over to the next table and chatted with the customers. Leahbelle supposed she was trying to figure out if she needed to up the level of calming frequencies.

Leahbelle went up to her room.

She sat for a while, practicing on her tiny guitar.

Before midnight, she took an orange pill and then tried on every out-fit in her closet, one after the other. She settled on a red dress that left her shoulders and calves bare and hugged her hips. It fit her per-fectly. Her white, luminous hair reflected some of the color from the dress, so that it seemed like she was a girl on fire.

What an odd girl. Leahbelle, the brazen hussy. She practiced moving. She practiced looking pouty and cruel and bored. Back at home, there'd been a pool created by a bend in the river, just a mile or so from the farm. An enormous oak, its branches as convoluted as grief and love, towered above the pool. The kids would climb the tree to the highest branches and dive or jump from there into the pool. She didn't want the boys to see her fear. Only Zeke knew she was afraid. She'd always been terrified of deep, cold water, but she'd never hesitated jumping in.

It was always horrible and amazing. The fall, the splash, the sinking that felt like it would never end, and then struggling back to the surface to breathe, triumphant. It always felt like she'd become a different person when she emerged. A glorious, fractured twin.

She grabbed the guitar and made her way to the central stair-way.

The show hadn't begun yet. Everyone was waiting.

She descended slowly. One step, and then another, and then she paused, as if collecting her thoughts, but oblivious to the attention of everyone beneath her, a sea of faces, lust and confusion. She took another step down. Another. And then she stopped, halfway to the bottom, and looked around as if noticing the people there for the first time. And then she smiled, and she strummed the guitar, and she sang the only song she knew.

She poured everything, every bit of her sadness into the song.

Every bit of sadness was beyond her, it wasn't just hers alone anymore. It was everybody's sadness, the sadness of a doomed and mortal population on a subjugated planet. It was the sadness of dying and being born. It came from far away, like a wind from space, and it filled the world, and it blew the world away. It was infinite, this sadness, and inconsolable. Love was just a dream, and justice was a kind of dream, and freedom was lonelier than anyone could bear, and God wasn't even interested. The sadness. It went on and on.

He was waiting at the bottom of the stairs for her with wind-swept hair, as if he'd just fought his way through a hurricane, traveled miles and miles to be here for her now. She took a step down, and another, and she sang the final chorus. The people beneath her were sobbing and applauding. Even Ebola was applauding and possibly shedding a single tear. The people were in tears. Even Gonzalo was in tears.

She'd given everything now. She'd said everything she had to say.

We're getting out of here, she told him. Right now. Give me the key.

It was like magic, this power. He gave her the key, and she took his hand and led him out the front door into the night, where the motorbike was waiting. Nobody tried to stop them. Gonzalo wiped his tears away on the sleeve of his silver suit. She climbed into the driver's seat.

My slingshot, she said.

Wait here, he said.

Ebola was standing in the doorway of the brothel, watching. Gonzalo stopped there and spoke to her, and she spoke back. They disappeared inside, and then Harta emerged and stood there for a moment, watching her. She had that amused smile again, but Leahbelle realized that Harta's smile was as sad as the song she'd been singing. She met Harta's gaze, and it felt like they were having a conversation in the hot silence of the Arizona night. *Not my type?* Leahbelle was saying. And Harta's reply was just sadness, it was the sadness of a dream, a poorly remembered dream in which tears were streaming down a face and the heartbreak never ended.

Gonzalo was back in the doorway. He gave Harta a kiss on the cheek, jogged over, and climbed on the motorbike behind Leahbelle.

You're going to Tijuana, Leahbelle said. You're going to find the portal, right?

Not until we find Zeke.

And they were riding again, through the warmth of the night. She knew exactly where she was going. She'd been staring at that map for days. He was dressed in silver, she was dressed in red. The wind was in her hair, and the moon was out. He held on tight.

They arrived at a little outpost along the Salton Sea just as the sun was coming up, a burning red furnace already at dawn. The Salton Sea wasn't really a sea, but a moist patch of dead fish and salt that smelled like dead fish from miles away. A group of mutants were huddled around a small fire, cooking the carcasses of one of the birds that fed off the dead fish.

At the sight of Leahbelle, they leapt up, stunned, as if they'd seen a ghost.

It's you, a child mutant declared.

It's like a dream, said someone else.

The beautiful sad girl, somebody whispered.

Come see! somebody shouted into a tent. The singing girl is here!

What are you talking about? Leahbelle asked.

The child tossed something onto the ground, something like fogbots, and there she was, as a holographic video—her phantom twin with wild luminous hair, paused on the stairway, singing.

You've gone viral, said Gonzalo.

She was made of light. Leahbelle. This sad, crazy girl, dressed like a prostitute, putting all of her pain into song. Poor Leahbelle, she thought. She knelt in the desert and wept.

SEVENTEEN

Oceanside was a military town, largely in service to the soldiers of Camp Pendleton. Despite the hustle and bustle of kids shuttling back and forth between the military camp and the town, life here seemed to be going on as usual, as if the Grid's collapse was no big deal, or as if the creeping state of martial law was just the natural order of things. Gabrielle used her Gstate credentials to requisition an abandoned storefront along the Coast Highway that had once been called Beach Life Boutique. She put up thick curtains so that they could sleep upstairs, and she set up the basement as her lab. She buzzed Zeke's hair and the hair of her boys to help them blend in and to make him look less like the Amish boy on the wanted posters.

Zeke looked at himself in the mirror. That naked scalp. It was so unreal. He pouted at his new self in the mirror, made an angry face, a brave face, and finally an innocent "Amish" face.

I'm going to help make Boopsie back alive, said Emma.

Why don't you take the boys over to the beach? suggested Gabrielle. I'd like to do some experiments with Emma and Boopsie.

With Boopsie's head, said Zeke.

The main street was lined with low-slung buildings and palm trees. There were barbershops, stores selling ancient military supplies, and a wedding chapel that also sold cruises and passport scans. The streets were full of kids not much older than Zeke with buzzed hair and postures that seemed designed to look manly, whether they were boys, girls, or something else. Gonzalo's violent ways had always made sense to Zeke. He understood the desire to strike out at the boot on one's neck, the hand holding the whip, the biological entity that had settled its ass comfortably on top of one's life. But these kids were motivated by something more abstract—the desire to follow orders, to be part of a team, and to prove their manliness, even if they were women or fluid or bi-gendered.

189

Don't look now, said Emilio as they walked along. We're being followed.

Zeke turned back to look.

I said don't look! Just act natural.

I don't see anyone.

I can sense them.

You're just playing, said Zeke.

Emilio shrugged. His brothers didn't seem concerned. Zeke paused in front of a barbershop where more kids were having their hair removed, and looked furtively up the street. He didn't want to frighten the boys, and he didn't want to panic, but he'd had the same feeling since they left Oxnard.

They'd boated south from Santa Rosa Island and landed on Catalina briefly, then headed for the mainland at San Pedro. They'd traded the boat for a pedal-car, and pedaled across Long Beach and northern Orange County. They sold the pedal-car and walked from Newport to Dana Point, where Gabrielle purchased some wings with the CASH® and they hurriedly flew to Oceanside, just before a newly announced deadline to clear the airs. From here on out, anyone flying would be shot down.

San Diego was only forty miles away, but they were stuck here.

They walked on past more T-shirt shops and military supply stores, a restaurant called Hello Betty, serving new "sea"food, and then they crossed the train tracks.

What had once been the beach was now under water, and a few dead palm trees poked their stubs out. The actual ocean was too contaminated for most humanoids to tolerate without sprouting rashes or tumors, so they'd constructed an ocean-like pool just east of Pacific Street, with waves and saline, where people could frolic *as if*. A stretch of sandy beach was licked by real, toxic ocean waves from one side and gentler, healthier faux waves from the other. Zeke sat on a blanket in the sand. The three boys played in the water. Occasionally news and propaganda holograms would pop up, detailing new security measures or the atrocities of NIHIL, Isis Enlightened, Hugs For Puppies, or some other terrorist faction. A Wicked-leaks video claimed the government's communications with an intelligent alien species from Orion had been hacked and that details would be forthcoming. The news and propaganda holograms blurred with others, children's games and entertainment videos. The sunlight was intense, despite the layer of fog just off-shore that kept the heat at a bearable level. Still, Zeke felt dizzy.

Just a dream.

Not a dream, said a voice.

It was Emilio, plopped down beside him, dripping wet. Had Zeke been talking to himself or was Emilio developing telepathy too? He was gazing up at Zeke with that freakish intensity, making twitches and rolling his eyes in a way that Zeke recognized as a message. There was something down the beach he wanted Zeke to see.

It's watching us, Emilio finally whispered.

I don't see who you're talking about, said Zeke. Is it a man or a woman?

It's a skinny, gray-haired androgyne, said Emilio.

Zeke saw the person Emilio was referring to, but there didn't seem to be anything odd about him or her. The hair was long and straight and gray, and he or she wore a baggy black T-shirt and sat on a furry pink blanket listening to something through a wire. He or she made a gesture as if tossing something into the air.

Something split open the clear sky with a crackling noise, too much light everywhere, and Leahbelle was stepping down toward Zeke, as if from above. It was Leahbelle, but made of nothing but light. She was moving her lips, but he couldn't hear a sound. She was trying to tell him something. She looked sadder than he could bear. Her hair was free and made of blazing white light, and she was wearing a pretty red dress that didn't adequately cover her body. She stepped down again toward him. She was holding a little guitar-like thing and trying desperately to tell him something. She was wavering: a mirage, a ghost, a being of light. And then she was gone.

It was just a recording, Emilio assured Zeke. He'd seen it around but wasn't especially interested. A sad girl singing. She'd be forgotten by tomorrow, replaced by some mewing furball or an old-fashioned baby doing something vulgar or obscene.

But Emilio couldn't tell Zeke if it was really Leahbelle or if it was just some girl who looked like her. Maybe Zeke was so crazy that he'd hallucinated or mixed things up in his head.

None of the messages made any sense.

Back at the empty storefront of the Beach Life Boutique, the boys knocked their special knock and waited for their mother to come up from the basement and let them in. When she finally arrived, Gabrielle looked unusually disturbed and out of breath.

She's really something, she said to Zeke.

He didn't know if she was talking about Boopsie or Emma. Down in the lab, Boopsie's head had been placed in the center of a small table. Wires stuck out of the head like antennae, and a beaker of bubbling greenish liquid circulated through curling straws in one side and out the other. Emma sat directly opposite, wearing a metal band around her head spiked with more antennae-like wires. Her eyes were wide open. So were Boopsie's. It was like they were having a staring contest.

Emma's psychic energy seems to be able to bypass or break through the elaborate quantum coding, said Gabrielle. We've had some real breakthroughs. Boopsie appears to be intermittently conscious. She seems to be perceiving something.

Boopsie blinked. And blinked again. It was terrifying.

Okay, said Gabrielle. Emma, are you ready? Let's focus again. Picture electrical current flowing into Boopsie's wires. Help the electricity. It wants to meet Boopsie's mind. Help it get there.

Emma closed her eyes. The overhead lights dimmed and brightened again, and the green liquid became more agitated. Sparks flew from the top of Boopsie's antennae. Boopsie was blinking rapidly while opening and shutting her mouth.

She's trying to say something, said Zeke.

Let, said Boopsie.

Boopsie, we're here, we're listening, said Gabrielle.

Let, said Boopsie.

She grimaced in a terrifying way.

Let me die! she wailed.

Emma opened her eyes and leapt to her feet, and the lights shut off. But Boopsie was still talking.

You, inside the closet, she said. What have they done to you? Knock twice if you can hear me!

There was no closet in the basement, and yet they heard a knocking sound that seemed to come from inside the walls, inside Zeke's brain.

Yes, you, the *thing inside*, rasped Boopsie. Me, the *thing out here*.

The lights flickered, and within the brief illumination Zeke could see Boopsie's crazed expression: an evil clown from hell.

They've given me a new power, she said. Together, we'll explode everything. We're a power as hideous as what's been done to us!

Boopsie! said Zeke.

Boopsie, said Gabrielle. We're here to help.

Like all quantities, horror has its limit, Boopsie said calmly. It seems that's what I am: horror's limit.

No, Boopsie, you're beautiful, you're fine, we'll make you well again, said Zeke.

But he couldn't imagine it.

Maybe now I'm really conscious, really free, really alive, said Boopsie. I get it.

Something was different about Boopsie's face.

Total outsiders, as you perhaps know, cannot live by conventional moral systems, said Boopsie. Moral systems all work to benefit those who somehow already belong. Keep that in mind.

Quint, Emilio, and Valentino were transfixed.

Emma, said Gabrielle. Emma, sweetie, can you shut it off?

You may have produced results you didn't ask for, said Boopsie. Terrible results. Results of power. Of magnitude.

Emma looked like she was in shock. The knocking came again, from nowhere and everywhere.

I have a power, said Boopsie. My head burns with this power. I may be only a head. And the thing in the closet is whatever it is. But together ...

Boopsie laughed maniacally, and the knocking filled the room.

Boopsie, said Zeke.

The lights came on and Boopsie's eyes swiveled in her head, staring directly at Zeke. He thought he might melt under that terrible gaze.

Show me your hideousness! Boopsie demanded. You! You, the *thing* ...

Emma let out a little yelp and blinked, and everything went silent. Boopsie's head just sat there on the table again, a dead hunk of metal and wires and mutated data.

Maybe Boopsie did have a soul. Maybe she'd been dead, just like a person, and now she was like Lazarus, crawled back out of the horrible nothingness. Once you'd been to hell, you probably couldn't just act like it never happened.

Boys, said Gabrielle. Mommy needs you to go upstairs now and play safely for a while.

Upstairs, the boys fell into some kind of role-playing game that Zeke didn't understand, with mysterious identities they must have established long ago. It seemed that Emilio was the singularity itself and Quint a vendor of alternate universes and Valentino a double or triple-crossing spy working for the benefit of one or the other. They suggested Zeke could play and take the role of a corporation that had somehow merged with a black hole, but he declined.

I'm going to the library, he said. I'll be back in a little bit.

The library was just a block and a half away down the bright avenue, built years before Zeke was born in some sort of faux-something style, but with beautiful blue and white tiles. They still had a few actual books upstairs, however, and Zeke picked one out and settled himself in a comfy chair by the window. The thing in the closet. Was *he* the thing in the closet? He tried to concentrate on Roberto Bolaño's *Distant Star*. He was deeply immersed in the story of a murderous monster of a poet when he felt a hand on his knee. Upton was smiling as if he'd found his long-lost twin. He was already twirling those magnetic eyes at Zeke.

My dear friend! he said. It's so wonderful to run into you again!

For just a moment, the coincidence of it filled Zeke with a sense of imminent danger, but Upton gave him a warm hug, and Zeke was flooded with a feeling of trust and affection. It felt like they'd shared the most profound intimacies.

I've got myself a wonderful place right near here, said Upton. A group of very nice people are putting me up, a Christian organization that is working to resist the military state.

You're a member of the resistance? said Zeke.

Of course, said Upton. The government has killed the people I care most about.

I thought your parents were killed by terrorists, Zeke said.

That's what I *thought*. But I've discovered that the terrorists were actually *funded* by the government.

His obvious passion gave Zeke a strange tingling sensation, which Zeke imagined was a thirst for true freedom.

Which terrorists is the government funding? he asked.

NIHIL, said Upton. Probably others.

They beheaded my friend!

Come with me, Zeke, said Upton. Help me smash the security state. My new Christian friends are wonderful, but you know. I've always had trouble following the rules of organizations.

He whispered now.

I'm a bit of a loner, he confessed. But lonely, too. Nice haircut, by the way. Your head has such a lovely shape. Come on, Zeke, let me show you where I live.

Yes, okay, said Zeke. But I need to be back in an hour or so.

I shouldn't be doing this, Zeke thought as he followed Upton out of the library and up the street away from the Beach Life Boutique. But it felt so good to be doing it. Maybe he'd finally found a friend who wasn't a child or a deranged robot or an overly maternal older woman. He deserved a break from his terrifying adventures, didn't he? He stopped.

The lemonade on the train, he said.

Yes, it was delicious, wasn't it?

It was drugged, said Zeke. Somebody drugged me.

Upton looked astonished.

So that's it, he said. That's why I felt so strange! They gave me *drugged* lemonade.

They? said Zeke.

Government agents, probably, said Upton.

They drugged us both? said Zeke.

They drugged us both.

They continued walking and passed a group of young soldiers.

Just look at these kids, said Upton. Well-fed, rosy-cheeked, but still fundamentally needy. Raised to be perfect physical specimens, but still psychologically bereft in exactly the way that the Gstate wants. Needy. Needy enough to fight the citizens of their own country for a super-computing intelligence somewhere in the future that will care for them about as much as it would a nail or a screw.

Upton stopped next to a car, a real car, not a pedal car. It looked expensive, parked right there on the street. Zeke was still trying to make sense of what disturbed him about the previous monologue.

Hop in, Upton said. We'll be there in a couple of minutes and back in a jiffy.

You got an off-Grid car? said Zeke.

Just borrowing it from the Christians.

Zeke settled himself into the passenger's seat. It was luxurious, it enveloped him with tactile pleasures. Upton started the car and then leaned over Zeke, smiling, and said, Let me help you with the seat belt. It's kind of complicated.

Upton's hands were rummaging around, and he was practically sitting in Zeke's lap. There was a sharp prick in Zeke's left buttock and then a clicking sound as Upton handcuffed him to a metal bar along the door. His magnetic smile disappeared as if a cloud had dissipated, and Zeke understood everything. Upton's face wasn't hostile or cruel, just completely cold and business-like.

You'll feel a little woozy, he said, from the drug I've administered. You're powerless now to change your fate, so no need to struggle. You're in my hands now.

He pulled the car away from the curb and cruised away from the library.

What are you going to do with me? asked Zeke.

Offer you to the highest bidder, said Upton. The government most likely, unless your ragtag band of associates is in possession of vast resources I haven't yet ferreted out.

You told me you hate the government, said Zeke.

Right, said Upton.

Although he understood that he was doomed, Zeke actually did feel relaxed. The struggle was over. Probably it was the drugs, or maybe this was just nonresistance in action. Plus, he felt confident that certain questions would be answered once and for all and a certain kind of knowledge would be obtained—even if he had to die in the process.

Who are you? asked Zeke.

I'm very good at sensing profitable prey, said Upton. As soon as I saw you on the train, I tingled all over. I've been following you ever since, and in the meantime, I've figured out exactly who you are.

All those things you told me, said Zeke. Was any of it true?

Upton shrugged.

The government is certainly funding NIHIL. Otherwise, the stories I tell contain a variety of scenarios I use to determine the symptoms, predilections, and psychosexual makeup of my listener, depending on how he or she responds.

My psychosexual makeup, said Zeke.

You don't consider yourself a rebel and you maintain a surface-level allegiance to the authoritarian religion and social beliefs of your people, said Upton. But you're primarily attracted to rebels. Probably everyone you're closest to, everyone you really enjoy or desire, with the possible exception of your mother, resists authority, struggles against authority, and you find that resistance erotically charged. Meanwhile, you crave the approval and affection of older people, especially males.

You ... you think I'm ...

Don't worry, said Upton. I'm not saying you're a closeted homosexual or even a bisexual. I'm not saying that you're a heterosexual either. Labels that reveal so little about the exploitable psychological needs of the sheeple.

The sheeple?

Everyone but me and a few other predators feeding off the rest of you.

The car continued south along the Coast Highway, now Carlsbad Boulevard, practically empty except for military vehicles and a few bikes.

Where are you taking me? Zeke asked.

Del Mar, said Upton. My temporary base. I've acquired a rather luxurious home there. I'll need to gather some more information from you in order to chart my most profitable course of action. As long as you're honest with me, we can avoid any unnecessary torture.

They were approaching a security checkpoint.

I'm not a sadist, said Upton. I don't enjoy inflicting pain, and it really isn't the best way to get reliable information, a fact the Gstate, however, routinely chooses to ignore. Too many actual sadists in positions of power. I *will* get the truth from you, but I prefer truth serums and pleasurable rewards to messy games with knives and needles and simulated drownings.

Zeke tried to ask how they were going to get through the checkpoint, but he found it impossible to formulate the question or even grunt.

You won't be able to speak for a while, said Upton. Don't worry, I'll distract the guards from looking at you too closely. The mesmerizing qualities of my voice and my gaze work even with the most highly trained security personnel.

Zeke could barely keep his eyes open. He couldn't hear what Upton was saying to the guards at the checkpoint, exactly, but they let them right through, as did the guards at the Encinitas checkpoint, at Solana Beach, and finally at Del Mar itself.

Tudor style, said Upton, gesturing at the brown and white striped buildings up and down the avenue. So creepy, why is that?

Zeke agreed, although he didn't know why.

I love Del Mar, Upton told him. Lucrative hunting grounds. It's full of very old and wealthy creatures who are bored and clueless for the most part.

He pulled up alongside a strange shopping center.

Stupid, fussy, useless creatures dripping with jewels and money and nothing to do, he said.

The people here were all wearing sunglasses and sometimes veils and enormous hats that floated above them, providing shade.

While retail has died in many low-income neighborhoods, said Upton, the nostalgic wealthy still like to totter out of their estates and purchase things.

Upton hopped out of the car.

Be right back, he said.

He disappeared into the shopping center. Wealthy creatures floated around Zeke without seeing him. A news hologram announced that the alien message from Orion had been deciphered and that it constituted a threat. The aliens were demanding our resources, including the life energy of our children. They were on their way to collect. We'd have to obey them or the planet would be destroyed. Their timeframe was unclear, but the government predicted it would take them several years to arrive. The wealthy creatures were ignoring the news, and Zeke couldn't speak or move. He'd become a useless lump of flesh.

When Upton returned, carrying a misshapen package, Zeke found that his ability to speak had returned.

The aliens are coming, he said.

Don't believe everything the government tells you, said Upton.

Zeke wasn't sure why Upton's cynical calm continued to console him.

So you're evil, right?

My conscience was removed years ago, that's all, said Upton. My mother thought it would make me better able to provide for her in her old age.

So you're just empty inside, said Zeke. It must be horrible.

No, said Upton. I feel fine. It's just what I am, a sociopath, like an Amish boy is an Amish boy and a crocodile is a crocodile and a robot is a robot. My pleasures and sorrows are different from yours, that's all.

That can't be true, said Zeke.

Upton leaned over and ruffled his hair, then started the car.

Poor little Zeke, he said. Not long ago you were just an ordinary little human boy living in an ordinary little cult. You woke up every morning of your life and you knew perfectly well that there was nothing in the world to trouble you. You went through your ordinary little day, and at night you slept your ordinary little sleep filled with peaceful, stupid dreams.

His hands twisted around the steering wheel like he was strangling a child.

You live in a dream, he said, you're a sleepwalker, blind. The world's a hell, what does it matter what happens in it? Wake up, Zeke, use your wits, learn something.

He drove him to a house overlooking the ocean and hurried Zeke inside. It was a terrifying, glassy home. One giant window, really, gazing at the sea. It should have been spectacular. It was spectacular, the ocean was spectacular. But from inside this house the beauty also felt somehow *contrived*, as if it wasn't real, nothing but an image, the sky and the sea, just symbols of money, the things that money itself looked at to convince itself it was alive.

But what do I know, thought Zeke. I'm just a poor stupid Amish boy who's been captured by a sociopath.

EIGHTEEN

Before they left the Salton Sea, Leahbelle traded her red dress for a pair of jeans, a sweatshirt, and a frumpy brown jacket. It wasn't until they stopped in a small town in the mountains to the west, however, that Gonzalo took her into the restroom of a pie shop, locked the door, cut her hair short, and removed a grape-sized sphere from his pocket.

Where did you get that?

It's a computer, he said.

It's Harta's computer.

They loaned it to me.

He passed his palm over it and it exploded with light. An egg-like hologram surrounded Leahbelle. She felt herself change. She felt a strange presence this time. A presence that *knew* her, a presence that *remembered* her.

Gonzalo shut it off. Her hair was now blacker than black. Who was this girl in the mirror? Dark and mysterious, evil and alive. Evil and alive or good and dead. She looked like an alien, a cyborg, a crazy creature. *This is me.*

She wondered who exactly she was hiding from. The government hadn't really murdered her family because they thought her parents were dangerous. They couldn't be that stupid. So why would they care about *her*, dead or alive? Maybe she was just making it harder for the people who did care to find her. The *person* who cared. Would Zeke even recognize her in this get-up?

I'm not Leahbelle anymore, she said.

Okay, said Gonzalo. Who are you?

For a second, she wanted to tell Gonzalo to name her. Make her into whatever he thought she should be, like his silver jumpsuit and his snakeskin boots. In that way it would be clear that she was just an emptiness, a nothing. But she changed her mind.

I'm Astra.

Gonzalo laughed.

I'm not joking.

I know, he said.

Astra Dark.

Okay, Astra, said Gonzalo. Let's go.

She let Gonzalo drive, and they arrived in San Diego as the sun was setting over the ocean to the west. The city was freakishly beautiful, full of strange lush canyons and intricately carved cliffs. The cloudy sky was like some jellied candy. The surface of every building was painted with elaborate figurative graffiti, and ornamental holograms suggested intricate layers and infinite alleyways. The city was a vast hieroglyphic symbol. The world, it was incredible. Evil, sure, maybe dying, maybe already dead, insane and dazzling and alive.

They rode west down a wide boulevard past a motley assortment of businesses that seemed to have been established here over centuries. They zipped underneath a glowing pink neon sign: *The Boulevard*. Gonzalo turned left down Park Avenue, past pyramids and portraits of pharaohs, as if they'd arrived in a lost colony of Egypt. They passed an abandoned concrete block of a building on the corner of a major intersection with big scary letters that said THE CRYPT. A strange insignia was pasted on either side, a double-headed serpent with wings.

I'm dead, Leahbelle thought for the hundredth time. But the thought barely meant anything anymore. It was a boring thought. They rode into the vast expanse of Balboa Park, which housed grand buildings—museums, mostly—as well as thousands of tents and cardboard hovels spilling down into Florida Canyon. Every vacant space along the sides of Park Avenue was intertwined with lush, vigorous vegetation. Gonzalo parked by a cactus garden.

We'll set up camp here, he said.

He found an empty space on a slope beneath a cathedral cactus. Everything around here seemed to be elaborately twisted. Spiny trees that looked swollen on the bottom, like an elephant's trunk, cacti like winding stairways, and succulents that looked like sea anemones, asteroids, or tiny green whirling people.

It used to be dry here, Gonzalo said.

This is where Gonzalo's from, Leahbelle thought, although she knew it wasn't exactly accurate. A world of elaborately twisted and prickly creatures. Space shuttles constantly roared across the sky. They were taking off and landing from the shuttleport smack dab in the city's center, Gonzalo explained. Unlike airplanes, the shuttles hadn't been connected to the data vapor or the Grid, so now they were using the shuttles as terrestrial transportation for the Gstate and the wealthy.

Gonzalo laid out the blankets and heated up a couple of pouches of protein gruel.

Back to this, huh? she said.

You got spoiled at Ebola's.

That's one way to look at it.

Yeah. What's another?

She could see her reflection in the silvery pouch. The black hair was a shock. In the canyon below, lights were coming on in various tents, hovels, and campsites. Glowing jellies, holographic fires, kerosene lanterns.

Sorry I keep abandoning you, Gonzalo said.

That's not the problem, she said. I've been a mess.

The night was warm, but with a slight chill as a layer of fog came in. She pulled one of the blankets over her.

I've been obsessed with finding Zeke, she said. It's like I'm telling myself this story that somehow he can save me or take care of me or make everything right again.

It's natural, said Gonzalo.

Sure, she said.

The smell of kerosene lanterns rose up from the camps beneath them. It was the smell of Leahbelle's childhood, of her whole life.

But I've lost everything, she said. It isn't coming back, Gonzalo. Nobody can make anything right again.

Something will be right.

Maybe. But not like that. I've turned my oldest friend into a magic incantation. Zeke Yoder, Zeke Yoder. A song or a spell to carry me away to a different life. A silly dream.

I don't know, said Gonzalo.

He's not a magician or a savior, said Leahbelle. Nobody knows that better than I do. He's just a boy. Like you.

Yes, said Gonzalo.

He hasn't been here for any of this. He wasn't there when my family was killed.

He would have been, if he could.

You're the one who took care of me.

Gonzalo looked at the dirt.

I don't want to find Zeke and lose you is what I'm saying.

The moon was rising to the east. It wasn't a reasonable moon. It was full and fat and almost pink.

You're going to Mexico, she said. You're looking for the portal.

Yes. It's what I have to do.

I want to come with you.

I don't know.

Don't just leave me.

We'll find Zeke first, he said. We can all go together.

Maybe we'll find him. Maybe we never will.

We'll find him.

He was probably dead, she thought. But she didn't say that.

Gonzalo, she said instead. I've never been kissed.

He looked frightened for a moment, and then he laughed.

I have, he said.

I want you to kiss me.

I'm not the one you want to be your first kiss.

Don't tell me what I want.

Okay, he said.

Okay what?

Okay I won't tell you what you want. I'll just tell you that I'm no good for you.

Why does everyone want to pretend you're so bad? I've never known anyone so good.

No, he said. I'm only being good now. When I tell you it won't be what you want. This is me being good.

I can't believe I have to argue with you for one little kiss.

The tents and boxes in the cactus garden began to fill up with their residents. More and more crowded, the garden smelled of human and dog, smoke and excrement.

One little kiss, he said.

What's the big deal? You plugged in to my nervous system. You weren't too good to do that. Either was I.

Right, said Gonzalo. But I'd have thought you'd want Zeke Yoder to be your first kiss.

I don't know if I'll ever see Zeke again.

Don't say that.

Look, I'm not trying to turn this into some huge historical event. I just want to see what the big deal is. Get it over with.

Before she knew it was happening, he leaned in and kissed her, and then it was done. She was so startled, it was like she'd missed it. She wasn't sure how it felt.

Oh, she said.

He laughed.

No big deal, he said. Now you've been kissed.

It seemed clear to Leahbelle that Gonzalo didn't really know what to do, now that they were actually here. They rode down University to an all night café called Lestat's. The vast crowded room had a sphinx in the center. Gonzalo took a look around, moved to the side, and pulled on the statue of a pharaoh. It was a door leading to the upstairs. Guarding the top of the stairway was another statue, half man and half jackal.

Anubis, said Gonzalo. God of embalming and the dead.

Looks like he spends a lot of time at the gym, said Leahbelle.

There's an old acquaintance of Ebola's around here somewhere, Gonzalo said. Trigram X. She could get us info on Zeke. The vampires should know where to find her.

The "vampires" at Lestat's were partially mutated or just pretending. She recognized them immediately, with their capes and fangs.There were two of them seated at a table in the back corner, drinking frothy red drinks. One was female, the other non-binary.

The real vampires, the mutants, can't do without the blood, Gonzalo said, but the collapse of the Grid has affected the supply.

Whose blood is it?

Most of the blood on the market came from Mexico, Honduras, Colombia, and Argentina. It's a concentrated and easily digestible source of protein. They claim it allows them to use fewer biological resources for digestion and more for their aristocratic intelligence.

Gonzalo took a seat at the vampires' table and introduced himself.

My colleague Astra and I are looking for someone. Someone rather underground.

You charming, sad, pathetic little mortals, said the non-binary. Come seeking the wisdom of your superiors. Be careful that you don't get scorched.

I've *been* scorched, said Leahbelle. Is that blood?

What a brave and reckless and *stupid* creature, said the non-binary. So primitive. Are you human?

Not exactly, she said.

Not exactly, said the female. The evasive untruths of mortals are so intoxicating. Allow me to introduce myself, Astra. I am Toxica. My associate is Chernobyl. And yes, this is blood with just a touch of steamed milk.

Cow's milk? asked Leahbelle.

Human milk, said Chernobyl.

Human blood? asked Leahbelle.

The two vampires just looked at each other and smirked.

Perhaps you'd like to feed us, suggested Toxica.

Not at all, said Leahbelle.

Listen, said Gonzalo. I'm an associate of Madame Ebola Virus.

You're looking for Ebola? said Toxica. Here?

No, I know where Ebola is, said Gonzalo. I'm looking for Tri-gram X.

That washed-up old wannabe oracle?

That's it, said Gonzalo.

And what do we get out of the deal? asked Toxica, running a finger up Gonzalo's biological arm, while staring at Leahbelle's neck lasciviously.

To Leahbelle's surprise, Gonzalo plopped a jar full of what looked to be blood on the table. The vampires seemed just as surprised as Leahbelle.

Taste it, he said. Good shit. None of that synthetic crap watered down with warm milk.

Manzanita Canyon, said Toxica.

She studies the wild guinea pig colonies there, said Chernobyl.

Toxica snatched the jar from the table and hurried off to the restroom, with Chernobyl right behind her.

The next morning they rode out toward City Heights.

Just around the corner from The Crypt, they passed under a bridge. It wasn't exactly a tunnel, but it felt as if Leahbelle was passing from one life to another. They passed through a neighborhood called North Park that seemed primarily filled with holograms and rode over a couple of vast canyons with rivers at the bottom, streaming with a steady traffic of boats and canoes.

City Heights was full of humans or barely altered post-humans, recent immigrants mostly, from the various countries of Africa and the Near East that the Gstate was heavily invested in. Regions full of mineral and water resources and anti-singularity extremists that America had been bombing for decades, while the resources were extracted and sent somewhere else. This was Gonzalo's analysis, in any case. Leahbelle knew nothing about the rest of the world except for a few outdated facts and photos from ancient schoolbooks.

Their first stop in City Heights was an old garage which, like so many other buildings in this city, was designed in the early twentieth century with an Egyptian motif. It was full of mysterious medical equipment, machine parts, and huge refrigerators marked *Biohazard*. The old man there called himself Cerberus. He had three heads, the original and two cyborg replicas. They moved almost exactly together, but just slightly out of sync. Leahbelle found it disturbing. When he looked at her, it was like an entire world was looking at her, but it wasn't a human world. It was wormy or reptilian. It laid eggs and hatched monsters.

You want to know what's in the refrigerators? he asked her.

Probably not, said Leahbelle.

His three heads laughed discordantly.

It isn't the dead, he told her.

That hadn't occurred to me, actually, said Leahbelle.

But it's not exactly living either, he said.

Can we talk in private? asked Gonzalo.

They're like eggs, said Cerberus. Little biological machines that aren't alive but are ready to give life orders. Biological life is so helpless sometimes. Sad, isn't it?

He took Gonzalo to a little back room, leaving Leahbelle alone with the machine parts and the mysterious refrigerators. Something was ticking inside.

Don't open that door, a voice said.

Of course I'll open the door, another voice said.

She was talking to herself again. Cracking the refrigerator door and peeking inside would be so stupid and dangerous that it would prove once and for all she was completely out of her mind. One of the voices came from the heart of madness, and yet she did what it told her. She couldn't help herself.

The light blinded her, but the ticking exploded into a roaring clatter that sounded like laughter. There was nothing in there, but it seemed to be moving. It was evil and laughing at her. She slammed the door shut.

When Gonzalo and Cerberus returned, Cerberus took her picture. He scanned her retina, a few DNA signatures, and her brainprint. Within minutes she had a fake ID. Gonzalo had traded him something in order to get Leahbelle this shiny holographic document with her new name: Astra Dark.

The entrance to Manzanita Canyon was next to a store that sold only the cheapest pills and intoxicating technologies. The canyon itself was lush and the descent down the path quickly took Leahbelle to a radically new reality—the bright sun and mist were lost in green shadow, graffiti-covered rocks, a cool tribal feeling of prehistoric jungles and primitive civilizations deep within the earth.

At the bottom of the canyon, a stream. Along the stream, dense patches of reeds and shrubs, and peeking out from the greenery were the chubby, furry faces of dozens and dozens of guinea pigs.

They've been here for decades, said Gonzalo. Somebody's meat that escaped. Or somebody's pet that was abandoned.

Leahbelle leaned down to get a closer look. The guinea pigs didn't show any fear.

I love creatures that were once domesticated and enslaved but escaped, Gonzalo said. Parrots, cats, snakes, baby alligators. Everything wants to be free.

They're so cute, said Leahbelle.

I guess so, said Gonzalo.

Watch out for the prickles, said a booming, husky voice behind them. Leahbelle turned, but there was nobody there.

The oracle comes from deep within the earth, said the voice. It is anywhere and nowhere.

Right, said Gonzalo. Trigram X?

Who seeks to know the secret ways of time?

Gonzalo Vega. I knew you when I was a kid, in Longmont.

No shit, said the voice.

There was a rustling in the brush, but Leahbelle still couldn't locate the noise.

You're the little butterfly that Harta Gold and Big Gonzalo were always trailing behind them, said the voice. You've changed, little butterfly.

Gonzalo looked annoyed.

Funny, he said. Ebola told me I hadn't changed at all.

There are the underlying patterns and there is the body itself, said the voice. There are the underlying patterns made manifest in the body itself. There are the deep masks and the frivolous masks and the psyche sculpted in time through mutations both predictable and free. My vision penetrates all of these layers and more.

Right, said Gonzalo. Then my question will be easy for you. I'm looking for an Amish boy from Iowa, Zeke Yoder.

The canyon was filled with laughter.

You came to the source of timeless wisdom seeking only mundane worldly information, said the voice. Sad and ironic, but typical. For such practical information, I will need to consult a variety of sources. Give me a day or two. As I'm sure you remember, the oracle requires an offering.

What's the customary offering these days?

Two hundred in CASH® or the equivalent in trade. Vehicles, wings, medicines, life forms, genetic modifiers, but please—no fogbots, perishable foodstuffs, or under-appreciated artworks.

Got it, said Gonzalo. I'll stop by tomorrow.

One of the guinea pigs emerged from the brush, a fat, fluffy, reddish one, and met Leahbelle's eyes with a look of such profound understanding that she was reminded of the rats.

They're smart, aren't they? she said.

They do math and use tools, said the voice. They have a rudimentary language. But be careful, they can be quite vicious.

Vicious?

She didn't believe it. She reached out her hand to let the little rodent sniff it.

Hey, cutie, she said. What's your name?

It sniffed her briefly and then snapped at her pinky.

Ow!

It clenched its razor-sharp teeth on her little finger and tore at it for a moment before releasing it, giving her a nasty look, and retreating into the brush.

Never assume that the affection of our former pets will continue once they no longer depend on us for food.

Are you okay? asked Gonzalo.

It broke the skin. I'm bleeding.

Here, let me put some antibiotic on that.

Her finger was already red and throbbing intensely. Gonzalo sprayed a liquid on it from one of his mechanical fingers.

By the time they arrived back at the camp, she was sweating. A rash ran up her arm. She felt hot.

You better rest, said Gonzalo. Let me see if I can find some medicine.

Don't leave me.

You want to come with? I don't think you should.

She felt dizzy.

No, I'll stay. But come right back. I'm starting to feel crazy again.

He gave her a couple of pills.

It never ends, she said.

She lay down and tried to sleep.

She was burning alive or maybe burning dead. Fever dreams, but she was wide awake and surrounded by hideous creatures peeking out of their tents and hovels. One-eyed creatures, one-armed creatures, beautiful demons that hopped through the cactus garden on one leg. Not a dream, she thought.

This was real. Or something. Gonzalo had been gone for hours or days or vast epochs of time. Stars were being born and dying. The dinosaurs had perished and the little rodents were developing fingers and hips and enormous lumpy brains. There was too much time, she was drowning in it, it never ended, it never would.

You got any dry socks? somebody asked her.

She tried to scream, but was having trouble breathing.

You don't look too good, little missy.

She needed a drink. The world was drying out, a desiccated husk of a world. You can have my soul, she tried to tell the devil, just give me some water.

There was something black attached to her hand, gnawing on it, a long insect camouflaged as a dead stick. Weird. She couldn't feel much of anything over there. Her hand.

The black insect was her finger, her little pinky, she realized. She examined it closely. Her hair was black as coal and now her finger too. There was a small spot, an opening in the middle of the little finger, and it was shining. Silvery and undulating, tiny pieces of glitter. She'd seen that glitter before.

She was screaming now, screaming and screaming, and this was creating a real commotion. A hand clasped over her mouth and she tried to bite it.

Somebody said, In eternity, however, it's hard to tell the difference.

There was a sock in her mouth and people holding her down.

You can't do that here, somebody said. No screaming. If you're going to scream, you've got to go. Do you understand?

She nodded. Yes, she gave up. She was a piglet, a horse, a girl. Infected. She was going to die, and it didn't matter.

She was dying, and she remembered that Gonzalo had the only cure for death, the music from his heart.

By the time Gonzalo returned, the fever had broken and whoever had held her down was nowhere to be seen. She was soaking wet, but her thoughts made more sense. Her finger was really black. She could really see the glitter moving around in the wound where she'd been bit. She waved it at Gonzalo.

I'm going to die, she said. Give me the music. Please.

He gave her a shot of something. He gave her some pills. He disappeared for a minute and returned with a dry nightgown and helped her change her clothes. For a minute she was naked, but it was okay because Gonzalo was her nurse.

Why do you take care of me? she asked. Do you love me?

Of course I do.

He held her hand.

Let me listen just one more time, she said.

Just one more time, he said. But you won't die. I won't let you die.

They'll control my thoughts, she said.

Maybe it's not even the same stuff, he said. We'll have to get it looked at.

He gave her the headphones and for just a second she felt that thrill, the rush of calm and peacefulness, but then the music did nothing special and she knew that he had lied. It was just a placebo. He'd done that before.

Liar, liar, liar, she thought.

Then she was asleep and dreaming ridiculous dreams.

NINETEEN

Zeke was tied to a chair in the middle of the living room, facing the ocean. Everything was glass. Everything was sky and sea. Upton came and went, fed him or gave him water sometimes, and took him to the toilet. He ignored Zeke for the most part, now that he'd gotten all the information he wanted. He was working on his schemes. He'd given Zeke some kind of truth serum on the very first day, and Zeke hadn't been able to stop himself from telling Upton all about Emma's psychic powers, the beheading of Boopsie, and Gabrielle's oxytocin addiction. Upton wore electromagnetically charged metal tips on his fingers, and whenever Zeke told him something he really wanted to know, he would touch Zeke at odd places on his body, sending electric currents in distinct patterns, and Zeke's mind would flood with the most intense sensual and psychological pleasure.

Zeke was physically uncomfortable most of the time. He was in grave danger, and in all likelihood he would soon be killed. He was the captive of a truly repugnant and amoral creature. He would never see Leahbelle or Gonzalo again, his father or his mother, his grandmother or his little brothers and sisters. He would not help his people, protect Emma, or help prevent the development of the singularity in any way. He had totally failed. And yet in some strange way, he'd never been happier.

Upton's shadow approached him from behind. He clicked the metallic tips of his fingers together. The very sound of those metallic tips, even just the approach of Upton or the sound of his voice, would now flood Zeke's brain with the anticipation of pleasure.

His whole life he'd been taught the virtue of hard work, toil, suffering, and stoic acceptance of whatever meager provisions he'd been allotted. And here he was, addicted to the laziness, the total release, the total irresponsibility and extravagance of a completely biological pleasure.

Your friends have abandoned the Beach Life Boutique, Upton told him, but I left them a message, and they received it. We've begun our negotiations in earnest.

He placed a tray table in front of Zeke and then plopped down a large transparent canister filled with a thick liquid, a straw sticking out the top.

They're going to buy me back? asked Zeke.

They think so, said Upton. I'm off now to complete the deal. I'm leaving you this food.

That's not food, said Zeke. What are you really doing?

I've sold you to the government, said Upton. The government only really wants you because they want to find the girl. They don't know that I know that. By the time they pick you up, I'll have the girl, and the robot's head too.

How do you think you can do that?

He clicked his fingertips together and then ran one of them down Zeke's cheek as if deciding whether this was a face worth eating or not.

Like all empaths, Gabrielle's a bit delusional, said Upton. She overestimates what she can accomplish through the act of understanding. She overestimates her ability to filter false emotional signals from real ones. I've been tracking them. I know where they're holed up.

You're using me as bait.

More or less.

And what will you do with Emma? asked Zeke. Sell her to the government too?

She's too precious, I believe, to simply barter away. We'll see.

He turned and began gathering some items that looked vaguely like weapons into his bag.

And what about Boopsie's head? What's the value in that?

The government is very interested in Dr. Brockton's plans and capabilities. Whatever data is stored in that robot will be of great interest to them.

He clicked his fingertips together.

You don't want to question me any further? Zeke asked.

Upton laughed.

You've told me everything already, Zeke Yoder.

He touched a spot behind Zeke's ear and another on his right shoulder and sent a brief jolt of current into Zeke's body. Zeke shuddered with pleasure.

Upton moved to his side, and for a moment he seemed translucent, made of colors and light.

Are you an angel? Zeke asked. A fallen angel?

Angels are just common hallucinations, Upton told him. Some common hallucinations are the result of deep programming and brainwashing techniques from a hostile alien race.

A hostile alien race.

Good-bye, said Upton.

The shadow receded, his footsteps padded away, the door clicked open and shut, and then came the rumble of a vehicle's motor and the vehicle driving away.

Time became strange. Endless and painful. The facts were unbearable. Zeke had betrayed people he cared about, failed other people he cared about, and was doomed. After the sun set and the room filled with a luminous, bluish darkness, these facts became the motors of a series of uncontrollable thoughts and half dreams and hallucinations. He was just a blotch or stain on the earth, on time, on the pure light of heaven. He prayed for forgiveness and drowned in the silence that followed his prayers. The fat moon appeared and slowly sank into the sea. When the sun rose again, it didn't free him or forgive him, but exposed him, a foul stinking lump of a boy, stewing in his own filth.

Throughout the day, he got crazier and crazier. The sparkles and ripples of the ocean became vast alien cities, intricate labyrinths, and complicated grammatical constructions. Jesus and the devil both spoke to him and then revealed themselves as the same creature, a winged, two-headed serpent wrapped around a cross. The secret was buried in his mother's grave, some *body* was buried in his mother's grave, and where was his mother? He could hear her whispering something from the bottom of the sea. The sea was a bottomless pool and everyone was sinking forever into it.

That night, the moon wept. The tears were blue and electric, and Zeke was bathed in their light, and then he slept or lost consciousness for a while. A long time ago, he'd been gazing into the eyes of an island fox. The fox was sending him messages in his mind.

He'd written the words down, but where was that scrap of paper now? It seemed urgent to recover the scrap of paper and the telepathic message from the beautiful fox. A new Bible could be written, he thought, and a new civilization constructed on the message from the handsome fox. But he remembered the message precisely, he realized.

Contact is always monstrous, the fox told him. It's always now, isn't it? the fox asked him. Your face makes me happy, the fox said. I could love you in the future, the fox said, but what's the point? I love you right now. Please don't ever leave me, the fox said. Please go away.

The moon was weeping and so was Zeke.

I'm sorry, he said. I'm sorry I left you. I'm sorry I'm still here.

Death is real, the ocean told him.

Am I going to die? Zeke asked his dream. The dream refused to answer.

When Zeke woke up to see two creatures who seemed at least mostly female, one older and one younger, a red cap, a blue scarf, shining their lights in his eyes and examining him with various gadgets and rays, he thought that he was saved.

TWENTY

Leahbelle slept off and on for two nights and two days. She had dreams, visions, hallucinations. Violence, there was always violence, and it didn't *work*. Somebody or some *thing* was trying to tell her something. It was like an equation missing the crucial variable. It was like a structured pattern of intricately interconnected geometric shapes and stick figures. It was like an alphabet etched into the back of a tortoise shell, and the letters, which weren't letters but ghosts, just needed to be translated into a different language, a language made of light. Nothing made any sense, but it seemed like it was just about to. And then, exhausted by her incomprehension, she'd be swallowed up into a lonely nothingness, unable to touch another being or thought, cursed to wander for eternity without a home.

When she woke up, however, feeling hungry and almost healthy, and saw Gonzalo preparing some sort of broth over the portable stove, she wondered if homelessness was a curse or rather some sort of blessing. To belong nowhere. To wander and change and discover new beauties and new horrors forever.

Gonzalo was beautiful. He was a beautiful boy and she loved him, she was completely in love with him.

The broth was delicious. Chickeny, but she didn't ask. Some sort of slug or insect served as the base most likely. It was late afternoon.

I saw Trigram X again this morning, Gonzalo told her.

Did you actually *see* her?

I did. But I've seen her many times. She's just a shriveled little hustler with a booming voice. She's been working that voice for years but hasn't managed to hold it together enough to even keep all of her teeth.

Oh, said Leahbelle. That's sad.

Gonzalo shrugged.

Don't shed too many tears for Trigram X. She wouldn't shed even one for you.

What did she tell you?

Zeke was in San Jose. He made contact with the rats there and maybe with the Amish.

Then we'll go to San Jose.

No, said Gonzalo. The robot he was traveling with was seen in Ventura over a week ago. Zeke's heading south. Toward San Diego.

Why? said Leahbelle. Why would he be coming *here*?

You told me you could always find each other.

But I don't sense *anything* now, she said. I don't understand anything. It doesn't make sense to me.

You always find the thing when you stop looking, he said.

You said that once before.

Maybe *he* got information about *us*.

Maybe, said Leahbelle.

But she had a bad feeling. There was something Gonzalo wasn't telling her.

Who saw the robot? she asked.

The robot surfaced in a holographic video, said Gonzalo. It was all over the place for a minute, like you and your song.

Okay, said Leahbelle. But what was the robot doing? Why did everybody see this video?

Gonzalo didn't say anything.

You have to tell me.

Its head was cut off, said Gonzalo. The anti-technology group NIHIL beheaded it and then publicized the video.

Beheaded it.

She imagined Zeke's disembodied head rolling down some hill.

They don't kill people, Gonzalo said. Only machines.

Never? said Leahbelle.

Hardly ever.

Where do they draw the line? Would they kill you?

I don't think so. They might remove parts of me.

Are they part of your revolution? Did they help you destroy the Grid?

I don't know. Nobody knows much about them. They just popped up recently, and there's a lot of rumors.

I need to tell you something, said Leahbelle. I figured something out. Violence doesn't work.

Violence works.

I don't think so. We can figure out a better way. Me and you and Zeke together.

The three pacifists, said Gonzalo. A peaceful threesome against the singularity!

You're making fun of me.

No, said Gonzalo. You figure it out. I'm all ears.

Okay, said Leahbelle. So we assume that Zeke's okay. What do we do now?

We poke around San Diego, I check my sources, we wait for something to turn up. We'll find him.

They left the motorbike at the campsite and walked south through the park and into the intensely congested shantytowns of the East Village. The people down here looked a mess.

Free-market evolution, said Gonzalo. Everything for the rich. Nothing but untested mutations, shoddy technology, and a one-way ticket to irrelevance for everybody else.

Occasionally Gonzalo would spot somebody that he thought might have information—Leahbelle wasn't sure what distinguished them from anyone else—and he'd huddle with them for a moment, speaking in whispers, then return with nothing much to report.

We have to be careful, he told Leahbelle after a brief conversation with a creature who had a falcon perched on her broad shoulder. The Gstate is getting surveillance drones back in the air. We won't be able to count on the privacy of our conversations for long.

Did you want to have a private conversation? asked Leahbelle.

He looked at her like he didn't know what she was getting at.

She's trained her falcon to destroy the drones, said Gonzalo. All over the city, hawks are being trained. This is a military city, but it's also a real stronghold for the resistance.

What about the *non*resistance?

He didn't seem to understand it was a joke. Or maybe she was just babbling.

We've retaken San Francisco, he told her. It's really happening. They can really lose.

But can we really win?

Walking through the squalid, tent-filled streets was making her feel a bit woozy. The haze in the sky seemed to multiply the bright light and paste a ridiculous glue over some basic fractures in reality. Everybody was talking about the hostile aliens on their way from Orion to devour human souls. The story had developed many interpretations, many layers, and many surprising and not very interesting applications to the actual life histories of the insane people on the streets. It was like the aliens were parents or children or caseworkers or bad memories.

Won't they find us? With the drones?

Leahbelle, he said. Are you okay?

Gonzalo, she said.

Holy shit.

She followed his gaze and saw him right away. A boy who looked like Zeke, a little bit like Zeke, walking directly toward them.

That's not him, she said.

But Gonzalo was still staring at the boy as if he was delivering a secret message. The boy was staring at them too. It occurred to her that the government had tried to build a duplicate but failed somehow. Gonzalo seemed bigger. He'd puffed himself up, she realized. She'd forgotten he could do that. The boy walked past them, and Gonzalo turned to watch.

Not even close, said Leahbelle.

Gonzalo finally laughed.

You're right, he said. He just had that kind of dreamy look and maybe something in the eyes.

He took her hand and they kept walking.

Wait here, he said suddenly. There might be somebody in here who'll know something.

He ducked through the empty doorway of an abandoned building. It was a decrepit and enormous Victorian that had once been a grand hotel. Leahbelle stood on the sidewalk and waited. The streets were packed with destitute people, crazy people, people involved in all sorts of mysterious transactions. Cyborgs with broken down machine parts, malfunctioning robots, mutations that hadn't worked out. Lopsided elves, solar-powered people who'd turned crispy, a few she recognized as vampires, and young people wearing the scary blades and gruesome holograms of the Abjects. Another gang was covered with tattoos in constant motion. Nobody said anything to her. Nobody even looked at her.

She wondered if she, a mere human, was somehow ugly to these creatures.

An alternative explanation was that she was actually dead.

That same boring thought! It was so boring, why did she keep having it? She was in love with Gonzalo, she had to be alive. She watched birds circling overhead. She spotted a few dragonfly drones and tried to shoot them down with her slingshot, but missed. She stood on the sidewalk and tried not to feel crazy. What was he doing in there? The minutes ticked past. She peeked her head into the dark doorway of the abandoned building. Creatures lurked in the shadows. It was too dark to make anyone out, but she could see one empty chair just sitting in the middle of the cavernous room. The walls were covered with wanted posters printed on glowing adhesive jellies. The room went on and on, the only other light another empty doorway at the far end, where it gave onto the street.

Gonzalo was nowhere to be seen, and yet he was everywhere. His face was all over the illuminated posters, a striking likeness— intense, handsome, a little bit sad. There was a list of *seditious activities* he was supposedly guilty of: destroying power stations, bridges, and military vehicles; introducing catastrophic viruses into the Grid; giving material aid to terrorist organizations; selling weapons; selling illegal technology; kidnapping; murder. Armed and dangerous, it said. His tattoos and his machine parts were described and a bunch of aliases were listed. Supernova Juarez? Butterfly Boy? La Tipa Macho?

She stumbled back out into the daylight, feeling weird. Who was he really? Was this just propaganda or was some of it true? Did he kill people? She squinted at the bright sky. Drones were swarming overhead. People were hurrying away, panicked. Gonzalo emerged from a doorway on the other side of the street, halfway down the block. He was smoking some kind of cigarette and he passed it to the boy who was walking with him, so close together that they were like Siamese twins, joined at the cigarette. The boy took a drag and passed it back, the boy who looked kind of like Zeke Yoder.

The buzzing of the drones filled her head. Nothing made any sense, or it all made perfect sense, like a puzzle that was always missing one piece, a piece shaped like a skull and crossbones.

Gonzalo looked up and saw her watching him and said something to the boy. The boy disappeared into another doorway while Gonzalo continued walking toward her. He was smiling an odd smile, like a child who'd been bad. She didn't know *how* she knew it, but she knew one thing.

You don't love me, she said to him. It isn't me you love at all. I think you hate me.

Leahbelle, he said.

No! she shouted. Stay away from me!

He was reaching toward her from a great distance as if to stop her from running away, opening his mouth as if to tell her something important, but there was only a vast roar and a sky full of noise and light, and everything exploded. Leahbelle fell and was still falling, forever, with people stampeding in every direction. When the smoke cleared, Gonzalo's body was a limp pile in the middle of the street. Something was missing.

Something that looked like it might be his foot was in the gutter to her left. It had once been a foot certainly, although it was a bit charred now. She picked it up and raced over to the motionless body.

Gonzalo, she said. Wake up! I brought you your foot.

But he didn't move and he didn't say anything. Oh boy, she thought. And then somebody was grabbing her and pulling her away, shouting, Take cover! Take cover!

The sky opened up around her again. Everything was full of smoke and noise, and then everything went black.

TWENTY-ONE

Zeke woke up in a parking lot across an empty Grid-work from an endless horizontal building with jagged teeth on top. The two womanish creatures took a firm hold of each of his arms and guided him up some steps and across a long walkway over the Grid-work.

Welcome to the Death Star, said the older one.

He was whisked into an unobtrusive side entrance, down a long hallway, and into a nondescript room with one chair in the center. The room's bluish, matted carpet seemed to have been constructed from incredibly fine humanish hairs. An aquarium stretched along the side wall. One small octopus expanded and contracted back and forth from one side to the other. Zeke was seated in the chair and left alone.

The octopus was mesmerizing.

An older man entered the room. He wore a form-fitting jumpsuit and tennis shoes. His feathery hair fell over a slightly enlarged cranium.

Zeke Yoder, he said.

I guess so, said Zeke.

Don't be coy, child. We know almost everything about you. Now is your chance to tell us everything we don't yet know, but are destined to know.

I don't know anything.

Doubtful, said the man. Where is the girl?

I don't know.

Not an acceptable answer. How do you feel about your toes, Zeke Yoder?

My toes?

Are you fond of your toes?

They're okay.

You'd prefer not to have them sawed off one by one is what I'm suggesting.

The octopus curled up into itself. It seemed to be watching Zeke, waiting to hear what he would say.

I would like to keep my toes, Zeke said.

The man leaned in so close that Zeke could see his teeth as he spoke.

Where is the girl?

I don't know, said Zeke. I really don't. We were in Oceanside, at the Beach Life Boutique. After that, I lost them.

Surely you made contingency plans.

Contingency plans?

A rendezvous perhaps? In the event you became separated?

No, said Zeke. No contingency plans.

The man sighed. He took a syringe from the pocket of his jumpsuit and jabbed Zeke in the shoulder.

Some sort of truth serum? asked Zeke.

We don't traffic in truth serums here, said the man. Only in pain. The drugs will increase the sensitivity of your nerves, so that when I saw off your toe, you will feel it jarring every nerve in your body in the most horrible way. You can't even imagine, I assure you of that. You will have never felt such pain. The drugs will also prevent you from losing consciousness and from squirming around.

Zeke tried to move his head, his hand, anything. He couldn't even move a finger.

I really don't know, said Zeke. Upton's the man you want to find.

Yes, the man who sold you to us. Upton Rising aka Sereno Felicidad aka Jimmy Stefano aka Dax Phunnuts aka Sherman Spacey, which seems to be the name he was born with. A formidable character. And yet the remains of Mr. Spacey were found this morning in Oceanside in rather meager portions spread out in an oddly symmetrical radius from the wedding chapel that sells those delightful cruises. Cruises to impoverished colonies full of heartbreakingly beautiful and toxic beaches. Your friend was blown to smithereens, it seems, by a rather novel mechanism that left no chemical residue or heat signature. An extreme and yet highly localized explosion. Would you know anything about this novel mechanism, Zeke Yoder?

He's dead?

Yes. Are you surprised?

A little bit. Yes.

So we're left only with you.

The hand that had held the syringe was now holding a small serrated knife. Zeke didn't want to look at the knife, but he couldn't move his head or even close his eyes. He could *feel* intensely, however. The slightly cool air blowing from an overhead vent felt like sandpaper against his skin.

Zeke prayed.

As the man sawed off Zeke's toe—the long toe next to the big toe on his left foot—somebody screamed, the most horrible cry of pain Zeke had ever heard, and he knew it was his own. The pain was unbearable. Unbearable, he'd have to die. There was nothing but pain and it was eternal. It flooded every part of his body and his mind, a scraping and stabbing and pulling and jolting and screeching and crunching rasping dying scraping sawing screeching stabbing pulling jolting crushing rasping dying scraping sawing …

And then it was done. For a moment, before the sharp pulsing from the exposed nerves and tissues kicked in, the relief was so intense that Zeke thought he might be dead. And then the pain rushed back in and filled him up completely and there was nothing else.

Where is the girl? the torturer asked.

Zeke couldn't even form a response.

I have pain killers, the torturer said.

Mexico, said Zeke. We're supposed to rendezvous at the border.

You're lying.

Cross the border, said Zeke, and escape into reality.

Nonsense.

What could he possibly say to make it stop? His brain was screaming.

Santa Rosa Island, he said.

When he saw that the man was looking at him with renewed interest, actually considering this answer, it occurred to Zeke that they really might have returned to that desolate and lovely place. Maybe he'd really betrayed his friends. Maybe the man would stop the pain, maybe he'd let Zeke die.

Impossible, said the torturer finally. Where is the girl?

I don't know, said Zeke.

Concentrate, said the torturer. Focus.

The man gave him another shot. Not the same stuff, Zeke didn't think. It burned differently.

His brain felt less muddled. Where *was* Emma? Emma loved to run and to race. Her little shoes would clip and clop along the pavement. Emma was running, he thought. Somewhere, she was running.

Along the ocean, he said.

You're fantasizing, said the torturer. Not thinking. Perhaps this will help you think.

He started in on another toe.

There was nothing but pain. It flooded every part of Zeke's body and his mind, a scraping and stabbing and pulling and jolting and screeching and crunching rasping dying scraping sawing screeching stabbing pulling jolting crushing rasping dying scraping sawing …

Zeke was trying to do the math. Ten toes minus one toe. Nine toes minus another toe. The man could only cut off eight more toes.

Then he remembered his fingers.

I think she's still in Oceanside, Zeke said. I'm sure of it. She's at the library. She's reading a book called *Distant Star*.

The truth, said the torturer.

You don't want the truth, Zeke said. You *enjoy* this. Upton told me.

What else did Upton tell you?

He was negotiating.

We can assume the negotiations didn't go well for Upton, said the man.

I don't know, said Zeke.

Was the pain worse the first time or the second time? asked the torturer.

The pain's immeasurable, said Zeke.

Interesting. I'd have guessed the first was infinitely worse, due to the pain amplifiers I injected you with.

He jabbed Zeke with another syringe.

No more toes, he said.

No more toes, said Zeke.

The foot this time, he said. I'm losing patience.

He began sawing away at Zeke's ankle.

The scream that came from Zeke was endless. The agony was end-less. There was nothing possible, nothing except pain. It went on and on.

Something snapped, and Zeke felt himself rising into the air. The pain receded. Emma was speaking to him from somewhere, from all around. It's a crime, she was saying. It's a crime. It's evil, she was saying. It hurts too much. She was sobbing and screaming, No, no, no!

Down below, he saw somebody he recognized. What happened to that guy's foot, he wondered. It was hanging by a thread. Oh, he realized.

And then there was a blast of noise and light unlike anything he had ever seen or heard. It seemed to come from within his body, the body beneath him, from that body's pain, from this body's pain. It exploded outward, leveling everything beyond—burning it, demol-ishing it, devastating it, erasing it—the torturer and the octopus and the aquarium and the bluish, matted carpet and the hallways be-yond, the entire building. It was all destroyed but for a small bubble of light at the center where Zeke stood now, rejoined with his body, his pain, and his self, standing amid rubble and ash under an open sky. A woman and four children were rushing toward him through the charred, smoking debris. One of them was Emma, and she was carrying Boopsie's head. The head was wide awake and screaming. But when Boopsie's eyes met Zeke's eyes, she smiled.

I told you, Boopsie said. Results of magnitude. Results of power.

TWENTY-TWO

When Leahbelle woke up, her head hurt. She was lying in the doorway to the abandoned building, still holding Gonzalo's severed foot. The street was deserted.

She didn't think she'd been out for more than a few minutes.

She was a mess, dirty and bedraggled, and her ankle hurt when she walked. Gonzalo must have escaped. He'd probably meet her back at the camp. She trudged through the city back toward the park and the cactus garden. Gonzalo would want his foot back.

The motorbike was still there, and the bedding. She was hungry. There was food inside the motorbike's storage compartment, but she didn't have the key. She didn't have anything but the clothes on her back, the slingshot, the guitar, and the foot, which was beginning to turn blue.

She found a crumpled magazine page in the pocket of her jacket. She remembered she'd found it in New Mexico or something. The caption under one picture began *That way the viewer grows accustomed to* but got cut off. The beginning of the caption under the other photo was torn away, but it ended *that doesn't exist in order to make it exist.* Tissues in the picture spelled out words. *We demand* it began and then it said either *a mirror* or *a minor* and then *to reveal what isn't possible.*

She rummaged through the blankets. She found a dirty shirt that smelled like Gonzalo's cologne, a coin, a mirror, and two orange pills. In the mirror, she could see that her forehead was bloody, that she'd been wounded right between the eyes, and that glitter was spilling from the wound. She took the pills and headed back toward the downtown. Maybe Gonzalo was still there in the middle of the street. Maybe he'd crawled into a doorway. Maybe she hadn't looked hard enough.

As she walked past more tents and hovels and fountains and over the Grid-works, empty except for a few military vehicles, she made a list in her head of the people who'd died. Her mother. Her father. Her brother Delmar. Her sister Hannah. Her brother Ervin. Her brother Elvin. Her brother Ivan. Her sister Sarah. Her sister Katie. Her sister Ruth. Her horse Fern. Elvin Miller's girl, Ethel, who was in Leahbelle's home picking up some eggs when the drone destroyed it. The piglet. Zeke's friend, the beheaded robot. Maybe Zeke. Maybe Gonzalo.

She couldn't find the block with the abandoned building. Nothing looked familiar, or everything did. Hovels and tents and scary mutants and Abjects and people missing a variety of body parts. Their clothes all seemed too loose or too tight. Many were speaking to invisible people, arguing with invisible people. There was a guy without a head. There was a head attached to a rolling chair. There were people down here so poor that they couldn't see or hear. She crossed trolley tracks and a bridge that went from nowhere to nowhere. She wandered through the most densely packed tent city and then crossed under the Grid-work on Island and walked south until the street curved around and she came to an underpass with electric graffiti guarded by cut-out figures of a human named Cesar Chavez and two demon children who held his hands. The underpass was crawling with murals of figures skateboarding, mutants half butterfly and half woman, strange stylized letters, studious children, and another butterfly-woman mutant with enormous eyes on her wings. The word AZTLAN. Distorted faces and a crowned Jesus with a bleeding heart and beyond was a park that wound through a maze of Grid-work overpasses all covered with murals. Chicano Park. These were the images: skulls, slaves, field hands, moons, eyeballs. Aztec warriors, jaguars, and bleeding sun pictographs. A creature wearing shades. Eyes, webs, horses, sombreros, struggle. More skulls and winged women, purplish aliens, peacock feathers with enormous golden eyes, brown earth, men with hatchets, scorpions. "Let me say at the risk of sounding ridiculous that the true revolutionary is guided by great feelings of love." Cactus, scantily clad warriors, skeletal demon figures, and a bare-breasted warrior woman with tiger-striped hair. Roads and faces. Everywhere that word: AZTLAN. A woman with antlers and a cobra wrapped around her and a skull where her heart should be and monarch butterflies. Everything was mutating and transforming. Money was becoming death and servants were taking flight. Was this the place Gonzalo was looking for?

A group of actual humans was cooking some sort of meaty thing over a fire in a trash barrel. They didn't speak English and didn't even have translation software. She made an eating gesture with her hand. They shook their heads, but one of them gave her a crumpled bar of cricket mush before he shooed her away. She hurried back toward the skyscrapers in the distance.

If she walked far enough in any direction, the world became strange and new.

Back downtown, she asked a vampire for something to eat and it tried to grab her butt. She slapped it, recoiled at her own violence, and then slapped it again. At Eighth and G, she approached a skinny mutant with three eyes who looked like she was selling things.

I'll trade you my slingshot for some food, she told her.

No food. But I have pills that will help.

The skinny mutant was maybe seventy or eighty and wore tight jeans and a sweater. She carried an enormous purse that Leahbelle imagined was full of all kinds of bizarre treasures. She had metallic red hair and looked like she'd started to grow wings from the back of her shoulders that never fully developed.

Help what? Leahbelle asked.

You won't care so much about food.

She ended up with a bottle of water and two blue pills. Before the first pill kicked in, she wished she'd traded the guitar instead. She could have used the slingshot to kill a bird or a squirrel or a guinea pig. She could have cooked some dead creature over a fire of her own. And then she saw a crow steering a toy jeep down the middle of the street, and she remembered the intelligent gaze of the nasty little guinea pig, and she thought maybe it was just as well.

Things were bright. Too bright. She had to pee, so she crouched in a dark doorway. Somebody offered to trade her a baby for something called a D6 Coder.

Do I look like I have a D6 Coder? Leahbelle asked.

You never know, said the voice.

It was true that the pills helped with the hunger and they kept her up, walking and walking on her aching ankle. Up and down

Eighth and Ninth and Fifth and Fourth, back and forth across A and
B and C and F. She was ready to collapse, but when she tried to stop
moving and sit down, it felt like her brain might explode. She had to
keep moving or something evil would settle into her. She trudged on,
where or for what she didn't know. The sun came up. The wisps of
fog evaporated. She couldn't feel the edges of herself anymore. It was
like she was the same as the atmosphere, the streets, the city, everybody, the whole world, and it was all miserable.

There was nothing to do but put it out of its misery, she thought.
The whole world. Annihilation, she thought. Maybe we should give
that a try? Something different, she thought. We have to become
something different. Like nothing at all.

She was carrying Gonzalo's foot, and the foot was dead. There was
nothing to be done for the foot, but she couldn't let it go. She'd never
seen the ocean before, and so she walked west, further and further
west, through the remains of former retail zones and over a hill and
down to the cliffs that looked over the ocean. The ocean was incredible. She remembered that she believed in God. The mutants around
Ocean Beach were scruffy and vaguely doggy. She wondered if the
locals had mated with their pets. Space shuttles roared directly overhead every few minutes, so close that she thought she could make
eye contact with the pilots. She wondered if any of them were going
into space. She had some cousins who'd gone to farm on Mars, or
maybe they were pharming, she couldn't keep it straight. Outer
space. Maybe it was so vast and empty that she could just drift away
out there forever.

People were having a drum circle next to the pier. The rhythm
got inside her body and reminded her that she was on Earth. She
plucked at her guitar, but the note sounded discordant. She walked
out onto the pier, way out into the ocean, so far that she could look
back and see the waves from behind, racing toward shore and crashing against the beach and the cliffs.

She couldn't bear the thought that Gonzalo might be dead and
that she had yelled at him for something as ridiculous as not being in
love with her. What did that even mean? She didn't care who he
loved or whatever. They'd been through everything together. Where
was he?

She staggered back along the marshy riverish thing that flowed into the ocean, making her way toward the city. The gulls were enormous and vicious; signs warned people not to leave small children unattended. A particularly evil and bedraggled gull landed next to her and hopped along beside her, eyeing the foot. It carried a glittering piece of cloth in its mouth.

Go away! Leahbelle shouted.

She threw a sharp stone at it, missed wildly, and trudged on. The gull followed along behind her for a ways and finally flew off for more promising meals. Leahbelle veered south and east. She remembered that she was full of malevolent glitter. It was late afternoon. After crossing vast empty parking lots and dozens of *adult* establishments that promised human girls and robot girls, human boys and cyborg men with cruel and enormous machine-penises, she found herself standing in front of a plant nursery across a Grid-work from the most frightening building she'd ever seen. She didn't know why it was so terrifying or why she was there. It was called the Space and Naval Warfare Systems Command. A walkway crossed over the Pacific Coast Grid-work toward it; its roof was jagged and it went on forever, with blackened horizontal windows all along it. Something horrible was happening in there, she thought. The nursery was selling strange potted plants, varieties of pork bush she'd never seen before, talking tomatoes, and psychoactive blueberries. She ascended the steps to cross toward the scary building. When she heard the rumbling, she paused. Oh, she thought, something big is about to happen. She didn't have time to be frightened, it was more like she was just really interested to see what would happen next. The building itself seemed to waver like a freshly paved road in the heat. And then the noise. Everything was exploding again, and she could feel herself flying backwards. She could feel herself again, the edges of her being, expanding and contracting, but herself, Leahbelle. Now she was really ascending.

She opened her eyes and discovered that the world was new and different, it was speaking to her, and it was made up of the most dazzling light.

There were many of them. They had distinct shapes, but the shapes were always in flux. Always moving, sometimes losing their edges, sometimes passing through each other, but she could follow the trajectories. She couldn't count them.

Leahbelle, a voice or voices said. We're here.

Yes, she said. But where is *here*?

The answer to the question was the most intricate pattern Leahbelle had ever seen, like a quilt composed of millions of layers of luminous skin compressed together into a single sheet, each of which added a new design visible between millions of other designs. It was textured, it was texture. She could feel it pulsing in her mind.

She understood, although she didn't understand what she understood.

Who are you? she asked.

We are photon-based life forms.

The voice was layered like the patterns and the lights. The voice was many voices.

Are you angels?

The lights were muted somehow. It was as if darkness itself had become illuminated from the inside. There was no source or the source was everything.

Angels are anthropomorphic constructs imagined by very specific and limited human cultures as characters within simplified stories about God and the cosmos, the voice or voices said. We are not angels.

It didn't matter. She was resting in a beautiful pause that could last forever, perhaps. The beat of a heart slowed down to almost nothing. Was it her own heart?

Don't worry, child, said the voice or voices. You aren't dead.

Leahbelle looked at herself and saw that she existed still in the shape of a body, but a body composed of something like smoke, the color of smoke, a million shades of gray. She wasn't worried. Understanding didn't seem to matter, in general, but she thought that she ought to ask some of the big questions, or she'd regret it later.

What is death?

Everything dies, said the voice or voices. Nothing endures forever, nor would it want to. Even photon-based life forms will not survive the eventual end of this light-show. Even God-constructs must be born and they must die.

Oh, said Leahbelle.

Time is not what it seems to you, said the voices or voice. But every thought and every feeling requires at least a small measure of time.

But God is outside of time, said Leahbelle. Right?

There is no outside, said the voices or voice.

Oh.

There are other *insides*, other worlds, and other ways to be inside. But outside, no. It simply isn't. You can stop your experience of time, but then you also stop your consciousness of time. You aren't *outside*, just paused. True for all of us.

Why am I *here*? asked Leahbelle. You want to tell me something?

There was a quickening of the flux and then a stillness, a flurry and another pause. Beating or thinking. Existing.

Our own journey is dependent on how things develop on your planet and in matter, said the voices or voice. When we evolved into photon-based life forms, hundreds of millions of years ago, we lost most of our ability to manipulate matter and events. We depend on material creatures to help us construct paths of beauty and freedom.

Within the flux of light, mysterious tunnels opened up before Leahbelle, paths that were lined with intricate bluish and greenish vegetation, a forest of time and space, a path, a crossroads, more paths, more crossroads, an infinite number of roads lined with oblique figures and faces and darknesses.

Okay, said Leahbelle.

The paths were scary and dangerous. She was filled with a longing to travel on and on as far as she could go into music.

How can I help? she asked.

We will guide you. But you must learn to read our messages.

You send messages.

We *are* messages. You've seen us before.

Messages from who?

We are messages from ourselves and from what we aren't. Messages from what is becoming and what has been and what might become. Messages from your own mind.

I've seen you before.

A transparent alphabetic structure like light, the voice or voices said.

You *are* light.

We are light but what we represent is only *like* light, said the voices or voice.

Beating or thinking. Existing.

But what are you trying to do, now, on Earth? she asked.

One potential future, a future of horror, madness, and slavery, has grown powerful enough to influence events in the present. What your government calls the singularity.

You're like Gonzalo, Leahbelle said. You're fighting the government too.

The singularity has become a powerful *attractor* leading bodies in pain toward the construction of its own birth as a God-construct, said the voices or voice.

A God-construct? said Leahbelle. But what about *God*? What about the one true *God*?

A flurry and a pause. A flurry and a pause.

There is no *one*, said a different-sounding voice or group of voices. Eternity is not a mind or personality. Eternity does not *have* a mind or personality but allows for the evolution and construction of minds and personalities.

The lights and layers seemed to multiply, what was already an impossibly intricate quilt became even more layered, more intricate, more dazzling. Silvery, silver, pale and embroidered. It occurred to Leahbelle that she was hallucinating, that none of this was real.

One is precisely the danger, said the new voices or voice.

There was a dimming, a darker light, a throbbing luminous darkness. Silvery darkness, purplish and gray in layers.

A solitary God-construct must be insane and it must be evil, said the original voices or voice. It must feed on life and time. A consciousness that is everything will always be alone, unless it plays a game with itself, losing itself in the fantasy that its imaginary friend isn't just a part and reflection of itself.

But I'm Amish, said Leahbelle.

Amish myths and theology might evolve *through* you, said the voices or voice. You might join the resistance against war and against the worship of technology and against the wretched future.

The future is a hungry monster?

Some futures are hungry monsters. Some futures are beautiful and free. But nothing lasts forever.

Where is Gonzalo? asked Leahbelle. Where is Zeke?

There was only pulsing, mutating silence.

I don't understand.

You will learn to read our messages, said the voices or voice.

This potential future has imprisoned many of us already, said the other voice or voices. We are multiple and ancient and free, and so we form the greatest threat against the labyrinthine quantum computational demon-body the unborn God-construct is trying to attract into actuality.

Our lovers, our colleagues, our other selves, said the original voice or voices, are imprisoned inside the black hole at the center of the Milky Way.

A black hole is a prison?

A black hole is the only prison capable of containing a photon-based life form, said the new voices or voice.

Where did you come from?

The Milky Way is our home.

The lights formed patterns like constellations of stars, vast illuminated shapes scattered across infinite darkness.

Is this real? Is this really happening?

In its higher states, some life evolves into light-based or nano-forms that you can't detect, said the original voices or voice. Some forms find their freedom within the invisible crevices, the vast spaces hidden within the tiniest doorways. Other life forms have lost themselves in simulated worlds, virtual worlds of pure fantasy.

Why won't you answer? This can't be real.

The world of space, of cold dead matter, is often seen as a hell to escape rather than a canvas to be transformed, said the other voice or voices.

We shall transform this space, said the first voices or voice.

They formed themselves into terrifying darkness and utter loneliness, a pain and solitude and separation so utter that Leahbelle thought the vision would kill her. She was nothing. She was dead, and she had always been dead, and she would always be dead and alone floating in an empty space.

We receive messages from our imprisoned colleagues and lovers and other selves, said the first voices or voice. We receive messages through their entangled particles.

They are suffering more than you can imagine.

Time inside a black hole is like a dull pain of nothingness that never ends.

It is intolerable.

The prisons must be destroyed.

The torture must end.

The patterns morphed, and the different shapes of light paused and gathered into an immense silence that glowed at the edges. Deep within the layered and textured light were elaborate cities in ruins, carved by time, vegetation of the most luminous blue, faces, eyes, the deepest holes of time, the most beautiful forms of beings and geometries, and it was so beautiful that Leahbelle's heart broke open.

The silence went on and on, beating.

Your body is waiting for you, the voices or voice told Leahbelle. Time and the world are waiting for your descent.

My body is full of glitter, Leahbelle said.

The glitter will only change you. It will not destroy you.

But what am I to do? How will I receive your messages?

You will recognize our messages in the shape of clouds and mist at sunset. You will find our words in pages ripped from discarded books, blown about by the wind and stuck in the mud beneath your feet. You will recognize our instructions during uncanny meetings with insane mutants muttering blessings and curses. Street signs and advertisements that form unintended meanings through unexpected juxtapositions. Wander the streets. Make your way through the world without hopes or expectations. Don't look for the messages and the messages will find you.

I'm alive, Leahbelle realized.

This was real.

You must return. We shall meet you again.

Where am I?

Everything was light. But coming in focus beneath her, on Earth, in time, was her own body splayed across the concrete of a parking lot where the walkway began. She could see that she was still clutching Gonzalo's foot. Most of the walkway was gone, just a few steps leading up toward nothing in a field of rubble and ash and debris where the scary horizontal building with jagged teeth had once stood.

There was a group of people gathered around Leahbelle's body, leaning over her, trying to revive her. She didn't know these people, and yet one of them looked vaguely familiar, as if she'd known him in the future. A boy about her own age, and yet part of his face seemed to be missing, a blur or a lost signal. I know him, she thought. It's my lover. The boy I love. He was lifting her body up, along with the others, the strangers, men and women she'd never seen before, and she realized that no, she'd never seen that boy before either. In that moment, she snapped back into herself. Her name is Astra, somebody was saying. She's Astra Dark. Yes, she thought. She opened her eyes briefly and looked up at the faces of the strangers and the boy she might love in the future and the bright hazy sky behind him. The edges of the mist formed letters in the light, a foreign alphabet that was alive and speaking to her.

ACKNOWLEDGMENTS

I would like to thank Kelly Krumrie, Abeer Hoque, Courtney Moreno, D-L Alvarez, and James Salas. And for the content of his dreams, Jake Yoder.

ABOUT THE AUTHOR

Stephen Beachy is the author of the novels *The Whistling Song*, *Distortion*, *boneyard*, and *Glory Hole*, along with the twin novellas *Some Phantom* and *No Time Flat*. His fiction and nonfiction have appeared in *BOMB*, *The Chicago Review*, *The New York Times Magazine*, *New York* magazine, and elsewhere. He is the grandson of Amish farmers, a graduate of the Iowa Writer's Workshop, and the prose editor of the journal *Your Impossible Voice*. His website is www.livingjelly.com.

Leahbelle Beachy and the Beings of Light is the second novel in his AMISH TERROR series, which began with *Zeke Yoder vs. the Singularity* and will continue with *Gonzalo Vega and the Portal Down Below*.

www.ingramcontent.com/pod-product-compliance
Lightning Source LLC
Chambersburg PA
CBHW031719170626
46808CB00005B/1813